"Are you scared, Liz?"

"I shouldn't be. I'm as tough as nails, remember?"

"But you came running to me," Brad said softly.

"Just tell your cousin to back off, Brad. I'm only doing my job. He doesn't have to threaten me. If he's got nothing to hide, I'll be the first to sing his praises."

"Okay, I'll talk to him, if that's what you want. But, Liz, we were discussing what happened tonight. I like the part about you coming to me for help. I like that a lot."

She'd asked for it, she thought, as he pulled her into his arms. And it had been inevitable—as inevitable as the moon's flight around the earth, as the stars' pilgrimage through the heavens. Liz's eyes closed, and Brad's mouth came down on hers, hard and insistent . . .

ABOUT THE AUTHOR

The writing team known as Eve Gladstone, Joyce Gleit and Herma Werner, first "visited" the fictitious town of Ramsey Falls in *One Hot Summer* and liked it so much that they wrote two sequels—*After All These Years* and now *Wouldn't It Be Lovely*.

"We thought of everything we love about Upper New York State—the charm and the elegance—and we put it all in one town," Joyce explains.

"Well, really, one county," says Herma. "Because we couldn't leave out the countryside, the Hudson River Valley, the horse-breeding farms.... All of that—it's just so lovely."

Books by Eve Gladstone

HARLEQUIN SUPERROMANCE
297–ALL'S FAIR
324–ONE HOT SUMMER
349–AFTER ALL THESE YEARS

HARLEQUIN INTRIGUE
23–A TASTE OF DECEPTION
49–CHECKPOINT
75–OPERATION S.N.A.R.E.
111–ENIGMA

Wouldn't It Be Lovely

EVE GLADSTONE

Harlequin Books

TORONTO • NEW YORK • LONDON
AMSTERDAM • PARIS • SYDNEY • HAMBURG
STOCKHOLM • ATHENS • TOKYO • MILAN

Published November 1989

First printing September 1989

ISBN 0-373-70380-5

For my sisters-in-law,
Cynthia Cowen and Joan Cowen,
and for Claire Gorelick

CHAPTER ONE

"LIZ, YOU HAVE the most extraordinary look on your face."

"Have I? I was concentrating."

"On what?" Celie Decatur asked.

"The truth is," Liz said after a moment, "I was really telling myself to cool it, to slow down. This isn't windy Chicago. This is soft, beautiful summery Ramsey Falls in upstate New York, and I'm in a different time zone entirely." She laughed in her warm, throaty way and added, "Do I make sense? Because if I do, explain it to me."

Celie shook her head. "I hate to be the one to say I told you so, but I told you so."

"Go ahead, spell it out," Liz said to the older woman. "I deserve it."

"It's the very first thing I warned you about, Liz. We're a gentle backwater, and that's the way we like it. This is Sleepy Hollow country with one exception. You may fall asleep like Rip Van Winkle, but when you wake up twenty years later, you'll find absolutely nothing changed."

"And nothing momentous happening in between— unless you consider the Ladies Auxiliary Dinner at the firehouse. Changed from Wednesday evenings to Thursday evenings. Did you know that? Heady front-page stuff for your newspaper, Celie. I'm going to get a nifty photograph to go with the story—half a dozen women smiling over a coffee urn.''

"You're incorrigible, you big-city reporter," Celie said in a faintly impatient tone. As the publisher and editor of a small-town newspaper, she had made it clear before to Liz, her only full-time reporter, that the *Times Herald* was perfectly in tune with community needs. "The Ramsey Falls Ladies Auxiliary helps support the Ramsey Falls firehouse," she went on, "which in turn keeps local taxes low. Yours, too, as soon as you settle in and find yourself a house you'd like to own."

"I'm sorry, Celie. Really I am." Liz smiled apologetically, although her dark brown eyes sparkled with undisguised humor. Trying to wind down in a hamlet in the Hudson River Valley wasn't quite as easy as she had imagined it would be. In fact, the world of Ramsey Falls as reported in the semiweekly *Times Herald* was physically and mentally light-years away from Chicago and the daily paper she had worked on there.

"I keep thinking there's a gigantic story I must cover before someone else does," she told Celie. "Only in this peaceable kingdom there are no huge, cataclysmic events, at least not the kind I'm used to. You know, riots, strikes, robberies, marches on city hall—the things I think of as the meat of newspaper life."

"In other words, you came to work for me in order to forget all that, and you can't forget it," Celie said. "You knew when you left Chicago that you were coming to a world where very little happens of the 'stop the presses' variety. I told you during our interview to think carefully about making such a drastic change in your life."

"I understand," Liz said. "The trouble is, I'm still on overdrive, even though I want to slow down. I was tired of the rat race and I can't even think of returning to it.

It's just that old habits die a little hard." She reached out and gently touched Celie's arm. "I promise, Celie, every day in every way I'm trying to slow down." She glanced around the soft green landscape. They stood near the paddocks of Bosworth Stud, the largest Thoroughbred horse breeding farm in Merriman County, owned by Victor Bosworth.

"Now where on this glorious estate is the horse auction going to take place?" she asked Celie, then saw a large striped tent behind the horse barn. "That's it, I suppose."

"Clever girl. Come on." Celie tucked her arm through Liz Grady's and drew her along the paddock fence. The horse breeding farm occupied a thousand soft green acres of rolling countryside in the Hudson River Valley, and on this warm and cheerful morning, mares and their young foals were to be seen grazing on the first fresh growth of spring grass. There were more than horses on the turf that morning, however. Buyers in elegant city clothes strolled about or sat on discreetly placed chairs and benches, partaking of refreshments served by waiters wearing white jackets and navy blue pants, the colors of Bosworth Stud.

"You'll have a chance to observe how a really first-rate horse auction is conducted," Celie said. "Buyers have come from all around the world to attend."

"Oh, it's posh, all right," Liz said. She hadn't yet come to terms with the unexpected world of horse breeding. Once again she was being challenged by what the remote, private world of Ramsey Falls offered an outsider from the big city. "I'm impressed," she said to Celie. "In fact, I've never seen anything like it."

"No horse on Bosworth Stud is valued at less than a quarter million dollars, and several many, many times that," Celie went on in a proprietary tone of voice.

"A quarter million dollars!"

Celie let out an impatient sigh, which clearly meant she was prepared for a lecture on the humane applications of a quarter million dollars. Liz, with her air of barely contained energy, was finding it hard to restrain herself. She impatiently drew her fingers through her thick dark hair. She was a long way from the big city, where there was a wrong that had to be righted everywhere she turned. Practice would eventually make perfect, and as Celie's only reporter she'd have to learn to keep her opinions to herself.

"Where is this fabulous stud, what's his name?" Liz asked. "Wouldn't It Be Loverly? They all look alike to me—sleek, shiny, chestnut-colored. And, anyway, it's an odd name for a horse."

"Blame it on Victor Bosworth's head trainer. He usually names them. After the first hundred names or so, you begin to get a little fanciful."

"I wouldn't mind doing a story on horse and owner."

"Uh-uh, out of the question," Celie said. "Don't even bring up the notion of interviewing Victor Bosworth. He's a modest man who doesn't seek publicity. In fact, if he even suspected you'd do such a thing, he'd have you run out of town."

Liz turned and stared at Celie in astonishment. "Have me run out of town? Wait a minute. This isn't the wild and woolly West, or have I suddenly entered another time warp? Run me out of town?"

Celie gave a sudden, embarrassed laugh. A widow who published the newspaper her late husband had left her, she was a very pretty woman in her late thirties with short blond hair that a warm wind had delicately ruffled. "I didn't quite mean that, Liz. I meant Victor could make things *uncomfortable* for you here in Ramsey Falls. There's plenty of national press around today to cover the auction, but Victor absolutely refuses to give interviews."

"Making things uncomfortable for me is the same thing, Celie."

Celie let out a sigh. "Come along, Liz. When I hired you, I had no idea someone so lively would show up, so...so..."

"Rambunctious," Liz finished for her.

"Determined, is the word I was searching for. There's Victor. Now be on your best behavior."

"I promise." Liz examined the owner of Bosworth Stud and said, "Well, he looks unprepossessing enough, considering he owns all of Ramsey Falls."

"Unprepossessing? I think the word is modest. And where'd you get the notion that he owns all of Ramsey Falls?"

"His name's all over the place. Bosworth Hall at the college, Bosworth Stud, Bosworth this, Bosworth that."

"Don't exaggerate. The name Decatur stands for something in this town, too. And the Kents and the Vanderheydens."

"Oh, of course I'm exaggerating," Liz said in an apologetic tone. She put a hand on Celie's arm. "I'll get my act together soon. I promise."

"Oh, I've no doubt you will. No doubt at all," Celie said. "And maybe that's what I'm worried about."

Victor Bosworth caught sight of them and waved. Of scholarly appearance, he was a tall, slender man in his forties, with thinning hair and shy eyes behind horn-rimmed glasses. With him was a man slightly taller than he, a decade or so younger, brown-haired, with a craggy face, an aristocratic nose and a brow Liz decided at once was brooding. An interesting face requiring further study, although far from handsome, she also decided. He wore a light, well-tailored suit, like Victor, which seemed very formal for a Saturday morning in the country. His jacket was open, however, his tie loose and the top button of his shirt collar undone. There was something about both men that struck Liz as alike, and for a moment she couldn't understand what it was. Then, all at once, she understood. There was a certain patrician quality about both of them. They were very sure of themselves. They had the world under their control. It was evident in the upright posture, the relaxed walk, the way they smiled.

There were elements of Ramsey Falls that were exactly like Chicago—worlds of entitlement, of people who lived above the fray and surveyed the world from their positions of privilege. In Chicago, though, she had never been invited into that world, and here in democratic Ramsey Falls, she was a guest. Well, a reporter, but a guest, too.

Liz turned briefly to Celie and realized that even Celie was dressed as though for the city. She was small and slim and her black-and-white print dress and black linen jacket were both elegant and correct. As for Liz, she wore what she'd thought were proper country clothes for a horse auction—jeans with a crisp white T-shirt illustrated across the front with a picture of the bearded Henry David Thoreau—but now she wasn't so sure. Her hair was thick and wind-tossed, and she put her hand up and patted it down, knowing the gesture would make no difference to its curly, tumbled appearance.

"Victor Bosworth, Brad Kent, this is Liz Grady," Celie began. "I was telling you about her, Victor. She's my new reporter."

. Victor extended a hand and gave Liz an unexpectedly sweet smile. "I thought we'd meet before this."

"Oh, I've been busy covering all the hot news in town," Liz said. When he frowned slightly, she was immediately sorry. Celie coughed.

Brad Kent smiled, however, and extended a hand. "His beard," he said, referring to her T-shirt and the picture of Thoreau, "does it tickle?"

His remark broke the ice, and Liz let loose her throaty laugh, noting with relief that all three joined in. "Not so you'd notice."

Brad Kent held her hand for a moment longer, then released it. She caught the interest in his eyes, which he made no effort to hide. "You don't mind if I feel a certain envy for Henry David Thoreau?"

His remark was so unexpected, and yet given with such charm and ease, Liz felt the heat rise to her face. "I'm going to send this shirt to the laundry and forget to pick it up."

"Speaking of Thoreau, how do you like our version of Walden Pond?" Victor asked.

"Ramsey Falls? Very much."

"Not quite up to the excitement of Chicago, I'm afraid."

"Then you know where I'm from," Liz said. "But gossip would travel unimpeded in these parts, I suppose, operating as it does in a near vacuum."

She heard Celie gasp and knew she'd done it once again: put her foot in it, pretended superiority when she didn't mean it. She didn't.

Victor, however, smiled. "You're perfectly right, Liz. Nothing much to talk about in town except who's arrived, who's departed, who's up, who's down. If you have a secret you plan on keeping, I'd suggest you forget the notion."

"You prefer the anonymity of Chicago?" Brad asked, studying her. His voice was deep and warm and relaxed, as though everything and everyone in his purview was in his control.

Liz thought with surprise that she had never met anyone so nakedly sure of himself. "Anonymity? In Chicago everyone's famous for at least fifteen minutes. Everyone gets into the act, political and otherwise."

"I suppose that's why they call it the Windy City."

She laughed, knowing there was no rancor in his remark, and that he had made it for the sake of a joke. Still, Liz had the unexpected feeling of having been picked up bodily by Bradford Kent, stuck on the end of a pin and been left wriggling. With unexpected clarity she understood he was a man used to saying what he thought, of perhaps expecting more than he was prepared to give. She was saved from having to respond by Celie, who asked Victor Bosworth what time the auction was scheduled to begin.

Victor consulted his watch. "Just about now." He took Celie's arm. "We counted nearly two hundred."

"Plenty of people from the press?" Celie asked. Liz noted that the question was asked in a very quiet, careful way.

"I set up drinks and food for them, gave them plenty of printed material to work from, and they'll go away happy."

"Clever," Celie said. "If you need my help..."

"I always need your help. Coming along?" he asked, turning to Liz.

"Yes, that would be wonderful," Liz said. "It's my first horse auction." The romance of buying and selling horses for racing eluded her, but she was determined to learn its lure.

Brad Kent, his hand lightly on her elbow, guided her across the lawn toward the yellow-and-white-striped tent. "Doing a story on the auction for the *Times Herald*?"

"Celie said she just wanted general coverage. Are you, um, involved with it somehow?"

"I'm Victor's lawyer."

"Ah. I suppose you've got a pocket of contracts to hand out as the horses go under the gavel."

"It's done on a nod and a handshake, Liz, and the whole business bores the hell out of me. Come on, let's get out of here."

She stared at him with astonishment. "Get out of here?"

"You know, fly the coop."

"The auction may bore you, but I'm a working girl."

"It's Saturday. Doesn't your boss know anything about workers' rights?"

"Well, she knows about this writer's work."

"Don't let her intimidate you. Celie's famous for her bark, which is never followed by a bite. I'll tell you what to write when it's all over. There's a very pleasant restaurant down the road apiece called Haddie's. They serve a mean Bloody Mary."

"I know Haddie's, but Bloody Marys in the morning," she pointed out, "are a little too mean."

"It's a perfectly respectable late morning." He stopped and turned to her. "How many times have you been told that your eyes are extraordinary?"

"Often enough. What's so extraordinary about them?"

"For one thing, they're enormous. One pupil is a tiny bit off-center, which is what gives you that vaguely dreamy look. The left. Or is it the right?" He lifted her chin with his finger. "Stare straight at me."

His face was close to hers. She could feel his breath on her cheek. "Your eyes are navy blue," she said. "I think."

"Same eyes as every male Kent in a line that goes back four hundred years. Dark blue. I'd say it's your right."

"Thanks," she said, disconcerted as she pulled away from him. "No one ever explained my eyes to me before. Four hundred years. Amazing. I've never met anyone with a line like yours. I mean, a line that goes back four hundred years. Well, I suppose mine does somehow or other, except it's not traceable, at least I don't think so. My parents didn't just spring up overnight like hyacinths or something."

"No, I suppose not," he said thoughtfully, still gazing at her.

"I'm Irish and half a dozen other things on my father's side. Italian plus Polish plus an assortment of religions on my mother's. I'm a mongrel—but it all has to go back four hundred years."

"Back to the first man and woman, I'm sure. Which means we're related. My car's over there." He pointed in the general direction of the main barn, where there was a sizable parking lot. "Suppose we continue comparing the theory of our relatives over Bloody Marys?"

Liz looked toward the yellow-and-white-striped tent where the auction was being held. There was a crowd at the entrance, but Celie and Victor were nowhere in sight.

"All you'll have to know is how many attended," Brad remarked, "and what was sold. I'll give you the complete rundown in time to make the evening edition. From the horse's mouth, so to speak."

"Evening edition," Liz said. "That's what I love about working on a semiweekly publication. The deadline's are nice and easy and the next issue we're talking about is Tuesday's."

"Is it a deal? Walking out on the auction, that is."

She looked curiously at him. "I have the oddest notion you've made up your mind for me."

He gave her a crooked grin. Far from handsome, she thought, but his smile was wonderful. And his navy blue eyes, stretching back in an unbroken line for four hundred years, were clear, friendly and decidedly interested. "It's a deal," she said, "except I'd like a cup of black coffee instead of that Bloody Mary."

Haddie's Inn, on the main road just outside of Ramsey Falls, occupied a comfortable turn-of-the-century house overlooking a small pond. Haddie herself, a robust woman with red cheeks and a talent for cooking, had arrived in town a year before to take over a restaurant whose owner had retired. Haddie believed in large portions, home-style cooking and moderate prices. The restaurant had been enlarged over the winter, and the room where Liz and Brad were seated smelled of new wood, of the plants suspended in pots from the ceiling and of spring drifting in through large, open windows.

"Haddie certainly knows how to make you feel at home," Liz said appreciatively.

"Sure all you want is coffee?"

"I think so."

They exchanged smiles and then Liz, feeling unexpectedly exposed to his unabashed scrutiny, turned her attention to the ducks in the pond and the small boy who crouched at the water's edge and threw them pieces of bread.

"Seth Whiting."

She turned back. "Excuse me?"

"Seth Whiting. He's the kid feeding the ducks. Seven years old. Son of Jemma Whiting Gardner. Jemma owns Whiting Printing. Main Street."

"Oh, right," Liz said. "I know Jemma slightly. Nice lady."

"Seth's stepfather teaches at Pack College. They purchased an old stone house over on Rock Hill Road and . . . shall I go on?"

Liz shook her head. "No, I get the point. Small-town pride. Everyone knowing everyone else. Everyone happy. Arcadian simplicity, et cetera, et cetera. A world of habit, of formal little events like the yearly firehouse clambake and the church penny social. No," she added, shaking her head, "I'm not knocking it. It's wonderful."

"And every hundred years a centennial," he said, smiling.

"Or every ninety-nine years," she amended, referring to the celebration the summer before when it was discovered the tricentennial was being celebrated a year early. "And just think, the Kents have lived through four of them. Navy blue eyes staring in wonder at the passage of yet another century."

"But still, knowing your roots and everybody else's roots has its bad points," he told her unexpectedly, looking out the window again. Seth Whiting, still at the water's edge, had been joined by another boy his age.

"Bad points?" Liz asked.

"Knowing who you are, where you come from, where you're expected to go and that you're only another knot on a long rope that comes out of the past and stretches to infinity. Stepping into a pair of well-shod but nevertheless worn shoes." He stopped and turned back to her, and Liz was caught by a dark look in his eye.

"Sounds good to me," she said. "My life's been full of ambitions and change and not knowing whether I'd get from here to there. I lived in Chicago all my life, in a high-rise apartment in a working-class section of the city. Grew up on concrete. Handball at a city park instead of Little League in a grassy dell. You didn't know your neighbors except to nod at on the elevator. Friends from my high school days disappeared into the great maw of education all over the country. Or married and disappeared. Or just plain disappeared. I stayed put because I had one simple ambition—I wanted to be a reporter, and that was that. I'm a big-city kid, streetwise, tough, and everybody's a stranger. No shoes to climb into unless I want to be a traffic cop like my mom or a blue-collar worker like my dad." She hesitated, wondering if she were bragging in her own way to show up the differences between them.

"How'd they take your coming east? Your parents, I mean."

"Weren't too happy about it. We're a noisy, brawling family. Arguments are always at top decibel, the way they should be, and followed by utter calm, all resentment gone, the way it should be."

"Is it?" Brad said. "In my family we're extremely civilized with one another. And, of course, resentments last entire lifetimes. Several lifetimes. Everyone's still mad at Great-Aunt Josefina who captured my uncle on a trip to Spain and married him for his money. She was a dancin' gal."

"And had plenty of progeny, I hope."

"Afraid not. The family interfered and sent Great-Aunt Josefina packing to Manhattan, where she became a pillar of society."

"And your poor uncle?"

"Spent the rest of his life walking around in a daze."

The waitress came by and served Brad his drink and Liz her coffee. Then Haddie herself came over to the table to smile benignly at them. "What you want is a muffin with that coffee," she told Liz. "And you know what I think about drinking it black."

"I know. It's bad for me, Haddie."

"Appreciated the mention in last Tuesday's edition," Haddie said. "You'd be surprised how many people read it and came in."

"You're four-star all the way," Liz told her with a smile. "Celie decided that I'm the restaurant reviewer, as well," she explained to Brad. "Nothing like Haddie's roast beef and home fries."

"Or her Bloody Marys," Brad said, raising his glass. "Bring the lady a muffin."

"Will do," Haddie said, walking away, her smile that of a mother hen having performed her proper duty.

"It has to be on the bill," Liz told him. "I can't continue to review restaurants and expect to be given a handout."

"Oh, by all means. Mustn't have muffin payoffs under any conditions."

"Oh, damn," Liz said with an exasperated sigh. "I haven't been able to say one thing right today. I'm coming off as an insufferable prig out to show the natives how to live.''

"On the contrary," Brad said, wrapping his hands carefully around his glass as though to keep from touching her. "You come off as an exotic species of flower with enough scent to capture every male within a hundred-mile radius.''

Liz felt the heat rise slowly to her face and hoped it wouldn't show. She thought she was able to handle just about anything, yet here she was being disconcerted by his steady gaze, his absolute certainty of her reaction. "I think I've had enough coffee," she told him.

He laughed just as the waitress appeared with an oversize muffin, a small crock of homemade butter and a dish of thick strawberry jam.

"Have some," Liz said, truculently slicing the muffin in half.

"With a Bloody Mary? And you're a restaurant critic?"

"A reluctant restaurant critic." As Liz carefully buttered the muffin, she made a promise to herself that all personal discussion was out-of-bounds. She was a reporter, and the first thing a reporter did was ask questions, not field them.

"Is your law office in Ramsey Falls?" she asked politely.

"I have a small office in town, but the main office is in Merriman, the county seat.''

"But you live in Ramsey Falls."

"As a matter of fact, I'm building a house above the river in Ramsey Falls.''

She thought carefully about her next question. After all, an invitation to a drink constituted politeness, not a commitment. "Present for your bride?" she asked.

His eyes glittered with amusement. "I'm not married, not about to be married, have never been married. I decided that I was tired of living in a three-hundred-year-old stone house and wanted something that was all glass and took in a wide view of the river."

She relaxed visibly. "Building it yourself?" She bit into the muffin, silently agreeing that Haddie was right: coffee with a muffin were very companionable at that time of day.

"With the help of a good architect and some committed artisans," he said. "I like working with my hands." His gaze never left hers.

"That so?"

"Care to help?"

"What would I be expected to do?"

"Lend moral support."

"Oh," she said, "I've plenty of that to lend. And no interest to demand whatsoever."

"No interest at all? Is that what you said?"

Liz hesitated a moment. No, he was far from handsome, she thought, but it didn't matter. He was... *interesting.* "I have an extremely charitable nature," she told him.

"You'd be surprised how grateful I can be over the least bit of help."

"Brad, I hope you build houses as smoothly as you talk."

"I'll undoubtedly keep on talking, but it's the first and last I'll ever build."

"Settling in for the duration?"

He frowned slightly and was a long time answering. "Maybe that's what it is—settling in for the duration."

They were parrying, talking about something else, something extraordinarily intimate for two people who had just met, and yet she had no idea what that something else was. To cover her embarrassment, she asked how many rooms the house contained, although she wasn't the least bit interested in knowing. At the moment, Liz occupied one room at a local boarding house, and she had no plans to change her mode of living.

"Kitchen, living room and bedroom," he told her, "but right now it's a gleam in my architect's eye. You can write an article about the project for the Home section of the *Times Herald*."

Liz laughed. "There isn't any Home section."

"That's the idea. Finish your muffin. I'll take you out to see the place now."

"The auction, Brad, remember? Celie wants the story. Yes, I know," she added when he shook his head, "for next Tuesday's edition. Well, at least let's stop at Bosworth Stud to see how it's getting on."

"Very well without us." He called for the check with seeming reluctance and was slow about finishing his drink.

When they were in the parking lot, a car drew up and Jamie Duboise stepped out, his eyes glistening with excitement. He was a local realtor whose business had doubled in the past year, due, he said, to the town celebrating its tricentennial twice. "It's not every town that has a bi-tricentennial," he liked to say. Liz was renting a room at his mother's historic stone house. "The sheriff's out at Scottie's," he told them. "Scottie's up to his old tricks, shooting up a storm. He won't let anyone on the property."

The rise of adrenaline was almost immediate. "A shooting?" Liz asked, reaching automatically into her bag for her notebook. "Where's Scottie's?"

"Mountain Road. Third turnoff on the left at the junction of Bridge and I-84. It's one-way. Keep on it until you see the sheriff's car."

"Thanks. I'll have to phone the paper, see where the photographer is. Oh, damn, he's at the auction. Brad, give me a lift to my car, would you?"

"Wait a minute," Brad said. "You're not going. The man uses live ammo in a real gun. You know, the kind that kills."

She frowned. "Of course I'm going. Come on, give me a lift." She swung into his car. "Brad, let's *go!*"

He climbed into the driver's seat but didn't put his key into the ignition. "Scottie goes off on a tear every now and then. When he does, he sits on his porch and shoots up the neighborhood. Harmless he may be—he's never done anything more than scare the chickens—but someday, however—"

"Brad, I don't want to argue with you."

He sat back and engaged the engine. "I'll take you there."

"I'll have to get along without a photographer, I guess."

"There's a camera on the back seat. You can use that."

"Wonderful, thanks."

"Don't thank me. It's a baby-sitting job. I'd hate to be the last person to see you alive."

"Give me the rundown on Scottie. First name, how old, that sort of thing."

"You're a cold-blooded number," he commented, glancing quickly at her.

"I'm doing my job, Brad."

"This what you left behind when you came east?"

"Yes." She held herself tightly. She had meant to leave it behind, but it took only a word to feel that welcome surge of adrenaline that meant a story. "I was on the police beat before I moved into the city room. I've been in a lot tougher situations than someone sitting on his porch taking potshots at the sheriff."

"You're even hoping it'll end with Scottie shooting at more than a chicken. It won't matter what the *Times Herald* prints. You have a feed into the news services, haven't you?"

"No," she said, without even admitting to herself that the possibility had crossed her mind.

"I'll bet."

They drove on in silence until the turnoff to the Scott house. "We'll stop here," Brad said, pulling up and parking at the side of the road. "The sheriff probably blocked the road about a quarter mile up."

"A quarter mile? It'll be over—"

"We'll ask them to play a rerun," he told her. He reached into the back seat and handed her his camera. "It's automatic. Just point and click. Fresh roll of film, too."

"Thanks."

"Save it."

"Brad." She had started up the road at a near run, but now stopped and waited for him. "Look, I'll manage a hitch back. Why don't you leave if it makes you unhappy?"

"Because they're going to collar Scottie and throw the book at him. They do every time, and I always end up arranging bail for him."

"A civic-minded citizen." She started up the road again, matching her stride to his. "I'm impressed."

"It's something we've always done," he told her briskly.

They heard the sound of a car around the next bend in the road. "Don't tell me," Liz said. "We're too late." She took the camera out of its case and held it up to her eye, locating the release.

The sheriff's car came into view. When he saw Brad, he pulled up. "Pal's in the back seat," he said.

Liz quickly stepped up to the window and photographed the grizzled man grinning toothlessly at her.

"Hey," he said, "Make sure you take my good side."

"Want to come along?" the sheriff asked Brad.

"I'll follow," Brad said. "You know Liz Grady."

"Sure. How are you? Sorry you missed the excitement, Liz."

"I'll come along, too, if you don't mind," she said. "What's the charge?"

"Drunk and disorderly and scaring the chickens."

"No one hurt?"

"Not even Scottie's feelings."

"Hey," Scottie called, "the missus is gonna have a fit. Let's pick her up and tell her the good news."

"Plenty of time for that," Brad said.

"See you in jail," the sheriff said, and moved on.

Liz followed Brad back down the road in the wake of the sheriff's car. "Okay, okay, that news would really burn up the wires. Scottie, whatever his name is, living on Mountain Road, arrested on Saturday for drinking and shooting. Missus has conniption fit when informed. The prominent Merriman attorney Bradford Kent had the culprit released on his own recognizance. Until the next time. Gosh, that plus the report on the auction should make the Tuesday edition of the *Times Herald* heady stuff. Should be an absolute sellout."

At the junction of the highway, Brad braked the car to a stop. He turned to her, his expression completely sober. "How long do you suppose you'll be in Ramsey Falls?"

"I'm not sure. I signed on with Celie Decatur to get away from Chicago. She has big ambitions for the *Times Herald* which is why she hired me in the first place. She wants to go daily, as a matter of fact. And I want to be around when she does. Anyway, why do you ask?"

"I just want to know how long I have to knock some sense into you."

She waited a moment before speaking. "I don't know what you're talking about."

He turned around and started up the car. "You will."

CHAPTER TWO

LIZ MADE the Ramsey Falls police station rounds daily and knew all the officers on duty. The most popular feature in the *Times Herald* was its court page, which listed local infractions taken from the police blotter. Just a few lines for speeders, car collisions, drunken drivers, loiterers, hunters caught trapping out of season and excessively loud parties late at night, but they provided the local citizens with gossip not otherwise learned over the fence, or else confirmation of gossip that was learned over the fence.

The one-cell jail was at the back of the station, which occupied a large turn-of-the-century clapboard house on Main Street. Scottie was sleeping it off on the cell cot when Brad and Liz rolled up.

It took Brad no more than fifteen minutes to procure Scottie's release, putting up the bail and handing him a lecture, before ordering a taxi to take him back home.

"Keep shooting up the neighborhood like you did today," he warned the man who swayed before him with his pleased, toothless grin, "and I'm going to have you do some time."

"Nah, you won't," said Scottie.

"Try me," Brad said.

For the first time that day Scottie looked cowed. Liz had followed his arraignment and subsequent release, and it struck her that Scottie held Brad in considerable awe.

"I guess I don't get my shotgun back," he said in a subdued voice.

"It's evidence, Scottie. You're not off the hook yet."

"That gun's worth a lot to me."

"You don't act it."

"Aw, come on, Counselor, quit treating me as if I were a kid."

"When you grow up, Scottie, I'll begin to treat you with a lot more respect. You've got a wife, kids. You might think of them once in a while."

Scottie grinned sheepishly, them moved off, carefully maneuvering down the stairs as he walked gingerly to the waiting taxi. Brad took some money from his wallet and handed it to the driver. "See that he gets some strong coffee down him while you're at it."

Later, on the ride back to Bosworth Stud, Liz spoke up. "Do a lot of that sort of thing?"

"Pro bono stuff?" Brad shrugged. "There's no one else to handle it around Ramsey Falls."

"There are other lawyers," she began.

"It's a family tradition."

"For the good of the community."

"It's a family tradition. You don't think about whether it's good, bad or indifferent. It comes with the territory."

Liz thought about that for a while. She had grown up with the idea of charity for its own sake. You have a helping hand, you lend it, even if you stand to lose it in the bargain. "I guess I don't understand," she said at last. "Your attitude strikes me as lord of the manor stuff. It . . . it lacks the milk of human kindness."

"Human kindness to Scottie? Man's never worked a day in his life. Wife supports him—"

"And obviously cares about her husband if she's putting up with him."

Brad laughed suddenly. "Would you support a lazy lout given to shooting up the neighborhood when he's had too much to drink? No," he added, "I already know the answer to that one. You don't like guns and you don't like liquor."

"I'm not sure I like being that transparent, either, but you're right about both. Next question."

"Hungry?"

"Celie's going to wonder—"

"I'll handle Celie. What's your favorite food?"

"Don't you know?"

"I think I do," he said. "You have eclectic tastes and will eat anything on a dare from sea urchins to calves' brains. Given your choice, you'd go for something exotic, but when you cook for yourself, you'll open up a can of soup and feel thoroughly satisfied."

"You're right, of course," Liz said. "Again. I hate being an open book."

"Ah, but what a book."

She cast a shy glance at him, and when he returned her gaze, she looked quickly away, embarrassed. The truth was, she had found herself wondering what his lips would feel like against hers.

"Got somebody?" he asked.

"You mean you don't know?"

"I'm talking about Chicago."

"In California," she said. "Berkeley, to be exact. He's working on a doctorate." Then, anticipating Brad's next question, added, "In philosophy. He's teaching also. At the university, I mean."

"Nice place to hunker down, Berkeley. Been out there?"

"Yes, just before I came here, as a matter of fact."

"And he let you go. Amazing." The words were spoken quietly, so quietly in fact that Liz wasn't even certain he'd said them. Then he added, "You came here, your friend's in California. That's a lot of distance between two people."

Liz shrugged. "So it is, but this job opened up and Doug's into teaching. He likes the benign climate. I like a change of seasons. He's kind of easygoing. I'm kinetic. There are a few things we have to iron out before we..." She stopped. Bradford Kent was a lawyer with a lawyer's talent for picking brains. At the moment she didn't want hers picked, not about Doug, anyway.

"Sounds like you disagree on all the important points."

"Not all of them."

It took him a long time to answer, and when he did, his words were terse. "I see."

No, he didn't see, she thought. Her relationship with Doug wasn't complicated. They had lived together in college, they had traveled to Europe together, and then they had separated. They had once been in love and now there was warmth and affection between them and sometimes they talked of marriage, but the need and the heat were gone. They were a continent apart through choice. Doug had gone west and Liz had taken a job on a Chicago paper. The question of marriage, of her moving to California, or his returning to Chicago was never discussed. They saw each other on vacations and when Doug came east to visit her and his family. There had never been any rancor between them, no threats, no disavowals. They were comfortable together and equally comfortable apart. She didn't expect him to live like a monk, not surrounded as he was by the young and the nubile. Perhaps he didn't expect it of her, either, although it had worked out that way.

"Why did you leave Chicago?" Brad asked suddenly.

She exhaled a sigh of relief. He'd asked the one question she didn't mind answering. "Because my job was getting to me. I would have stood for just about anything—in fact, I did stand for it. Tight deadlines, the seamy side of life, power playing, murder, mayhem—it was all grist for my hot little word processor. I was, *am*, ambitious and was quite happy working the wrong side of the law for a big newspaper. Except, one day I came across a really hot story and it was taken away from me. It's that simple."

She splayed her hands and held them up to show she'd came away from the whole affair empty. "Not because I was incompetent, either. The trouble was that the story had to do with corruption in the educational system. I was on the city desk and the education department of the newspaper felt it was their bailiwick. Result, the story was pulled away from me and subsequently won a Pulitzer Prize. That took the cake. I walked, deciding I'd had enough of big-city interoffice politics, and fished up here, thanks to my ex-editor who thinks I'm going to go running back to her as soon as I get the country out of my system. End of story."

"Not quite the end," Brad told her. "You traveled to a small town in the east. As far away," he added, "from the West Coast as you can get."

She shrugged. "Unfortunate coincidence. Can't be helped."

"How did you make your way to these parts?" Brad asked.

"My city editor knows Celie. The job opened up and here I am. Which, incidentally, brings me to another point. Do I still have a job, or has Celie fired me?"

"My guess is that the ambitious Celie Decatur is proud of her big-city reporter. You can write your own ticket, if you haven't already."

"I think you and I are talking about two different Celie Decaturs."

"I'm talking about the lady I've known all my life."

IT WAS CLEAR the auction had ended when Liz and Brad returned to Bosworth Stud. The grounds were still crowded, however.

"Wonderful," Liz said, noting everyone was either eating or drinking. "Food, I'm starving." She headed straight for the refreshment tent, working her way through a crowd gathered at the entrance.

"Liz, where the devil have you been?" Celie asked, descending on them just before they reached the food line. "The auction's over and I don't think you've been around to take down a single bid."

"Celie, I'm sorry," Liz began.

"I kidnapped her," Brad broke in. "We covered a shoot-up out at Scottie's place—"

"Anyone hurt?" Celie put in quickly.

"Only Scottie's feelings. They've confiscated his shotgun for the time being."

"The damn fool. He's going to hurt somebody one of these days."

"That's right," Brad told her. "It's about time he learned a lesson. I'm having him hauled up before the justice of the peace next week."

"Judge Vanderheyden, you mean."

"Probably. This time Scottie's going to be given a stiff
fine if I have anything to say about it, and he's going to
pay it himself."

"His wife's going to pay it, you mean. Poor soul, she
has her hands full."

"What does Mrs. Scott do, anyway? For a living, I
mean," Liz asked, reaching for her notebook.

"Don't bother. Police blotter stuff," Celie remarked
disdainfully. "You didn't have to go chasing after that
one, Liz. Brad should've known better. Nothing Scottie
would like more than having his name in the paper, and
nothing like mortifying his wife. Well, we can't help a
notice of his arraignment, but that's quite enough." She
motioned to Liz's notebook. "Victor got a record price
for Wouldn't It Be Loverly."

"Really? Now isn't that loverly! Who won it?" Liz
asked.

"No one's saying, but you know the rumors around
here. It's either the Queen of England or an Arab po-
tentate, although believe me, it's neither."

"Do *you* know, Celie?"

Celie shook her head. She turned to Brad. "Victor's
playing this one tight."

"Victor plays them all tight," he said, "and you know
it, Celie."

"Where can I find out?" Liz asked.

"You can't," Celie told her. "Just say Loverly was
sold for a record price paid for a colt at auction and that,
incidentally, he won the Breeder's Cup."

"You mean write the story but leave out all the juicy
parts?"

Celie shook her head. "We're not talking about juice. We're talking about one man's right to privacy. And the right for the new owner to anonymity if he wishes."

"Oh, Celie," Liz groaned. "What's the use of a newspaper that doesn't carry the news?"

"The record price paid for the colt is news. The fact that he won the Breeder's Cup is news. His noble line is news. The exact amount is irrelevant, and so is the name of the buyer."

"Celie, you don't mean that."

Brad touched Liz's arm. "Don't press it, Liz."

But Liz paid no attention to him. "Celie, are you the publisher and sole owner of the *Times Herald* or—?"

"What kind of a damn fool question is that?"

"Nothing, I guess," Liz said with a sigh when she saw the anger that colored her boss's face. The revelation surprised her. Celie was protecting Victor Bosworth for something far more personal than mere friendship.

"There's Victor," Celie said to Brad. "He's been looking for you."

Brad gave Liz a smile that told her to be patient and cautious. "I'll catch up with you on the breadline."

Liz nodded and said to Celie, "Okay, I'll handle the story. Don't worry. It'll be the picture of discretion. One picture, in fact, worth a thousand words. Of the horse, I mean. I hope Victor will part with a photograph."

"Jake Martinez was around taking pictures," Celie snapped, referring to the free-lance photographer whose services the *Times Herald* used. Then she added in a curious voice, "You're being awfully friendly with Brad, aren't you?"

Liz shrugged, but deliberately avoided a direct answer. "Just adding to my store of acquaintances."

The remark clearly didn't satisfy Celie, but all she said in a more kindly tone was, "Have you eaten?"

"No. It's amazing how many people are worried about whether I've eaten or not."

"Better help yourself. I'll see you later."

"Thanks, Celie." Liz gave her a spontaneous hug, then looked around for Brad and found him with Victor Bosworth just outside the tent. Hands dug into his pockets, tie undone, he was talking earnestly to the horse breeder, who seemed to be listening with rapt attention. She gazed at Brad for a long moment, at his tall figure, at the way his brown hair never seemed to be quite smoothed down. She was trying to decide just how attractive he was or wasn't when he turned suddenly and smiled at her, as though he had known all along precisely where she was. She flushed and pointed at the food table, which took up the far side of the tent. He nodded and she went quickly to the table, not daring to look at him again.

Bradford Kent had descended upon her as though he were a horde of gypsy moths and she a vulnerable oak tree. He had kidnapped her, questioned her, dragged her all around the county and dumped her unceremoniously back on the original site, no ransom required.

He was, as her mother might say, a fine figure of a man. No, not good-looking, but his face was all sharp angles that caught the light well. And his mouth. She liked his mouth. Yet he wasn't good-looking, not in the way Doug was, but she felt his charged-up energy, which she thought matched hers. The food line snaked forward. A new feeling of peace had come over her, as though Ramsey Falls were taking her into its vast, comfortable green bosom at last.

There was a soft touch on her shoulder, and when Liz turned she found a young woman smiling shyly at her. "You're the new reporter for the *Times Herald*, aren't you?"

"Yes, I am."

The woman was a plump brunette in her early twenties with clear, friendly blue eyes. "I'm Marion Nelson."

"Liz Grady. Hi." Liz's hand was firmly shaken.

"Listen, if you're looking for a good story, I've got one."

"You mean on who bid for and won Wouldn't It Be Loverly?"

The woman shook her head. "No, I wasn't even thinking of the auction. It's something else far more interesting."

"Selling for the highest price ever paid at a horse auction is pretty interesting," Liz said. "Who purchased it is even more interesting."

"Well," Marion said, "I work here in the office. Maybe it wouldn't be so difficult to find out."

"I *would* like to know."

"Sure, but I mean I'd have to wait until Monday or whenever. You know what I mean."

"Anytime. I can always do a follow-up," Liz said almost automatically. Celie wouldn't allow a follow-up, but by now her curiosity was piqued and she intended to chase the name of the new owner of Wouldn't It Be Loverly as far she could—just for the sake of the chase. And as Brad had correctly hinted, there were always the news services to contact.

"What's the other interesting story?" Liz asked.

"It's my father," Marion began.

"Your father? He bought . . . wait a minute. Begin at the beginning."

The line edged forward and Liz found herself in front of the waiter. The table was set with a variety of salads and pâtés, and if Liz hated anything, it was making a decision about food, in spite of Brad's summation of her tastes.

"The shrimp salad," Marion said. "I'm coming back for seconds."

"Right," said Liz, who then moved down the line for a cup of coffee. When Marion caught up, they made their way over to the terrace where they found seating space on a low stone wall that overlooked the grounds and rose garden. Liz glanced back at the food tent to find Brad waving at her and pointing simultaneously at Victor, who was several steps ahead of him. She nodded, as though she understood perfectly well what was going on.

"My father owns a small house on I-84," Marion began, once she had taken her first mouthful. "The house sits on a spot that isn't zoned commercially."

"Meaning?" Liz asked. Having grown up in a city where commercial buildings and private houses existed cheek by jowl, she wasn't certain of the intricacies of country zoning laws.

"Well, part of the highway is zoned for commercial use—restaurants, gas stations, supermarkets and the like—but I-84 began as a one-lane road that grew like crazy. Town zoning laws have always been very strict about the uses made of the road. Where my father lives, it's still the way it was at the turn of the century—full of private homes and no stores or garages or whatever."

Liz reached into her bag for her notebook, and in her own private shorthand quickly took a few notes.

"I don't live at home now," Marion continued, "but I grew up in that house. We moved to Ramsey Falls about twenty years ago, so that means we're not natives. And I guess," she added as an afterthought, "they'll never consider us natives."

"They. An old story," Liz said, putting her pencil down and picking up her fork once again. She speared a shrimp and held it in midair. "Rather typical of small towns—very parochial, that sort of thing. I don't exactly feel at home here, either. I'm new in town as everyone keeps reminding me and will probably keep reminding me from now until the end of my life."

"Ordinarily we wouldn't care what they think about us," Marion said. "You let them lead their lives, we lead ours and everybody's happy. The trouble is with the Vanderheydens."

Liz looked at her in surprise. The Vanderheydens, Liz had learned when she'd first come to Ramsey Falls, comprised one of the oldest, most reclusive families in the area. "Somehow the word trouble and Vanderheydens don't seem to go together. I thought they were the backbone of Ramsey Falls, and except for Judge Vanderheyden, out of the public eye, so to speak."

"The Vanderheydens only talk to the Vanderheydens, but actually that's the old generation," Marion said with some disdain in her voice. "The ones coming up are a lot more aggressive. Then of course there's Judge Vanderheyden. He's a special case."

"Hanging Judge Vanderheyden."

Marion gave a sarcastic laugh. "Oh, he'll hang you and me and my Aunt Martha. He'd never hang a Vanderheyden or a Vanderheyden relation or someone who married a Vanderheyden or who's descended from someone who married a Vanderheyden six hundred years ago in Holland."

"That bad, huh?"

"It's only bad if you cross one of them. Or if one of them wants to cross your property line. Anyway, to make a long story short, the judge's son, Will Vanderheyden, wants to put up a bar-restaurant next door to my father's house. Not only isn't my father happy about it, but Will is circulating a petition among all my father's neighbors to say it's okay with them."

"And they're signing the petition?"

"They're afraid not to."

"What?" Liz shrieked the word.

"Afraid."

"Just a minute. You mean, afraid like afraid for their lives?"

Marion shook her head. "No, I don't think that. No, not that definitely, but afraid anyway. Maybe afraid because of something that might happen in the future."

"But what can Will or the judge do?"

Marion shrugged. "They don't put a contract out on you," she said, suddenly giggling, then turning serious. "If you go up before the judge for a minor traffic infraction, well, you can imagine the outcome. And Will is a volunteer fireman. Try working up his enthusiasm when your house is on fire."

"Come on, you're talking as if they're a combination of Al Capone and Dirty Harry."

"It's just that you don't cross Vanderheydens. Except my father. He's hiring a lawyer to fight Will. It's going to cost him a bundle, and I wouldn't care since it's his money, but what I do care about is the fact that my father has a weak heart and all this isn't good for him. That's what has me worried."

Liz shook her head slowly, knowing there was no real story in a minor border dispute. "The property isn't zoned for commercial use, so how can Will Vanderheyden get away with it?"

"I don't suppose that matters if you're a Vanderheyden."

"You mean they're above the law?"

"No, they'll go about getting all the right variances. They'll manage to have that part of the route rezoned for commercial use. They won't be sneaky about it. In fact, they couldn't be sneaky if they tried. After all, we have a town zoning board that believes in doing things in a very legitimate way."

"Legitimate because nobody takes them on."

"Exactly," Marion said. "How about meeting my father? He can tell you what's happening. Don't you think it would make a good story?"

Liz popped the shrimp into her mouth and chewed thoughtfully. There was no real hook so far, and besides, every story had two sides. She'd have to interview Mr. Nelson *and* Will Vanderheyden. Of course property disputes sometimes escalated into much headier battles. The hook depended upon something happening: threats, violence. Bloodthirsty, that's what I am, she thought. In Chicago or any big city you only had to look under the nearest rock to find violence. Here one had to dream of it.

"Could you see him?" Marion asked.

"I could, but I can't promise anything."

"That's okay. Just talk to him. It's about time someone stood up to Will and the judge, only I don't think my father ought to fight it alone. If the *Times Herald* did a story... wow!"

"No promises," Liz reiterated. She thought about Celie and how Celie might want to protect the oldest clan in town.

"My father's place is about two miles down from Haddie's, and it overlooks the river across the road. The road is zoned for commercial use until about a quarter mile past Haddie's. Then you'll see the firehouse and past that a diner, and from there on it's zoned for private housing." She reached into her bag and extracted a pen and a notebook. "This is my father's address. It's a stone Dutch Colonial with a small garden in front full of tulips. His name's on the mailbox."

"I'll stop by and see him," Liz said. "But please understand that my editor makes the final decisions."

"You couldn't be fairer than that," Marion said. She put aside her plate, stood and dusted off her dress. "Listen, after you see him, call me and tell me what you think. Meanwhile, I'll try to find out who bought you-know-what for all that money. But if Mr. Bosworth plays it close to his vest, I'll have to be very careful about what I do."

"I always protect my sources."

"Wow," Marion said, her eyes widening. "You mean you'd go to jail rather than tell?"

"Sure," said Liz, aware that she was grandstanding but unable to resist it. "That's what people in my profession do if they have to."

"I don't want you to go to jail for me."

"It's okay. I'll hire the best lawyer in town." She looked around the lawn below the terrace, but Brad was nowhere in sight.

"Bradford Kent. He's neat," Marion said, nodding sagely. "Well, it was nice meeting you, Liz. I'll do what I can to help you."

"Thanks," Liz said. "Where do I call you?"

"The office. That's the little building just opposite the main barn. It's where the farm manager and head trainer have their offices. We're listed under Bosworth Stud in the phone book. You won't get through to Mr. Bosworth, so don't worry. His number is private."

Private. Too bad, Liz thought. A reporter was only as good as the phone numbers at her command. "Right. I'll let you know what happens after I speak with your father."

Liz sat for a moment and picked at her food, then put her plate down and, skirting the edge of the terrace, went around the side of the house and down the steps. Brad was nowhere in sight, which was just as well. She was about to take out her car keys when she saw that the gate to the stable was ajar and that the main barn was filled with people wandering around. She joined the crowd, stopping dutifully at each stall to examine the beautiful animals within and to read the placards identifying them.

Wouldn't It Be Loverly occupied a center stall. He turned out to be a shiny, handsome horse with a gleaming, coppery chestnut coat and bold, sassy patches of white along his flanks. He had white stockings on all but his right front leg, a star in the center of his forehead and a narrow stripe running down his nose. He was big and precocious and his eyes held a gentle sparkle that made Liz think he knew all about the risky business of horse racing. There was an admiring crowd in front of the stall.

"How much did he go for?" she asked the woman next to her.

"Thirteen million," the woman answered in an awed voice. "Won the Breeder's Cup, which is why so much was paid for him. His sire was Risky Business, out of Savannah,'' she added, referring to the colt's noble lineage.

Thirteen million, just like that. Celie's penchant for secrecy didn't work very well when it came to the public auctioning of horses. Everybody in town would know about it.

"Of course that's a bad-luck number," the woman added.

"Thirteen? He's going out to stud, isn't he? Sounds like the luckiest horse alive. Now who do you suppose bought him?"

"The Queen of England," someone close by said. "He won't go out to stud quite yet. They'll race him for a couple of years."

"For thirteen million? Why take chances?"

"Come *on*," someone else said. "Queen of England, my foot. I'll bet it's what's his name, you know, the one who owns all of Las Vegas. *He's* the one."

"He doesn't collect horses. It's some Arab oil minister."

"Come on, those oil ministers are all broke. You can't count on them anymore. The Japanese, the ones who buy oil paintings. *That's* who bought him."

"Syndicate. Half a dozen millionaires. They put in shares. It's big money buying horses and putting them out to stud."

Liz glanced at the horse again. He seemed no different from the others in the stable—shiny, huge and handsome. Well, horses were somebody else's turf, not hers. Only the name of the new owner was interesting and she'd find that out eventually. She turned and went on her way. Someone signed a check for thirteen million dollars for a shiny chestnut horse; another someone was fighting the establishment for trying to turn his front yard into a parking lot. She'd see Mr. Nelson, then call Marion, then interview Will Vanderheyden, then offer the story to Celie. *If* there was something to show, and *if* Celie said she could go ahead. Then if Marion showed her appreciation with a clue to the spender of thirteen million dollars, Liz would have something a little more interesting than a minor problem between a homeowner and the builder of a bar-restaurant.

Brad came over just as Liz was climbing into her secondhand Volvo. She reached for the seat belt, which was difficult to unwind and usually took her half an hour to wrap around her. "Hot on the trail of another story?" he asked, bending over and smiling at her through the window.

"You said it." She gave the belt another yank, and it moved out of its socket a quarter inch. "I thought you were going to help me write who bought what at the auction."

"I wouldn't even try to find out who purchased the colt. Nowadays people don't like to advertise their expensive peccadillos."

"What about Victor Bosworth?" Liz asked. "Everyone heard that the horse sold for thirteen million badluck dollars."

"The money will wind up in the Bosworth Foundation."

"Of course," she said with a smile. "To be contributed to Ramsey Falls' own Pack College, for the cause of education, for helping the young to stay away from the racetrack and improve their minds. He's a very generous man, Victor Bosworth."

"A quiet man, a bachelor, a man without issue. The foundation's his future."

"What he's in want of is a wife, as any man with a suitable fortune must be."

"Liz, don't waste your time trying to find out who bought Loverly."

She stared at him in amazement. "I have enough trouble with Celie telling me what I should or should not do. There's no law against my poking around for information. What's the big secret, anyway? There's no crime involved, is there?"

She threw the question out and was startled to find a look of anger blacken his face. "Liz, we value our privacy here in Ramsey Falls. We don't shout what we have or even what we don't have."

"Then what good is a newspaper?" She realized she had almost yelled the words, that her arms were rigid and that her hands were gripping the ends of the seat belt.

He shook his head and smiled. "Gossip. Small-town gossip. Clambakes and penny socials. You know that. Big ads from the local supermarket and who graduated from college and who joined the army. And who's engaged and when the next meeting of the Ramsey Falls Barbershop Quartet will be."

The seat belt gave and Liz managed to press it closed. She slipped her key into the ignition. "If you won't help me, I guess I'll just have to find out on my own."

"Good luck."

She shook her head. "You know where the article would end up if I found out who the horse's new owner was—in the wastebasket. You stick together, don't you, all of you Ramsey Falls movers and shakers?"

"We have to against the muckrakers. Speaking of which, how about dinner tonight?"

She laughed. "Dinner? I just ate."

"You can hang around and watch me eat."

"I'm sorry, Brad. I don't know when I'll be finished."

"Seven at Mrs. Duboise's."

"How do you know where I live?"

"You told me," he said.

"I didn't."

"Funny, I could've sworn you had. Incidentally, Victor gave me the list of horses sold and to which stables. With an exception, of course— Wouldn't It Be Loverly." He reached into his pocket, pulled out a slip of paper and handed it to her.

"Thanks." She tucked it into her windshield visor and switched the ignition on, then added, "You're full of surprises."

He looked quizzically at her and smiled. "Am I?"

"For a Ramsey Falls boy, yes."

"Seven?" He reached out and touched her hand briefly.

"Ever not have your own way, Brad?"

"Over the important things, never."

She turned the key and engaged the engine. "Well, we'll have to see about changing that, won't we?"

"You're in alien country, Liz. You're way out of your league. Seven?"

She laughed and gave in. "Seven."

LIZ SUCKED IN HER BREATH. She had no idea the view would be so dazzling. She stood on I-84, with the great silvery river snaking south below the mountains on either side like behemoths touching toes delicately in the water. To the north the river widened. She could see a bridge in the distance, and a barge made its way slowly upstream. In the late afternoon the mountains had changed from viridian to a Prussian blue that faded at the edges to a pale, smoky purple. The sky had a soft green cast where the mountains touched it, while overhead it was pale blue, like icy satin.

Across the road lay an oval pond that reflected the late-afternoon sky like a lady's dressing mirror, and beyond that stood an unoccupied turn-of-the-century clapboard house. The builders, she thought, must have once dreamed they'd come upon paradise.

And so apparently had Marion Nelson's father. The large white Dutch Colonial house with black shutters that she took to be his sat close to the road, as if to take maximum advantage of the view. Small evergreen shrubs skirted the building, and at each side Liz could see the fresh spring greening tops of oak and maple trees.

A small front garden was filled with multicolored tulips as bright as lollipops. Window boxes of ivy and early red geraniums were in front of each ground-floor window. It was a fat, comfortable house that showed the care and love of its owner. A bar-restaurant as its neighbor would ruin the setting and add to the traffic, with its attendant noise and pollution.

Right next door a surveyor's iron post was wrapped with a bright orange ribbon. There wouldn't be enough parking space, she saw, if the restaurant turned out to be a success. Cars would almost certainly park in front of the Nelson home, further irritating its owner. Progress, she thought. But some people might welcome commercial zoning and the added value to their property. It was time to meet Mr. Nelson and learn just how serious his gripe was.

There was a mailbox out front, homemade, in the same Dutch Colonial style as the house. She pushed the wooden gate open and walked along a small stone path.

Four stone steps led to a bright red front door with a highly polished brass knocker on it.

From inside the house she heard the strains of a Mozart concerto and breathed a little more easily. On the way over from Bosworth Stud, she'd had time to think about what Mr. Nelson would be like. Curmudgeon was possible. Or he could be a man with a grudge, a man who battled his neighbors for perceived hurts, real or otherwise, which could count for their hasty signing of Vanderheyden's petition. Mozart made her feel a little more optimistic that she might be dealing with someone quite sane.

Liz was used to knocking on strange doors. She was equally used to seeing people at desperate times in their lives, to steeling herself in order to handle her job correctly. Even with this simple errand, she felt her usual rush of anticipation. She lifted the knocker, but before releasing it the door opened.

"Marion said you'd come, but I doubt she expected you'd race right over." The man who stood there was white-haired with white furry eyebrows. He was as rotund as his daughter, and had her blue eyes, as well, and a very cheerful aspect. He was younger, she realized almost at once, than his white hair would indicate. "You're Liz Grady." His voice was deep, warm and pleasant.

"I am."

"Come on out back. I've got a carafe of chilled wine and some cheese and crackers. We can talk there." He led her through a foyer into an old-fashioned dining room with landscape paintings on the walls, then through a sunny kitchen and at last out back to a screened-in porch with a view of a wide lawn that dropped slowly away to a farm below.

"Your view out front is spectacular," Liz said, "but then so is this." She settled into the Adirondack chair he offered her.

"Both about to be spoiled by progress, I'm afraid. Traffic in the front and music and tables out back. I'll have diners as company whether I want them or not."

"Can't stop progress," Liz said.

He poured her a glass of wine. "The problem with progress is that you'd think it would be equal for everyone. *Prosit*." He raised his glass and saluted her.

She smiled, sipped the wine and nodded appreciatively. "Nice and dry."

"Local brew," he told her. "Have you done a story about the Ramsey Falls wine industry?"

Liz shook her head. "Wanted to but the editor—"

"Celie, you mean."

"Right. She said it was done to death last year during the famous bi-tri." Celie was stopping her at every juncture, she thought a little angrily, and wondered if her boss was up to something.

"You'll have to find a new angle."

"If you hear of one," Liz said. "I'd appreciate learning about it."

"What's happening right here ought to be good enough for Celie," he told her.

"Will Vanderheyden and his bar-restaurant, you mean?"

"About Vanderheydens thinking they own Ramsey Falls and every square inch of ground on it."

Liz put her glass down very carefully. "Don't you think you're exaggerating a bit, Mr. Nelson? I've been in town working for the newspaper for two months, and it's the first I've heard of it."

"Because I'm one of the rare ones not to knuckle under. Will wants the piece of land next to mine for commercial uses. He'll get it. Furthermore, he'll put up the building, go into business and then, if and when he's called on it, the authorities will cave in."

"What authorities are you talking about?"

"Judge Vanderheyden. We don't need more than that."

"There's a zoning board," she offered.

"There are also the moon and stars. Doesn't make them relevant to whether Vanderheydens want something or not."

"I understand you've hired a lawyer, Mr. Nelson. What does he suggest? I mean, lawyers don't take on cases just to lose them."

Mr. Nelson shrugged. "He says what I'm paying him to say. That we can fight the case and win. Trouble is, it's coming before Judge Vanderheyden in the first go-around."

"For certain? Isn't there something about conflict of interest?"

"He'll see to it, the judge will. If he doesn't hear the case, someone close to him will. If you check the histories of anyone on the bench in these parts, they all tangle up somewhere. They're related one way or another."

Liz was quiet because she could see the man's despair.

"Speaking of lawyers," Nelson went on, "since the judge's sister is married to his father, the hottest attorney in these parts is sure to represent Will Vanderheyden."

"And who," Liz asked, treading very carefully, and somehow knowing the answer before she even framed the question, "is the hottest attorney in these parts?"

Mr. Nelson screwed up his eyes and stared at her in amazement. "Two months in this town and you don't know?"

"It's time-consuming to learn who's who around here," Liz said. "I'm sorry. I didn't catch the lawyer's name."

He shook his head. "Bradford Kent, that's who."

CHAPTER THREE

LIZ HAD SUBLET her small Chicago apartment to a
friend, uncertain before she left for Ramsey Falls
whether or not to burn her bridges behind her. She came
east with a couple of suitcases and a trunk to follow.
Celie Decatur arranged for her to board with Mrs. Duboise who, according to her whim, occasionally rented
out rooms in her old Huguenot stone house just outside
of town.

The room Liz occupied had been recently remodeled
into an austere re-creation of the original bedroom occupied three hundred years before by the first Duboise
daughter to live in the house.

Small and low-ceilinged, its furniture authentic and
intimidating, the room forced Liz into a neatness that
was completely alien to her. Her usual style of living was
among piles of books, magazines opened to unfinished
articles and scraps of paper with notes on them that
seemed important at the time of writing. She usually had
her typewriter at the ready, with a sheet of paper in it,
and erasers, pencils and paper clips close at hand. She
liked an old sweater draped on a chair, and a silk scarf
over a lamp to cut down glare. At Mrs. Duboise's, however, the slightest misalignment seemed an affront.

Her window looked out on a re-creation of an English cottage garden, spurting with spring flowers. Off
to the side were the neat borders of an herb patch, send-

ing up fresh shoots, and next to it a newly planted kitchen garden.

At seven that evening Mrs. Duboise tapped lightly on her door. Her voice held a hushed, impressed tone. "Mr. Bradford Kent is here, Liz."

"Tell him I'll be right down, Mrs. Duboise." So he came after all, Liz thought with some surprise. After her interview with John Nelson, she had discovered a Brad Kent not revealed earlier that day. Old family, Vanderheydens, privilege. If she decided to take up the cudgels for Mr. Nelson, she might have to square off against Bradford Kent, as well. The idea was an intriguing one; she liked a battle, but she wasn't quite certain she wanted him as an adversary. In fact, she wasn't quite certain just how she wanted Mr. Bradford Kent, if at all.

That morning when she had awakened her first thought had been of California, of Doug and the letter she owed him—the one she'd been finding it increasingly difficult to compose. The time she'd been with him in California had been a little strained. It had smacked of indecision most of all. Doug had asked her to reconsider going to Ramsey Falls. He'd wanted her to stay with him a little longer, yet Liz had had the feeling his life was edging away from hers, that his request was mere formality. The trouble was she'd understood and hadn't cared enough to commit herself one way or the other. Yet, even if they were both leading other, more satisfactory lives, for the moment neither had the energy nor the will to end their relationship. Doug, in fact, had promised to come east in August. It was time and distance enough for Liz to learn whether she wanted to keep the relationship going or not.

And to get to know Brad better. Gazing at herself in the mirror, Liz realized that the odd excitement she felt knowing Brad Kent was waiting for her was unexpected and strange. She pulled a comb lazily through her hair, staring at her dark, faintly exotic image. She wasn't Ramsey Falls stock at all. Suddenly she wanted to be blond and blue-eyed. She wanted to ride horses and be very elegant in silk dresses, instead of tawny-skinned with eyes so dark that they matched her black unruly hair. And one eye slightly misaligned to boot. Which had he said? The right? The left?

"Lizzie, love, don't keep the man waiting," Mrs. Duboise said through the door. Her voice held a slightly quizzical tone, as though she couldn't understand her boarder's casual behavior, as though Liz should have come flying out of her room all aflutter.

Liz, who was far too cautious, wasn't about to fly anywhere for the moment. She and Doug had been slow about falling in love, slow about living together, and were now slow about deciding whether everything between them was over. In contrast, Brad's fast moves were disorienting. It was too soon to decide whether she was flattered or not, but she was decidedly interested.

"Would you like me to serve some tea?" Mrs. Duboise asked.

"Oh, you're so sweet but no thanks," Liz called back, putting the brush on the dresser top and aligning it carefully with the comb. "We're going out for dinner, Mrs. Duboise."

Liz sprayed herself with a touch of the only perfume she owned, and that a gift. She had decided to wear navy pants and a white blouse with a collarless navy jacket. At the last minute she grabbed a red, white and blue scarf, which she knotted hastily around her neck as she ran out of her room.

Mrs. Duboise stood on the second-floor landing and smiled approvingly at her. "You look very nice, my dear. You see ... when you dress up ... ?" She left the sentence unfinished, as though it were part of a conversation they had held before. She was a middle-aged woman with a warm, intelligent face. She continued to smile, and with what Liz took to be a subtle wink, added, "He's in the drawing room."

"Thank you, Mrs. Duboise."

When she reached the open drawing room door, she found Brad Kent at the window, his back to her. There was a little catch in her throat that prevented her from calling out to him. Perhaps it was the casual way he was dressed—in jeans and a corduroy jacket, as though he expected her to come down wearing her funny T-shirt. And Liz hadn't realized before how broad-shouldered he was, nor how lean and strong his torso was. His hair looked very dark in the fading light of the day; it was a little long, just brushing his shirt collar. His hands were stuffed into his pants pockets, and she heard the faint jingle of some coins. She stood for a long moment, gazing at him, not quite certain what to make of his being there or even of his interest in her. She knew only one thing certainly: she was glad he was there, no matter what the differences were between them.

Brad turned suddenly as though he'd known all along what she was thinking. "Decided to abandon Henry David, I see."

She creased her brow. "Henry David? Oh, right, my T-shirt. I think Ramsey Falls has seen the last of Mr. Thoreau." With an unexpected surge of happiness she couldn't explain, she said, "I take it back, incidentally—my saying I wouldn't be hungry. I'm famished.

That's the trouble with not having your own place. No refrigerator to raid."

"We'll have to see about getting you new digs. I don't think they ever rented Jemma Gardner's old apartment on Main."

"No, it's all right," Liz protested. "I sort of like the nomad life even with its drawbacks. I'm not ready for the amenities."

"Stay light, packed and ready to leave if the going gets rough?"

She gazed evenly at him. "Or if it doesn't get rough enough," she said.

"There's the stone house I'll be abandoning before summer's end. It'll need a new tenant."

Liz laughed. "I'm committed to Mrs. Duboise for the time being, Brad. I like it here, and anyway she feeds me all the time, even if it wasn't part of the original arrangement. Shall we go?"

"Hold still a minute." Brad reached for the scarf she had grabbed just before leaving her room and tied without checking the results. He undid and carefully reknotted it. "I'm an old sailor," he told her.

"You seem to have an odd predilection for dressing me," she remarked, and to his hastily raised eyebrows, added with a laugh, "I mean, insulting Henry David Thoreau and then rearranging my scarf to suit your taste."

He stepped back to admire his handiwork. "Liz Grady of the Chicago Gradys, I'm glad you made your way to Ramsey Falls."

"Oh," she said flippantly, if merely to hide the unexpected pleasure his remark had given her, "It was written in the stars."

"Makes a man a believer, doesn't it? In the stars, I mean." He took her arm and led her to the front door where Mrs. Duboise was hovering with a wistful smile on her face.

"Enjoy yourselves," she called as they headed down the stairs.

"And exactly where are we going?" Liz asked, once they were on the highway.

"You'll see."

After a while he took a turnoff. The road narrowed as it edged toward the river, becoming a dirt road that was smooth and well maintained. Trees and bushes on either side were wearing their shiny spring leaves, small and yellow-tinted in the dusk. Below, wild violets gave the underbrush a soft mauve shadow.

"Odd place for a restaurant," Liz murmured.

Another turn off the narrow road took them under a bower of low, overhanging branches and down a dirt path that was scarcely wide enough for his small sports car. The path ended abruptly at a wide clearing. Dead ahead, high above the Hudson River with a dramatic view that took in the green curve of mountains and steep cliffs that pawed the water, was a small, half-built, slickly modern house.

Brad turned to her, his hand still resting on the wheel. "Welcome to Kent Manor."

"Setting's gorgeous." She exhaled, then in a quick movement, opened the car door, stepped out and ran over to the house.

"Beautiful, day or night," he told her, following her up onto the terrace. "Rain or shine. It might make a poet out of me."

"The view from my window at Mrs. Duboise is of a pretty little garden out back bordered by trees. I like this.

I like a view, but all my life my views have been cramped by other buildings, by trees, even by mountains."

"You're welcome to admire my view anytime."

"Small, compact," she said, looking the exterior of the house over. "Obviously not out of a kit."

He smiled. "Ty would like that remark. He's been talking about designing a line of small, modern prefabs that don't look rubber-stamped."

"Who's Ty?"

"Tyler Lassiter, my architect. Married to my distant cousin, Sarah. Moved here from California, as a matter of fact. Great believer in inexpensive housing for the disadvantaged."

"You, however, aren't disadvantaged."

He laughed. "No, I'm afraid not."

"Tyler Lassiter," Liz said, remembering. "I've seen his picture. I've called him up a couple of times, too. He's working on that renovation of the Merriman waterfront. Celie seems to think a lot of him."

"So do I." Brad unlocked the front door and waved her in. "What you're going to see is merely the shell."

"When are you planning to move in?"

"Late summer, if everything goes as planned. Incidentally, my current abode," he told her, "is the old stone icehouse on my parents' property. So is this—on my parents' property, I mean."

"Icehouse," Liz mused. "Must be pretty cold."

"No, I manage to keep it warm one way or another."

"I'll bet."

"Watch your step," he said, going in ahead of her.

"Oh, I intend to, Brad, all the way."

The wooden floors hadn't been laid, so they had to walk along the cross beams. "The floors are going to be pine," he told her. "Random width, natural color. Approve?"

She laughed. "Does it matter?" Then, almost afraid of his answer, she added hastily, "Yes, I love the idea, although they'll be a devil to keep clean."

"We'll coat them with polyurethane. The fireplace," he added, pointing out the most obvious feature in the room, a huge fieldstone fireplace that took up all of one wall.

"Is that what it is? I was wondering."

"Scientifically devised so that half the heat doesn't escape out the chimney. This way to the sleeping quarters."

Liz carefully followed him to an open space marked off for the bedroom. The view out of glass doors was of the river. "Nice," she said with no idea of either the layout of the room or its actual size. "Is it big enough?"

"For what I have in mind."

"I asked for that."

"And now the kitchen. I'm warning you," he told her. "I like to fiddle around in the kitchen."

"Really? With the cook or with food?"

"Both, now that you mention it. I'm having some pretty mean equipment put in. Restaurant stuff. The faint of heart are asked to step back."

"I'm afraid you can count me out then. My mother's the cook, not I. Still can't make a proper spaghetti sauce, but then why bother when you can buy it in a jar?"

He shook his head. "Philistine, but then I believe in only one cook in a family."

His remark brought her up short. She stared at him, aware of the surprised look on her face. "What did you say?"

He gave her a crooked grin. "I believe the word I used was philistine. The floorboards are coming this week, ditto the wall panelling. Once they're installed, I expect you around for moral support."

"I don't know. I generally charge for moral support. Well," she said, giving the shell of the house a cursory glance. "It's a bachelor pad, all right. No room for expansion, is there?"

"Meaning?" His smile was quizzical.

"You know, taking up housekeeping with a significant other, like a wife or something. Followed by nurseries and plenty of those navy blue-eyed babies that should seed the next four hundred years."

"Ty Lassiter's a great believer in add-ons, like nurseries and such. The house is guaranteed to grow as I need it. Right now I want to shake myself free of gray stones and brooding windows and rooms that have no function except as dust collectors."

"But not of your ancestors."

He frowned a little. "I'm afraid I don't see the point of your remark."

"You said you want to shake yourself free of the ice-house and you said you've moved from one spot on your parents' property to another spot. Which means you're running fast and hard to stay in the same place."

He was quiet, the frown unerased, and Liz, suddenly aware of having said something he didn't want to hear, quickly added, "I'd love to see the grounds before it gets dark."

"Good idea. I'll catch up in a few minutes. I want to check over what damage my carpenter did today."

He was annoyed with her. She felt it. He didn't want an instant analysis by someone he scarcely knew, and he was right. Liz let herself out of the house, and after gazing around briefly, she wandered along a dirt path that led to a stone wall overlooking the river. A quick glance at the house found Brad at the window watching her, hands deep in his pockets. She waved. He smiled and turned away.

Still annoyed. Well, that was an end to it. They'd have dinner, say good-night and she'd get on with being Liz Grady, new girl in town. She trailed a finger along the stone wall, following the path to a copse of trees that could have been a natural barrier between neighboring estates.

She picked her way through the trees and discovered a clearing beyond. What she saw took her breath away. Around a steep ravine that divided the property and high above a wide, clear lawn overlooking the river, stood an enormous and forbidding stone manor house with a turreted roof.

She stared at it as if it were a ghostly apparition. Then she heard a rustling behind her.

"Kent Hall."

She turned and found Brad standing a few feet away. "Kent, as in Brad Kent?"

He nodded. "Brad Kent, as in senior. I'm Brad Kent, Jr. and I occupy the icehouse, remember? You can't see it from here."

"A brooding battlement," Liz said, aware of being acutely uncomfortable with the knowledge of Kent Hall, but she went doggedly on. "Have we stepped back into eighteenth-century England?"

"Be it ever so humble," Brad said, "that's been home to generations of Kents."

"It's a little scary."

"That's what my friends thought whenever I brought them here from school."

"I don't blame them one bit. Does it have a resident ghost?"

"The only sound is of people tiptoeing around each other."

Although they were a couple of hundred yards away, Liz could see a formal front garden and a wide driveway that circled up to the house. To live in such a place required more than the services of a weekly maid, she decided. It would need battalions of servants and gardeners.

"There's nothing at Kent Hall in the way of ghosts or a sorrowful history," Brad told her. "Only my parents, my sister, Fran, an old German shepherd named Lady and a frisky Pekingese."

Liz stared at the great gray pile. She thought of her rough-edged father and her laughing, down-to-earth mother and their small, crowded apartment on the seventh floor of a redbrick pile in South Chicago.

Brad came over to her and gripped her arms. "What are you thinking?"

"You wanted me to see it, didn't you? Kent Hall, I mean. You wanted me to trip lightly through the woods and come upon it in all its heavy glory."

"Yes," he said, as if the thought had surprised him with its clarity. "I suppose I did."

She stared across the ravine. A door opened and a figure stepped out—a woman.

"That's my sister," he told her. "Want to meet her?"

Liz shook her head nervously, suddenly intimidated. It was a new feeling. As a reporter she had learned a lot about aggression, a lot about suppressing her feelings. No, she didn't want to meet his sister, not quite yet, not until she thought more about Brad, about Kent Hall and about divisions in the way people lived.

"No," he said quietly, "I can see now isn't the time."

His sister saw him, waved, then went down the stairs to a small sports car and stepped inside.

"She doesn't bite, you know," he added. "In fact, I think you'd like her." The car moved slowly around the driveway.

"I know I would," she said, gazing at him.

For a moment she thought he was going to kiss her, but instead he turned her gently around. "Come along, Chicago, you look faint with hunger." He took her hand, and holding it tightly, brought her back to the car.

IN KEEPING WITH the general tone of signs in Ramsey Falls in its three hundredth year of incorporation, the sign that came up on the highway appeared weather-worn and old-fashioned. In reality it was brand-new and informed the traveler that Lotus Vineyards was a quarter mile down the secondary road and to the left. In smaller print it announced lunch, dinner and special parties. A bed of petunias and marigolds surrounded the sign.

"I'll be darned," Liz said as the car swerved left. "I've seen that thing a dozen times, but it never registered before. Lunch, dinner and special parties."

"And you the restaurant critic for the *Ramsey Falls Times Herald*," Brad chided.

"Give me a break. I just took the job, and the column is weekly."

"And the owner of Lotus is a friend of mine, Liz. This is strictly a social dinner. Notebooks and antennae left outside the front door."

"Oh, Scout's honor," she said with a laugh. "My palate isn't particularly discriminating, and I figure anyone who cooks for a living deserves four stars." Liz, who was an indifferent cook and an equally indifferent diner, hadn't been able to convince Celie that she was the wrong person for the job of restaurant critic. Once she accepted it, however, Liz went at the assignment in her usual way: she was thorough, evenhanded and didn't want to put anyone out of business.

Lotus Vineyards was set well back from the road, which wound through several hundred acres of vine plantings. The main house was a white Victorian clapboard and the owner a bearded ex-army colonel who had planted the vines a dozen years before upon retirement.

His latest addition was the restaurant housed in a new barn tastefully painted inside and out and decorated in the Victorian tradition. A noisy wedding party took up half the restaurant. The bride and groom sat demurely and bright-eyed at the head table as a toast was given by the best man, who held up a glass and stumbled through a prepared speech.

"Hey, Brad, welcome," Colonel Humphries said, greeting them and smiling appreciatively at Liz. "I was wondering what the devil happened to you."

"Been busy, Al. I'd like you to meet Liz Grady."

Liz shook his hand and remarked warmly how attractive the restaurant was.

"We're trying," he told her, beaming. Her name as the *Times Herald* restaurant critic obviously didn't ring a bell. Nevertheless, he brought them with great ceremony over to a seat near a window. "Wedding party," he said, nodding in the direction of the noise.

"Who's the lucky groom?" Brad asked.

"They're from downstate," Humphries told him. "Latest fad is being married in a vineyard. Never figured there was that much romance in the sight of grapevines, but I'm not objecting."

"What wines do you specialize in?" Liz asked with interest, wondering if she had her syntax correct.

Brad reached across the table and put his hand over hers as if to stop her from whipping out a pad and pencil. "Uh-uh, none of that."

"You're right," the colonel said. "Duty calls. I think it's about time to roll out the wedding cake."

A few minutes after he left a bottle of the vineyard's estate wine was brought to the table and poured—a dry white with the characteristic, faintly grapey taste of New York State wines.

Liz nodded her approval. "Umm, let's see, witty and eclectic, I'd say, with a distinct touch of class around the edges. Am I close?"

"As close as you are to the moon."

She looked out the window. "The moon hasn't even risen."

"Lazy lug."

"Are you a wine connoisseur, Brad?"

He held the glass up to the light, turned it in his hands and examined it. "What makes you ask?"

"Oh, you strike me as the kind of guy who'd know everything about his clients, including the kind of wines they make and whether they're good, bad or indifferent."

"You seem to think I'm the only lawyer in town."

"I seem to think you're the only lawyer who matters."

"Not true. Check the yellow pages. You'll find a couple of dozen names in Ramsey Falls and Merriman, all of them thriving."

"Thriving. Of course. The way lawyers do."

Brad didn't respond quickly. Instead he gazed at her for a long time, as though taking her measure. "What's got your dander up, Liz? Or is this a side of you I don't know?''

She laughed loudly, and when several people at nearby tables turned to look at her, she clapped her hand over her mouth for a moment. ''You don't know any side of me. We just met today, remember?''

He smiled. ''You're right. So we did. Odd, I had the feeling we've been together for a long, long time.''

''It's been a remarkably long day. In fact, it reminds me of college. I went to class, worked in a diner and then came home to study at some god-awful hour and got to sleep at three in the morning, only to wake up at seven and begin again.''

''That bad?''

''I had to,'' she told him. ''Keep my marks up, I mean. I was on a full scholarship. I never had time to turn around to see if anyone was gaining on me. I couldn't afford to.''

Liz remembered that on her first day of classes, her parents had kissed her and wished her good luck as though she were going away forever, but, of course, they'd see her at home that evening. There were no dorms, no gorgeous campuses set amid rolling country-side, no parties or sororities to join. It was all ambition and hard work. ''No it wasn't that bad,'' she mused.

''For a minute I thought I saw a mote of resentment in your eyes, as though maybe you thought the world owed you a living but you didn't have a shred of a chance collecting.''

His remark startled her. He was wrong of course. The lot had fallen to her the way it did, and after that expensive, hard-won education, she had landed in Ramsey Falls. Nothing to resent, nothing at all.

She looked around the room and let her gaze rest on the bride and groom. The cake had been rolled in, and they were posing in front of it, his hand over hers as they pretended to cut into it while the photographer snapped pictures. "I feel good being here," she said softly. "Thanks for asking me."

Brad followed her gaze. He, too, stared at the proceedings across the room, then turned back to her. "And when you graduated—with honors—you were tough Liz Grady ready to take on the establishment and everything about it."

She laughed. "You betcha. I'm out to right wrongs, and I won't worry about whose toes I step on."

"Ah, it's a bird. It's a plane. It's Superperson out to help the underdog against the big bad guys." He gave her a crooked grin.

"Okay, Brad, I get your message. I'm trying to stir the dust and all it does is settle in the same old place. Everybody's happy and nobody needs my help, not even the Scotties of this world."

"Reporting the weekly school menu, church dinners and penny socials won't win you the Pulitzer Prize, Liz, but then again neither will Scottie and his drinking problem. Maybe sulking in our neck of the woods is the wrong place to be."

She studied him and wondered if he was hinting that she should get out of town while she still had her big-city wits about her.

Liz thought of John Nelson and of the appointment she had made for the next morning with Will Vanderheyden. She might have given up all thoughts of writing the story of the year, but it wouldn't be for lack of trying.

"Liz."

The waiter stood at their table, menus in hand. "You order," she suggested.

"I just did."

"Thanks. I hate making decisions about what goes into my stomach."

"And I won't ask what's on your mind," he told her once the waiter was gone. "I'd just like to offer you a little sage advice. Ramsey Falls is a tight little community. You're an outsider. Come on big-city aggressive and you'll get nowhere. I wonder," he went on, "just what possessed Celie to reach so far to pluck out her ace reporter."

He left the thought unfinished. Liz wasn't even angry over his remark. Since she had come to Ramsey Falls, she had wondered the same. "I'm here," she told him. "Celie knew I was a relentless digger when she hired me. She hopes I'll slow down, hopes I'll take her advice, but I'm no child and I know the game."

"Tough as nails, are you?"

"Tough as nails."

"Odd," he told her with a smile. "I sense a heavy dose of vulnerability in your eyes. We may look like easy marks here, but believe me, our patterns of resistance were set down hundreds of years ago. And I'm afraid," he said, reaching for her hand, opening her palm and kissing it, "you'll find us as romantic as hell, because we've got the time and will to think about who we are and what we want."

She was saved the trouble of finding an answer to his remark by the arrival of their first course. She extricated her hand from his, still feeling the imprint of his kiss. No, she thought, maybe the denizens of Ramsey Falls had the time, but they also had a way of moving a little too quickly.

CHAPTER FOUR

AN ORIGINAL OIL PAINTING above the Sheraton side table, a respectable copy of a Remington bronze near the window and a perfectly groomed secretary oozing propriety—Will Vanderheyden's real estate office in the center of town impressed Liz and wasn't at all what she expected.

His secretary's starched smile reached across her desk. "Mr. Vanderheyden will see you in a few moments."

Liz went over to an upholstered chair, picking up a magazine along the way. She leafed through its pages, not really reading. Her mind was on Bradford Kent. As a matter of fact, it struck her that she had thought of little else since the day before. That, she decided, was a cause for concern.

He had, in effect, *rushed* her, and she had, half fascinated and half against her will, gone along. That he had power in the community, she had no doubt. That the particular world he lived in was insular, she also had no doubt. It was a world of privilege and possessions, of rolling green acres, stately mansions and colts that sold for thirteen million dollars. It was a world where outsiders couldn't get in.

Then why, she wondered, had he been so interested? She was, after all, an outsider—with no name, no family, no background, no money... and a chip on her shoulder the size of a thousand-year-old redwood.

"Mr. Vanderheyden will see you now, Miss Grady."

Liz was brought up short by the secretary's announcement. She quickly brushed her skirt down, straightened her blouse and followed the other woman down a short corridor to a huge mahogany door that slid effortlessly open to reveal a stark white office hung with a series of black-and-white photographs of the local landscape. What she couldn't square was the big-city opulence in a turn-of-the century building on Main Street, Ramsey Falls, with a projected bar-restaurant on I-84.

Will Vanderheyden stood behind a carved desk completely empty of papers. He was about forty, of medium height, broad-shouldered and obviously in good physical condition. There was no resemblance between him and his cousin Brad, except for an air of self-possession she was beginning to think of as ingested with mother's milk.

His hair was thinning on top, and his smile was broad, clearly intended to put Liz at her ease. Liz relied on her first impressions when sizing someone up. Her instincts were acute at that point, before other factors could influence her. But this time his smile worked, and so she reserved judgment.

"Good of you to see me," she said, taking the seat he offered.

"Well, I wanted to meet Celie's star reporter," he said in a jovial fashion. "You're the one who's going to help her take the *Times Herald* into the twenty-first century. It's about time she went daily. What with all the growth in these parts—"

"Some say too much," Liz said.

"You've been talking to the wrong people." He laughed, but deep behind his eyes she caught a wary note. The sense of ease sloughed off her, and she sat a little more erectly in her chair.

"What can I do for you?" he asked abruptly. "You wouldn't be looking to invest in a house yourself, would you?"

She gave him an astonished smile. "Me? A house?" The idea was an extraordinary one. Neither she nor her family had ever owned anything in their lives but their furniture and a succession of secondhand cars. "Good heavens, a house means *roots*."

"And what's wrong with roots? Best investment you could make would be a little house on an acre or so of land. I've got plenty of listings that would fit the bill."

Her father had always talked of retirement to a lake-side community where he could fish and watch the world go by. "Maybe so," she said slowly. "But I haven't come to talk to you about real estate. Or rather I have, but it's as a follow-up to a story I'm thinking of working on."

He looked interested. "Shoot."

"Well, it concerns the rezoning of a portion of I-84."

"Ah, that's it." He slapped the top of his desk. "John Nelson. He's at it again. He knows as well as I do—and you should learn the facts if you think there's a story in it—that variances are given all the time. Legitimately. By the local zoning board. It's called progress." He gave her a suddenly cautious look. "I saw Celie at the auction and she never mentioned doing a story, and that's because it's a nonissue."

"It's part of my job as a reporter, Mr. Vanderhey-den, to check out potential stories. A lot of what I do is footwork that never sees print."

"Then, for your information, John Nelson is a born troublemaker. He's a gadfly. If he could, he'd put up a barbed wire fence around Ramsey Falls and allow no-body in. But he's a newcomer himself."

"Newcomer. I heard he's been here for two de-cades."

"Newcomer," Vanderheyden said derisively. "Miss Grady, you're new yourself. You don't know the play-ers yet. On the other hand, our family has been here for centuries. We helped build the place from scratch. We've donated land for parks and we endowed the local col-lege. And along the way we've always met opposition from some character or other who thinks we're stepping on his tail."

Liz listened to his tirade with an expressionless face. When he finished, she said, "You're planning a bar-restaurant next to his house, although the area isn't zoned commercially. What makes it so valuable that you'd risk a court fight over it?"

"Court fight? There won't be any court fight. The zoning board will issue a variance and that will be that." He stood and put his hand out to Liz. "I don't think I'd waste any more time with this business if I were you. You want a story about growth in Ramsey Falls, you come to me. I'll talk to you about growth."

"Good day, Mr. Vanderheyden," Liz said, shaking his hand firmly. She went steadily to the door. As she strode past the secretary's desk, she heard the buzz of the in-tercom. Then she heard Vanderheyden's brusque voice. "Get me Celie Decatur."

LATER THAT AFTERNOON Liz's phone rang just when she was putting the finishing touches to her article about a new addition to the Merriman animal hospital.

"Liz, can I see you for a minute?" It was Celie. Liz had been waiting to be summoned into her boss's office. It didn't take too much intelligence to know what Will Vanderheyden's call meant. Liz had her response ready. In fact, she had been practicing it all morning and afternoon.

Celie didn't smile when Liz let herself into the office. "Shut the door, please, and sit down." She pushed her glasses on top of her head and waited silently while Liz drew a chair over.

"Don't say another word," Liz said, perching on the end of the chair, her back absolutely straight. "I know what it's about. It's about some guy trying to fight the establishment when he doesn't have a chance in hell of winning. Will Vanderheyden wants a bar-restaurant where he wants it and that's that, folks. Don't even try to fight the establishment if you know what's good for you."

Celie shook her head during Liz's recital. "Are you finished?" she asked when Liz paused for breath.

"For the moment."

"For your information, it's a nonevent. John Nelson feels wronged. He's hired a lawyer to express his ire. It'll go before the zoning board and a fair decision will be made, by the zoning board, not by you or me through the medium of the *Times Herald*. Nor will it be made by Will Vanderheyden. Nor, for that matter, by John Nelson."

"You're talking about a zoning board afraid of its own shadow."

She saw Celie color and knew she had hit a raw nerve. Her first impulse was to apologize, but she waited. There was more in the air than was being discussed.

"That's out of line, Liz. You haven't been around long enough to make such a callous remark."

"I wasn't being callous."

"I see. And you've got evidence to back you up?"

"So far the evidence of what I hear. It should be easy enough to check on."

"Go ahead," Celie said, not unkindly.

"Then, if I find the town council has issued biased judgments in favor of certain families, you'll give me the green light to follow up on the John Nelson claim?"

"Liz, I want you to rid yourself of any previous *bias* and approach this story objectively. I don't think I have to tell you it's the first dictum of good reporting."

"No, you don't, Celie. I merely want to get what you're telling me straight. I'm not being hauled off the story? I'm just being told to approach it objectively?"

"What I want you to learn is how we do things in Ramsey Falls. It's merely a dispute over a zoning ordinance and will turn out to be a very short, undoubtedly boring assignment."

Liz stood and grinned at her boss. She had won some sort of victory but didn't think it was time to get out the funny hats and party favors. She had a feeling she'd have to be subtle in her approach. She was certain Will Vanderheyden didn't appreciate being called on his actions. The thought came to her, although she quickly dispelled it, that if she looked under enough rocks, someone might get hurt, most likely the outsider from Chicago.

BRAD WAS IN his Merriman office when the call came in from Will Vanderheyden. He had just returned from court and was knee-deep in papers when Will's querulous voice grated in his ear.

"Where the hell have you been? I've been waiting all afternoon to hear from you. Didn't you get my message?"

Brad automatically put his signature to a letter held out to him by his secretary. "Messages," he corrected. "Got them along with a dozen others. What's up?" He didn't like Will much, even if they were cousins. In fact, Will had been the source of some of Brad's anguish as a kid. He'd been a practical joker and hadn't known when to let up.

"I hate like hell to have a mosquito buzzing around my head that I can't quite slap down," Will said.

Another letter was placed under Brad's nose. He read the contents cursorily, then scrawled his signature across the bottom. Whisked away by his efficient secretary, the pristine white sheet with its immaculate print was replaced by yet another. "Who's the mosquito?" he asked.

"Two of them, in fact. Flying in tandem. Of course I spoke with Celie and she promised to get her ace reporter Lois Lane off my back."

"Lois L— You're talking about Liz Grady, I take it. Mind starting at the beginning, Will?" He waved his secretary away, mouthing at her to give him five minutes.

A deep sigh traveled along the wire. "John Nelson seems to think he has a grievance over the zoning change on I-84. He's gone and hired himself a lawyer."

"That's the bar you're thinking of putting up there, next to his house, isn't it?"

"You know damn well what my plans are, Brad. Whose side are you on, anyway?"

"Will, I've got a lot of work ahead of me. Just tell me what you want me to do."

"And, damn it, it's not a bar. It's a restaurant, and we'll serve drinks like anybody else," Will corrected. "A *theme* restaurant, specializing in fish. There's a pond on the property—and the greatest view in the lower forty-eight. We're going to stock the pond, turn the place into a gourmet establishment and make something of Ramsey Falls yet."

"Congratulations. Zoning board give the okay?"

"You know it hasn't."

"Don't tell me you're sitting around, twiddling your thumbs and waiting for approval. That doesn't sound like your style, Willie."

"And don't call me Willie."

"I'm surprised the property hasn't been cleared and building started. Or has it? That what has Nelson exercised?"

"One thing about your sense of humor," Will growled. "I never laughed when you were a kid, and I don't find it funny now. I want you to see Nelson or his lawyer and convince them of the error of their ways. Let the zoning board do its business and let the business of Ramsey Falls be growth."

"Make that bit of poetry up yourself, Willie?"

"Will. The name is Will. Get back to me when you have something to tell me."

To Brad's relief the call was disconnected. Without stopping to think, he punched in the telephone number of the *Times Herald*. He didn't ask to speak to Liz, however. His call was to Celie.

"Looks as if we have a battle over zoning on I-84," he said at once.

"Battle?" Celie sounded nonplussed.

"I heard John Nelson has retained a lawyer." Brad didn't tell her he had already spoken with Will and that he knew Will had called her.

"Nelson's upset," she said in an offhand manner, "because he thinks Will's guests are going to park on his lawn."

"I know John Nelson," Brad remarked. "He's an evenhanded man. If he believes Will's guests will park on his front lawn, I'll take his word for it. And possibly pollute his well and make a general mess out of a beautiful area of town that should remain undisturbed."

"We're talking about two things," she told him in a careful voice. "We're talking about one of the oldest families in town. You know the Vanderheydens resist change and that they're very careful about what they do to disturb the equilibrium of things. We're talking about a gadfly who also doesn't want his life changed. And, incidentally, he doesn't own the terrific view."

"The most beautiful in the lower forty-eight," Brad remarked. "Did you pull your ace reporter off the story?"

There was a slight hesitation before Celie answered. "No, I didn't. I think the whole story's a nonevent. She'll yawn her way out of it. The request for a zoning change will go before the board, get a fair hearing and then they'll vote. If Nelson wants to fight the decision all the way to the Supreme Court, he's welcome to it."

"Does Liz know Will isn't an easy adversary?"

"Brad," she said impatiently, "that's a fool question. You're his lawyer. You'll handle his affairs whether you like him or not. I may not care about the man but his interests in progress coincide with mine and with a lot of other fair-minded people around here."

Brad nodded, although there was no one to see him. "Thanks, Celie" was all he could manage to say. When he hung up, however, he didn't summon his secretary. He swiveled his leather chair around and gazed out his office window. His view was only of the two-story building across the way and the lighted windows of an office opposite. An insurance agency, which was busy night and day, occupied the space. He had a nodding acquaintance with several of the people who had desks near the window and who were always on the phone. He stared at them for a while and then turned back to his own desk.

A nonevent, the change of zoning on I-84. It was long overdue. Progress was moving north. Home owners were itching to sell out and make a bundle. The town, which seemed mired in lassitude in spite of the hoopla of the bi-tricentennial, could use a continuous source of income. There were too many large landowners and too few jobs for the locals. He thought of Scottie, who raised Brittany spaniels but never made a go of it, and therefore spent a good portion of his time crying about his fate, drinking and taking potshots at whatever happened to wander into his view. Steady customers for his Brittany litters could give him the leg up he needed.

Progress had to come from within the town. If it didn't, it would come from without, and then the walls of Jericho would certainly come tumbling down. Restrained growth was needed, a plan that would keep the town moving forward at a reasonable pace. Who else had the town's welfare at heart, if not the Kents, the Vanderheydens and the Bosworths—the old families who had contributed to its growth?

Liz Grady could do all the research she wanted. With the establishment of I-84 for commercial zoning, John Nelson wouldn't come away a poor man.

There was a light knock at his office door.

"Yes?"

The door opened and his secretary peered in. She was carrying a folder of letters to be signed. He still had a little thinking to do. "Give me another five minutes," he told her.

When the door closed behind her, he leaned back in his chair, hands locked behind his head. Liz Grady. He smiled, remembering their first meeting. He'd been deep in conversation with Victor Bosworth when he'd first seen her at the auction. She was a thin, lithe figure in T-shirt and jeans, walking alongside Celie Decatur, who had been dressed in her usual, expensive, absolutely correct chief-executive manner.

Her hands stuffed into her pockets, a big leather handbag slung on her shoulder, her gait firm and faintly pigeon-toed, he'd sensed almost at once the way she was in touch with her sensuality. And at the same time her insouciance was charming. Her smile was playful and a little intimate. Her large dark eyes were at once penetrating yet exotic and dreamy. And then he had found Thoreau's beard resting between her breasts.

She had laughed uproariously at his remark, "Does it tickle?" Her voice was throaty, a little rough. In the elegant, studied atmosphere of the horse auction, with its Thoroughbreds, human and otherwise, Liz Grady was the cocky little winner of unfathomable value. Was it possible he had fallen for her then and there, knowing nothing about her except that he liked her lines? Or was it something else, something in the soft spring air he couldn't quite identify that threatened to turn his life and his world upside down?

He didn't know, and he thought, reaching for the telephone receiver, that he'd be a fool if he didn't find out. Then, just as quickly, he put the receiver back in place. He'd wait. Let a couple of days go by. Find out if the fever lasted. Then he'd call her and ask to see her. Ramsey Falls was a small town. There was no use rushing things; it would only get local tongues wagging, and they'd wag soon enough.

"THIS ISN'T the same car as the one you used the day of the auction."

"Isn't it?" Brad mused absentmindedly as he opened the door of the steel-gray Porsche for Liz.

She settled in, pulling the seat belt tight, marveling at the same time how nice it must be not to remember which car one used on what occasion.

"Been to Ramsey Falls yet? I mean, the falls themselves," he said.

Liz shook her head. "I've been meaning to. I even started out once but got sidetracked. Celie made it perfectly clear that one more word about the falls in her paper and circulation would drop away to nothing."

Brad laughed. "True, the place has been done to death in all the brouhaha surrounding the bi-tri. However, I don't recall talk ever ruining something that's perfect."

"Part of your childhood, the falls?"

He started the car engine, then slowly eased into traffic. "They're part of everyone who came from around here."

"Sounds pretty romantic."

"You're right," he told her. "We're unashamedly romantic about the place."

There was a turnoff from the highway toward the river about a mile outside of Ramsey Falls. It led to a well-kept two-lane road that took them down a quarter mile or so to a tertiary road.

"The nice thing about the falls," Brad commented, "is that they've avoided becoming a tourist attraction."

"So far."

"So far. There have been occasional feints at development, but the powers that be have decided to keep the view hidden and intact."

"The powers that be, meaning the mayor and the planning board?"

He turned to her, and after gazing at her with a curious smile, as though trying to ascertain just how innocent she was, said, "Yes, of course, the mayor and the planning board."

"Oh," Liz groaned. "Of course, the powers that be, the Decaturs, the Vanderheydens, the Bosworths. And, I suppose," she added after a moment's hesitation, "the Kents."

He slowed the car to a crawl and took the first right, which led to a one-lane road that snaked through a natural forest of deciduous trees just beginning to display tiny leaves.

"Have you heard the legend of the falls?"

"I'm afraid so. And I've seen postcards, posters, paintings, children's books and reviews in the theater column about pageants."

"We're coming up to Painted Creek," he explained, "where the fateful events took place." He eased the car around a curve, pulled into a copse and cut the engine. When they stepped out of the car, Brad pointed to a narrow gorge spanned by an old wooden bridge. "There you have it."

"I'm impressed," Liz said. Below, a rushing stream had carved out a narrow niche in the gorge. Frail vines clung to the lichen-covered rocky walls of the gorge, while the ground was purple with wild violets.

"Pull in a deep breath," he told her. "It's like no other air in the world, and we sell it by the gram."

"Mmm," Liz said, obeying him. The fragrance was of fresh spring growth, and the underlying scent of decaying tree bark and a carpet of leaves that had been under snow for months. "I'd like a gallon to go."

"You can hear the falls from here," Brad said, taking her hand and leading her across the bridge.

She heard what seemed like distant, endless thunder, a roaring that drowned out all other sound and closed them off from the rest of the world.

He didn't say any more until they stepped off the bridge and rounded the cliff. And even then he didn't speak but led her to an overhang from which they could view the dramatic single tongue of water that spilled down the side of the cliff to the stream far below. There was an iron railing against which they could press for a good view of the falls. The faint mist thrown off was cool against their cheeks.

The rays of the sun cut sharp geometric designs across the treetops. Liz sensed Brad was sharing something with her that was significant to him. It wasn't a prize possession paid for with hard cash but clearly an enduring part of his past that he wanted her to know.

"Some say the spirits of the Indian maid and her warrior still haunt the falls. You'll have to be careful not to incur their wrath."

"Amazing," Liz said, looking around. "No graffiti."

He laughed. "Bite your tongue. If anyone tried it, I guarantee you I'd form a vigilante committee of one and track the miscreant down." He took her hand once again and led her from the outcrop and down a path through the trees to a small mossy spot surrounded by pine-scented deer fern and blueberry bushes. The sound of the falls was muted and pleasant.

"You know all the secret places, I suppose," Liz said as Brad spread the blanket out.

"I'd hate to tell you all my tales of derring-do. I once tried to scale the wall behind the falls, but all I got for it was a scraped shin and a good dousing. Didn't tell my mother about it of course. As a matter of fact, this was the only place I could run to when I wanted to escape my parents' notice."

"In Chicago when a kid runs away from home it's usually to the rails."

"Run away from home often?"

She shook her head. "Saw no reason to. Nor did my brother, for that matter. If we had something on our minds, it never rested there for very long. We all have short fuses. We go bang and then subside. I mean, it's either that or riding the rails. We don't have the luxury of falls around the corner, not even the privacy of great estates or baronial mansions with a hundred rooms. It was ease up or go sulk in your room."

"You're a show-off," Brad told her good-naturedly. "You don't miss an opportunity to let it be known you're not one of the landed gentry. You're from good old working class stock and you're not about to let anyone forget it."

Liz gave him an abashed grin. He was right of course. Only it wasn't showing off; it was a kind of self-consciousness that made her defensive about her origins. She had felt a little out of it at school. She had kept quiet about discussions of clothes or vacations or families. Experience had taught her, however, that what she had, the love of and for her family, were riches without end. And yet in this atmosphere, this world of privilege and history and everything in its place, she felt, once again, defensive.

"Maybe I am a snob," she admitted. "I was brought up to care about other people. I was taught that it's important to contribute to society, that it's important to be a voice against the abuses of power." She stopped, knowing how arrogant she must sound.

Brad reached over and took her hand, which she had been waving about to make her point. "Hey, I believe you. I'd want you to take up the tomahawk on my behalf any day. You've got an awful lot of passion tucked away in that beautiful frame of yours, and I'd like to see it put to some other use some day. For instance." He stopped, and as he had before, lifted her chin with his finger. "Never mind the for instance." In a movement that was at once surprising and graceful, he bent over Liz and touched her mouth with his. It was a quick, soft meeting of lips, yet in spite of his light touch she felt the unexpected raw power behind the sensation.

A small clue at the back of her mind told her that with Brad Kent she could let all barriers down, and the notion frightened her. She pulled back, knowing she had to get away from his touch.

Brad still held her, and for a long moment he gazed deep into her eyes. "The left one," he said at last. "No, maybe the right."

"Oh, that again," she said, laughing in spite of herself. He had quickly, efficiently, defused the situation. She longed to put her hand to her mouth, to touch the imprint of his kiss.

"Come on," he said briskly, getting up and pulling her to her feet. "I think we've had enough of Ramsey Falls for the day. All this peace and beauty is getting to me. I could continue to kiss you till the cows come home, and they're not due for a couple of hours. We're better off in public where I'm obliged to behave myself." He picked up one end of the blanket and handed it to her.

"Obliged to behave yourself?" she asked, stepping back a pace with her end of the blanket. "You and I could be at the deepest, darkest part of a cave and I'd oblige you to behave yourself."

He came toward her, folding the blanket with each step. "Fellow in California follows you everywhere, does he?" he asked, grinning. "Even into dark caves."

"We're not talking about friends in California. We're talking about the behavior between two comparative strangers."

"It's all up to you, Liz, just how comparative we're going to be. It's Saturday," he told her, heading back in the direction of the car, "and I know it's your day off and mine, as well, but if you wouldn't mind driving with me into Merriman, I promised to drop in on a client of mine. Take just a minute. We can go on from there."

Liz consulted her watch. "As a matter of fact, I haven't taken the day off, either. I'm following up on that business of the rezoning of part of I-84. There's somebody I could see right about now. Mrs. Randall."

They were walking single file across Outcrop Rock, Brad behind her. He took her arm and pulled her around. "Are you talking about the business with John Nelson? I thought you were backing off on that."

"Wait a minute. Wait a minute!" Liz said, snapping her arm away. "What's it to you whether I follow up on a story or not?"

"Liz," he said patiently, "Willie Vanderheyden was on the phone to Celie two minutes after you left him. He followed up with a telephone call to me. If Celie's given you the go-ahead to work on the story, it's only because she believes you'll drop the whole thing sooner or later. I just thought that maybe you'd seen the light by now.''

She stared at him, openmouthed. "Celie's right in one respect only. It isn't a story yet, but I'm very interested in what's going on around here. Can't I make the simplest inquiry without half the world nosing in?''

"We believe you're wasting your time, that's all.''

"We? I thought I worked for Celie Decatur." She threw the words out with as much disdain as she could muster, then made her way over to the wooden bridge, which she crossed quickly, aware of the clatter of her footsteps.

She was back at the car, tapping her foot impatiently, when Brad came ambling along, looking as if he had all day.

"Don't get involved, Liz.'' He opened the trunk and threw the blanket in. "There are plenty of good stories around town begging to be covered.''

"Begging? The only story I remember begging is the local rock band that thinks it's been shortchanged, 'publicity-wise.' John Nelson has a right to fight the zoning change.''

"All he has to do is go to court, and if the variance goes through, file a request for a review.''

"He will, no doubt. Meanwhile, without even zoning board approval, trees have been taken down and the ground carefully staked. You know, like the front entrance here, the back entrance there. Yesterday a front-end loader was moved in, and they started digging what curiously seems to resemble a cellar. Very odd happenings for a piece of property that could conceivably not be rezoned.''

"Passionate stuff, Liz.'' He opened the car door and held it for her. She hesitated a moment before climbing in. She felt a stiff fight coming on, as suddenly as the kiss had, but it was a long walk back to town.

When he was seated beside her, he said in a deadly serious voice, "If the zoning board thinks the restaurant is a good idea—"

"Bar," she threw in.

"Then they won't be intimidated by an article in the *Times Herald*."

"I don't mean to intimidate anyone, Brad. I leave that to the Vanderheydens. I just want to report the facts, sir, the facts. We on the *Times Herald* don't intimidate. I mean, how can you intimidate the Ladies Auxiliary of the Fire Department for holding a bake sale? I mean how can you intimidate the spring sale at the local supermarket? Intimidate the local minister who wants to change the church supper from Thursday to the weekends during the summer? I mean, we're talking tough issues here. The *Times Herald* raises its voice, innocent citizens cower. Celie wants the newspaper to go daily. With what? Intimidation? No—" she was aware of her voice rising, losing its customary low, faintly rough edge "—with stories that are never run."

He reached over and straightened her collar, which she knew didn't need straightening. "Liz, calm down."

"I don't think the zoning board decides anything on its own. I believe the Vanderheydens are calling the tune," she said.

"That's a rather strong denunciation of the zoning board, coming as it does from someone who hasn't been here very long."

"I've been told by Will, by Celie and now by you to forget the story, that it's a nonevent. What do you think that suggests?"

"Corruption of the very highest order," Brad said with a laugh. "We're all in it together, and you're the crusading reporter who came into town to get the bad guys."

"The reason you don't take it seriously," Liz said, "is because you think it's your God-given right to dictate to the rest of us."

"You're overreacting," he told her in a soft voice.

"No, I'm not." Her voice was equally soft. "I'm going to find out what the law is, how the board has acted in the past, and whose interests were best served in each and every case. The operating words are *conflict of interest*. It's just your basic sort of investigative journalism."

"Noble causes are very romantic," Brad said, "if unrealistic and off-the-wall."

"Off-the-wall? Because you're related to Will?" She stopped, aware of her gaffe.

He gave her a crooked smile. "No fault of mine, Liz. Blame my mother, who's the Judge's sister."

"And Will is your noble cause, I suppose?"

"No," he said, shaking his head. He turned the key in the ignition. It was only when they were easing out of the copse onto the one-lane dirt road that he spoke again. "Will isn't my noble cause, but he's a client and he's tenacious. Tell Nelson to save his money. He can use it to build a fence around his property."

"That's a very callous remark," she said.

"Callous or kindly?"

"Doesn't it strike you that just because Will Vanderheyden wants something, that doesn't mean it should be his by rights? That kind of behavior is insidious. And corrupting. It corrodes people's respect for the law, for the idea of equal treatment. This isn't a rural democracy," she added angrily. "It's an autocracy."

"Pretty speech," Brad said in a tight voice. "Op-ed page stuff. The reality is a little different. Will Vanderheyden wants to build a restaurant on a bit of land he owns on I-84. Most of the highway is already commercially zoned. This is a small pocket, albeit with an especially stunning view of the river, but a small pocket nonetheless. If the restaurant goes up, it'll bring business and money into town, and it won't hurt John Nelson one bit when he puts his house on the market. He'll be able to retire to a sunnier clime with the proceeds."

"Perhaps he doesn't want to retire to a sunnier clime," Liz said, not trying to hide the sarcasm in her voice. "And, besides, that's not the point. Will Vanderheyden handed around a petition to Nelson's neighbors. Whether by intimidation or the universal knowledge that his father, the judge, handles traffic tickets, among other things, Will got them all to sign that it's all right with them. *They* don't mind a bar-restaurant in their backyards. Brad, you know as well as I that they have a right to not sign a petition if they don't want to, without fear of the consequences."

"Are you trying to stir up trouble? We usually settle our problems in a court of law. Judge Vanderheyden is evenhanded, and he'd distance himself from anything to do with his son."

Liz caught the angry flash in his eyes and had to restrain herself from biting her lip. She had done it again. She never knew when to keep her mouth shut and play the game by someone else's rules. No wonder she hadn't been able to make it up the corporate ladder. If she had stayed quiet in Chicago, she'd probably be managing editor by now. And if Brad wanted her fired, all he had to do was raise an eyebrow and Celie would undoubtedly send her packing.

Then his look softened and she thought she even saw a slight smile, signaling his irritation was short-lived.

"Can't talk you out of it," he said at last. "In that case, I trust you'll approach the story with an open mind and see that everyone involved has equal time."

"Yes." She was aware of the chastened sound in her voice. She'd have to learn to control her harping, self-righteous air that was apparently so off-putting. And yet she couldn't resist adding, "It's the way I always work. The only way."

"The only way? You might find yourself pretty alone in Ramsey Falls."

She felt a disappointment in him that was so thorough that her heart was heavy with it. "Exactly what are you trying to tell me, Brad?" She was aware of the truculence in her voice, the anger she couldn't have hidden if she'd wanted to. "Is that why you asked me out today, to warn me not to rock the Ramsey Falls boat?"

"Liz, if you weren't so damn—" He stopped, turned the car sharply to the left with a squeal of brakes and took the secondary road above the speed limit.

If I weren't so damn what? she wondered. There were a half-dozen answers to that question.

CHAPTER FIVE

IT WAS A NEAT little room, lovingly furnished with old maple pieces. Family portraits smiled out from the fireplace mantel, and on the tea table fresh spring flowers sprouted from an agate-blue vase. Through the lace curtains at the window, Liz could see John Nelson's house, beyond which was the disputed plot of land.

"Marion Nelson told me you were coming, but I still don't want to say anything." The speaker, Mrs. Randall, pursed her lips, her eyes wide and distrustful behind thick-lensed glasses.

"But I won't use your name," Liz said. She closed her pad and slipped it back into her bag. "If you'll just talk to me off the record, Mrs. Randall, I'd really appreciate it. It's still possible to stop Will Vanderheyden, you know."

"You can't do anything about the Vanderheydens, Miss Grady. They'll look you right in the eye and smile and agree to everything you want and then..." Mrs. Randall shrugged, as if her sentence needed no finishing.

"I'm not sure what you mean."

Mrs. Randall, who was perched on the edge of her rocker, leaned forward. "My grandson just got his driver's license. This was one, two months ago. He's a good kid, works hard, attends school, minds his own business. Anyway, there's this spot just out of town. You know where Main Street trickles down to gas stations and what not, just before the shopping center? There's this big kiosk that cuts off a really clear view of the road. My grandson was leaving the gas station, there was a truck behind him and the kiosk, both blocking his view.''

"I remember that accident," Liz put in. "It happened just when I came to Ramsey Falls. I covered it for the *Times Herald*."

"Well, his mother was frantic. She called up Judge Vanderheyden and complained about the poor visibility at that spot. He said not to worry. He knows Bobbie's a good kid."

"The case is coming up, right?" Liz asked.

"I've signed the petition already, Miss Grady. Anyway, that has nothing to do with the judge and my grandson. They live over the other side of town. You can't take your signature back, even if you wanted to."

"Did you sign the petition before or after the accident?"

"Oh, before," Mrs. Randall said hastily as though the question were an insult. "Of course you can't fight the Vanderheydens. I mean, you wouldn't even bother trying. They own practically everything around here."

"Still, your grandson's case hasn't come up before the judge."

"No," the woman admitted reluctantly.

"They don't own you," Liz said.

"Oh, well, listen, I make up my own mind. I really do. It's just that they have the lawyers. You know, in the family and all that. Doesn't cost them a red cent, and they can carry everything right up to the Supreme Court. They'd win no matter what. And then, if you get into trouble like Bobbie—well, it wasn't his fault—but if someone goes against them, they always manage to show their displeasure.''

''It just takes a few brave souls to fight them.''

Mrs. Randall looked at her blankly, as though unable to grasp what she had said.

''Okay,'' Liz said, ''don't tell me anything. Just nod your head if you agree with my next question.''

Mrs. Randall, still perched at the edge of her rocker with her back absolutely straight, watched Liz without blinking.

''Do you want the bar-restaurant built next to the Nelson house?''

When the woman didn't move, Liz got to her feet. ''Thank you very much, Mrs. Randall. I really appreciate your giving me so much time.''

The woman accompanied her to the door. Liz left, discouraged, but exercised at the same time. Mrs. Randall had been the last one to sign Vanderheyden's petition. Liz had had no success with any of Nelson's neighbors. She was certain none of them wanted the restaurant, but also knew they wouldn't lift a finger to stop construction. They treated Liz like the stranger she was—powerless to act but someone who could possibly make things worse with her interference.

''Celie Decatur's a lovely woman,'' one man had said, ''but she's one of them. You don't think she'd side with us against them, do you?''

''Celie's fair,'' Liz had insisted. ''She doesn't buckle under pressure.''

''That's just the problem. They think anything they do is fair.''

Heading for her car now, Liz wondered. She stopped and mentally measured the distance between the proposed restaurant and the Nelson house. Close, but

maybe a line of bushes could hide the restaurant sufficiently. Maybe diners deserved a beautiful spot in which
they could partake of refreshments and admire the river
view just as John Nelson could. After all, he didn't own
the view. She climbed into her car and closed the door
but still didn't leave.

Maybe no one owned the view or access to it, but that
didn't alter what appeared to be the facts. The zoning
board hadn't yet made a decision in Will's favor, but
work on the site had already begun as though the decision were a fait accompli. And *that* was wrong, whether
Nelson had a case or not. She was more determined than
ever to stick with the story. On a smaller scale this was
exactly the kind of story she had worked on in Chicago.
Only this time she was no green cub waiting to be pushed
aside. This time she would play it to the end, even if she
had to take on Brad Kent and the entire Ramsey Falls
establishment. Even if a tiny glitch in her heart told her
that with Brad she might be letting something wonderful slip through her fingers.

She checked her watch. It was nearly five o'clock.
Celie would probably still be at her desk, even on Saturday. Liz sighed. Saturday night was looming. She had
nothing to do and nobody to do it with. She had let Brad
go to Merriman, claiming the useless Randall interview
as an excuse to break up the party. A schism had opened
up between them at the falls. She didn't trust his motive
for wanting to see her, and though he had tried afterward to make light of their argument, she wasn't buying.

She hadn't forgotten his kiss or her unexpected reaction to it. It had been a kiss as sweet and chaste as any
she'd ever received, and she had liked the touch of his
lips against hers entirely too much. She had quickly put

the brakes on. Liz had a guy in California; she wasn't looking for trouble in New York State.

She put her key in the ignition and switched on the engine. Maybe Brad was all technique and very little substance. But she doubted it. *The trouble, girl,* she told herself, *is that you've had one lover all these years and you're still entirely too innocent in the ways of a man with a maid.*

Liz eased her car onto the highway. It was only then that she noted the gray Mercedes stationed well back off the road. She glimpsed the face of the man sitting behind the wheel before he ducked low. Will Vanderheyden. A chill slid down her spine that had nothing to do with fear of the man himself but with his silent presence at the site. Sitting, waiting, spying. The question was why.

She drove ten miles over the speed limit as she headed back to town and the offices of the *Times Herald*.

"Mountain out of a molehill," Celie told her twenty minutes later. "It isn't front-page stuff, Liz. And sit down," she added, gesturing to an office chair. "You're making me nervous. I keep thinking you're going to go chasing after a story about escaped prisoners or bombings when nothing of the sort could ever happen here."

Liz reluctantly took a seat across the desk from Celie. "Celie, I'm not so sure this is the peaceable kingdom you think it is. This week I interviewed all of Nelson's neighbors, finishing up with Mrs. Randall this afternoon. They signed Will's petition for a variance, but they did it in order not to rock the boat."

"Great headline," Celie said. "People Afraid to Rock Boat. You can't write a story on guesswork. They signed, and unless they want to be quoted as having been coerced, there's no story. Period. You ought to know that."

"Oh, it's coercion of the most insidious kind. I think they call it fear of consequences." When Celie frowned, Liz added, "I'm going to stay on the story. Will has already broken ground for the restaurant, but the zoning board won't make its decision for another month. Can I write a notice to that effect?"

For a moment Celie said nothing. Liz caught a gleam of interest in her eye, but it soon faded. Celie shook her head. "It's his land. He's clearing it."

"Maybe we should do an ecological article, then. He took down some mighty oaks and at least one sugar maple over a hundred years old and a walnut tree that was absolutely massive and perfectly healthy."

"His trees," Celie said.

"Well, there ought to be a law. Probably is," Liz said, knowing her argument was going nowhere.

"Liz, don't let your zeal get out of hand. It's a zoning dispute. We have them all the time, which is why we have a zoning board. It'll be handled the way these things always are."

"That's what I'm afraid of," Liz said in a muted voice.

They stared at each other, and then Celie leaned back in her chair. A slight smile lightened her expression. "I've got the feeling that if I tell you to throw in the towel, I'll never hear the end of it from you."

"I'll be fair and impartial and I'll keep you up-to-date," Liz told her earnestly.

"You'll have to fit it in with your other duties."

"Right—restaurant reviews, high school basketball scenes, et cetera, et cetera. You've heard about the brouhaha at last night's bingo game at the firehouse, haven't you? Don't answer that one. It seems Mr. Hart-grave's hearing aid wasn't working and he missed his number being called. His neighbor won the pot. The fight of the century ensued between two octogenarians using canes and fists. They finally wound up sharing twenty-four dollars and seventy-five cents.''

"Liz, you asked for this job, didn't you?"

"Yes," Liz said after a while. "I asked for it, but when I order a salad in a restaurant I always add a little extra salt for zest.''"

"The zoning story doesn't get reported until you come up with something concrete."

"When Will Vanderheyden digs the cellar, that'll be concrete," Liz said with a smile. The smile, however, didn't last long. She remembered the Mercedes out at the site and Will behind the wheel, watching her.

She left Celie's office and took a deep breath. On Monday she'd track down local zoning board decisions for the past two years. She had a lot of work ahead of her, and was on her way to her desk to check her telephone messages when she caught sight of Adriana Scott standing at the window, looking out over Main Street.

Apart from Celie's private office and the conference room, most of the newspaper's business took place in a large, square space on the second floor of the Decatur Building. The advertising department, which was now empty, took up the north window space, each salesperson with a small glass cubicle that allowed for privacy when making a sales pitch. The editorial department, consisting of a dozen usually unoccupied desks reserved for free-lancers and stringers, took up the central portion of the room. Liz had a small glass cubicle to herself, her perk for being the only full-time reporter on staff.

Celie was both publisher and editor of the *Times Herald*. With plans for the paper to go daily, she talked about hiring an editor. Liz sometimes thought she might like the job, but she had no doubt Celie wouldn't give up the reins of control easily. Except for Adriana Scott, who came by daily after class, the editorial department had a forlorn air, as if the big story had happened a century before or might happen sometime in the distant future.

Adriana Scott was a journalism sophomore at Pack College. She worked part-time at the paper, reporting college news, and recently Celie had asked her to write a column on subjects of interest to the paper's younger readers.

She was a beautiful, affectionate twenty-year-old with dark red hair, frank brown eyes and a sprinkling of freckles across her nose. Liz and Adriana seldom met, but their relationship as the only steady members of the editorial department was friendly and open. Adriana was invariably bent over her typewriter or had the telephone to her ear or was rushing in or out on her way to or from class. To see her standing at the window on Saturday, shoulders hunched, struck Liz as odd. She went over to Adriana and touched her on the shoulder.

"Hi," she said cheerfully. "I almost didn't recognize you. I don't think I've ever seen you standing still—" She stopped when Adriana turned toward her with a tear-stained face.

"Oh, hi, Liz. I didn't hear you come in."

"What's wrong? Can I help?"

Adriana shook her head and sniffed. Liz frowned and reached into her jacket pocket for a tissue. "Here, I think you could use this."

Adriana nodded and dabbed at her eyes and nose. Liz automatically put her arm around the young woman's shoulder. "Come on. Let's sit down in my office and talk about whatever's bothering you. Boyfriend troubles?"

"No, Reg isn't around right now," Adriana said, sitting in the chair opposite Liz's desk. "Otherwise I'd be crying on his shoulder." She was referring to her boyfriend, Reg Casedonte, who also attended Pack College but worked in Merriman.

For the first time, Liz saw that Adriana was clutching a typewritten sheet. "It's this," she said, pushing it across the desk to Liz.

Liz glanced at the page then realized it was the list of offenders taken that week from the police blotter. She looked down the list, not quite certain what she was expected to find. Then, when she hit the name Robert M. Scott, she understood. Scottie. Drunk and disorderly. She looked over at Adriana to find her waiting expectantly, as though Liz would express her disapproval in no uncertain terms.

"It's awful," Adriana said, dabbing away at a fresh infusion of tears. "Reg said to forget about it, that I'm stuck with my parents. But he can afford to talk. His parents are neat. His father w-w-works. Mine d-d-doesn't."

"Adriana." Liz sprang out of her seat and went over to comfort the young woman. "Look, we'll leave it out of the story. Nobody need ever know. Celie would be the first to agree." Liz remembered how Celie didn't want her to follow up on Scottie's arrest. Now she silently thanked her boss for her concern.

"I mean, it doesn't happen all the time. Just when he's sort of disappointed. About the dogs, this time. He had to sell off the last one on account of taxes."

"The dogs?" Liz looked at her questioningly.

"He raises Brittany spaniels. But they're pretty expensive. He c-c-can't even afford to replenish the stock. Then he goes off on a toot and shoots up the neighborhood and it's in the papers and everybody in school knows about it. And I'll never be able to take the scholarship because I'll always have to work . . ."

"Hold everything," Liz said. "What scholarship?"

"For my junior year," Adriana said through her tears. "To Columbia. To study journalism. I can't go. To begin with, the family needs the money I earn now. As it is, I should be working full-time."

"What about your mother? What does she want for you?"

"Well, she'd like me to take the scholarship, but it isn't possible. She holds two jobs, and we still don't have enough money. There are four kids, and I'm the oldest. It wouldn't be fair of me to take the scholarship and not help out."

"Did it ever occur to you that their turn will come in time? For scholarships and everything else? And what about your dad?" she asked quietly. "Won't he get help? You know the kind I mean."

Adriana colored, and Liz wondered if she had gone too far.

"He's a really good man," Adriana said. "He just . . . just . . ."

"I understand," Liz said.

Adriana looked at Liz and rubbed her tear-dampened eyes. "He loves us, all of us," she said. "He just can't seem to help himself."

"Come on," Liz said. "I want you to dry those tears. We're going out for a cup of coffee. You're going to stop feeling sorry for yourself, and we'll concentrate on all those things in your life that you can do for yourself. If you have a scholarship for your junior year to Columbia, you're going to take that scholarship, period."

Adriana shook her head, but Liz could see a certain amount of relief in the tentative smile she tried to show. It seemed to Liz that Adriana carried a far heavier burden than Liz ever had, and that she obviously could never share it with either her mother or her father.

It was an hour later when Adriana and Liz parted. Adriana returned to the *Times Herald* considerably cheered, although no real solutions had been reached. Liz had learned something of the girl's bleak home life, with a mother who worked as a waitress to support the family and a father who, even with certain lovable qualities, could never be counted on.

On her way to the parking lot where she kept her car, Liz passed Whiting Printing. She saw Jemma Gardner at the front counter and waved to her. Jemma beckoned her in. All Liz wanted to do was return home so that she could draw herself a nice, hot bath. She remembered, however, that Adriana had worked for Jemma, and curious, she stepped into the shop.

"You're working late," she said to Jemma, who was eight months pregnant.

"I've been lettering this sign for myself." Jemma turned a small cardboard square around so that Liz could read the lettering on it: Promptly at Six. "A little reminder I'm about to hang over my desk. The shop and my business brain close promptly at six, and it's past that already. I've got to learn to delegate work," she added, gesturing at her stomach, "since, in another month I'll want to spend a lot of time with the infant. How are you, Liz?''

"Busy with all the wrong things, maybe."

Jemma smiled, her green eyes twinkling. "No, not if you like what you're doing. Everything will happen in good time."

Liz thought of Hunt Gardner, Jemma's second husband. She had been impressed with him—his humor, his intelligence and his good looks. The one time she'd met him, she'd realized that unexpected treasures could be found in the quietest and most unlikely places.

She and Jemma had met when Liz first arrived in Ramsey Falls. Whiting Printing published a couple of shopping guides in both Ramsey Falls and Merriman. Celie's *Times Herald* competed with the guides for local advertising dollars, but there was no rivalry between the two women. In fact, they seemed extremely fond of each other.

"Adriana Scott used to work for you, didn't she?" Liz asked.

Jemma nodded, frowning slightly. "She works too hard, I think, but Celie offered her an apprenticeship and she accepted it, even with her heavy load at school. Besides all that, she takes every odd job that shows up in town. But she's a terrific student. The energy of the young, I imagine."

"I know," Liz said, leaning on the counter and laughing. "We're so tremendously old, you and I. Has her father always been a problem?"

"Oh, I suppose so," Jemma said. "It's nothing we ever talk about, to spare Adriana's feelings. Besides, we've lived with Scottie's peccadilloes for so long that we take them for granted. I heard Brad had to rescue him the other day again."

"No solution to his drinking, then?"

"He won't admit he drinks," Jemma said. "We all try to protect Adriana and her younger siblings. At the same time they put up with Scottie. I always thought her mother should pack it in and leave him."

"I'm asking you to gossip, Jemma, and I know you don't like that," Liz said. "Adriana has a scholarship to Columbia for her junior year."

"I know," Jemma said. "Hunt's responsible for that."

"She's going to take it," Liz said. "I'm going to see to it."

Jemma gave her a wide smile. "We've been trying to work it out, but maybe it takes someone from far away and just distanced enough to make it come true."

"It'll happen," Liz said, going over to the door.

"Come for dinner soon," Jemma called. "I'll give you a ring and set up a proper date."

Liz waved and closed the door behind her. She felt suddenly terrific, as though she was no longer an intruder, as though there was hope for her yet in Ramsey Falls.

Mrs. Duboise wasn't home when she arrived, but a pot of steaming coffee sat on the stove in the kitchen along with a fragrant stew simmering slowly on a back burner. Liz filled a cup with coffee and carried it up to her room.

There she stripped, donned a bathrobe, went into the bathroom and filled the cast-iron tub with hot water. She used some bubble bath powder sent by her mother in packages that dutifully arrived every two weeks. Sprinkling the powder near the faucet, she dreamily watched the bubbles rise and fill the tub.

Then she dropped her robe and sank into the fragrant water. There was something transitory about living in a boarding house, even one in which the ancient tub was supported by claw feet. She didn't predict staying in Ramsey Falls past a year; still, it would be nice to have her own place again. It needn't be furnished as artfully as her apartment in Chicago. She might scrounge up furniture from her friends; the rest she could buy at a discount store she'd heard about in Merriman. *If* she decided to stay a reasonable length of time. *If.*

The warm, soapy water was comforting, and she closed her eyes. Her thoughts automatically went to Brad and to the house he was building for himself. He told her he lived in a stone cottage on his parents' property. She wondered if he used up houses and discarded them like so many soda bottles. What would happen to the stone cottage? Would they rent it? Or was money no object to his parents or to Brad? Brad had said he'd be vacating the cottage by summer's end, and for a while Liz mused about the possibilities of renting it.

"Absolute opposites," she murmured to herself out loud about Brad. He even liked to cook, for heaven's sake. He worked on the other side of the fence, where money dictated whom he would represent. Scottie excepted, of course. He had called it pro bono work. Feel-good work was more like it. She, on the other hand, was anxious to take up the cudgels for the underdog, any underdog.

Damn it, John Nelson had a right to be heard. And his neighbors had a right not to sign a petition without fear of retribution. Traffic violations, indeed. From everything she'd heard, Hanging Judge Vanderheyden was the Attila the Hun of traffic violations.

She heard a light knock on her bedroom door, and Mrs. Duboise called out, "Liz? You there?"

"I'm in the bathtub."

"Phone call. Brad Kent, I believe."

Liz inhaled sharply. "Tell him I'll be right there." She stepped from the tub, dripping water and suds, and grabbed her terry robe. She ran barefoot past a sagely smiling Mrs. Duboise to the hall phone, grabbed the receiver and tried to still the breathless sound she knew her first words would have. "Brad? Hi."

There was a moment of dead air, then, "Who's Brad?"

The receiver slipped in her hand. She righted it, surprised at the odd feeling of disappointment that she felt. "Doug? Is that you?"

"Hey, Liz, good to hear your voice. I figured I'd catch you in around now. Saturday night, getting ready for a big evening on the town. How's the weather out there?"

"Fine. Doug, are you calling from California?"

"Right. Listen, Liz, I owe you a letter and I figured I'd call instead of writing this time around." He gave a small laugh. "Besides, I wanted to hear your voice."

They tended to write long letters to each other, spread several weeks apart, each opening with profuse apologies about not writing sooner. "Well," she said brightly, "I'm glad you called, and it isn't even my birthday."

There was another moment of silence. She was aware of a peculiar tension, the kind experienced by two people embarrassed about apologizing after a bad argument.

"Who'd you say Brad was?" he asked.

"I didn't. He's a lawyer I know."

Another laugh. "Thinking of suing someone?"

Liz laughed, too. "Oh, he represents the opposition."

"I don't get it. Something to do with the job? How is the job, anyway?"

"How's the job?" She was aware of Mrs. Duboise hovering nearby, not out of nosiness but good will. "I've been meaning to write you a long letter about it, Doug. I will, anyday now. That's enough about me. Tell me what you're doing."

"Same old thing," he told her in a jaunty voice.

"Keeping yourself busy."

"Yeah. I'd say so."

"All work and no play?" Liz put the question squarely, knowing he might fudge the truth. She no longer missed him, she realized, and she had been kissed that day and the memory still lingered. A chaste kiss, but one so full of promise that she could conjure it up now.

"Well, you know," he said.

No, she thought, *I suspect but I don't know.* They spoke a few more desultory words, then said goodbye. She stared at the receiver for a moment, but suddenly the chill in the hall made her realize she hadn't toweled herself dry. Hurrying past Mrs. Duboise, she threw her a smile.

"Not Brad Kent," Mrs. Duboise said apologetically. "My hearing's not what it used to be."

"An old friend from California," Liz explained.

"Oh, Liz, about dinner," her landlady said. "I expected my son and his wife, but they had to cancel. Meanwhile, I made a huge goulash. How about sharing some with me? I know it's not the most elegant way to invite someone..."

Liz put a hand on the woman's arm. "Thanks, I'd love to, Mrs. Duboise. You're an angel."

"Scarcely that," Mrs. Duboise said, hurrying toward the kitchen. "Say in about half an hour? That should give you the evening to do whatever you want."

A whole evening, Liz thought, heading back to her room. She'd spend it in front of the television, blocking her mind out to the fact that she had wanted Brad to be at the other end of the line, not Doug.

Liz had scarcely slipped into her housecoat when the telephone sounded again. Once more Mrs. Duboise called her. "This time I swear it's Brad," she said with the intimacy of someone who had known him since his childhood.

Liz hurried to the phone, yet when she picked up the receiver, it was with a certain amount of caution.

"Liz, glad I caught you," Brad said at once.

"Are you back from Merriman?" She thought with a little broken sigh how glad she was to hear his voice.

"Back. Did you see Mrs. Randall?"

"Yes."

"Everything squared away?"

"Are you asking that question as a lawyer or as a friend?"

"Withdraw question, Your Honor. How about dinner?"

There was a painting of one of Mrs. Duboise's ancestors above the telephone stand. There was a slight tear in the upper right-hand corner, and she eyed it curiously. Her own grandmother, who had an odd way with metaphors, had given Liz the same advice more than once. "Keep your mouth shut and you won't shoot yourself in the foot." It had never made any sense, although Liz understood what she had been trying to say.

"Liz? You there?"

"Yes."

"How about dinner?"

In Chicago a fellow might talk about going to the theater or to hear jazz or catch a night baseball game. In Ramsey Falls one was obliged to have dinner, to face one's companion across a dinner table and to reveal oneself without outside distractions. She thought of the goulash simmering in the kitchen and her promise to Mrs. Duboise. "Sorry," she said at last. "I'm busy, for dinner at least."

"Meaning you're not busy after?"

"Yes."

"Pick you up at nine, then. Give you plenty of time to digest your dinner and come back from wherever it is you're having it."

Liz didn't even try to explain where she'd be and with whom. "Nine is perfect. What are we supposed to be doing?"

"Going out on the town."

"In Ramsey Falls?"

"We're full of surprises. By the way, just dress comfortably. We don't stand on ceremony around here."

When she hung up, once again Liz stood and stared at the painting and its small tear in the corner. She supposed it would cost a fortune to repair. And what did he mean, just dress comfortably? She'd play it safe, she decided, and wear a jade silk blouse with black slacks.

Mrs. Duboise was standing at the door that led to the kitchen when Liz headed for her room.

"Brad?" her landlady questioned. "I did have it correct this time, didn't I?"

"You did, Mrs. Duboise."

Mrs. Duboise looked at her curiously for a moment. "Of course I always thought he and . . ."

Liz kept her face expressionless and waited. "Yes?"

The woman shook herself as though trying to get rid of unwanted thoughts. "Good heavens, nothing. Nobody listens to parents nowadays, and it's a good thing. Seeing him tonight?"

Liz went over to the staircase. "Seeing him tonight, Mrs. Duboise," she called out, taking the steps two at a time.

CHAPTER SIX

THE SHORE ROAD COUNTRY CLUB, just outside of Ramsey Falls, was a stately white building with two bronze lions poised on marble slabs guarding the entrance. Architecturally it was an oddity having been added to in varying styles over the years. And yet that was precisely what gave the building charm. Through huge casement windows on the ground floor, Liz could see crystal chandeliers glowing brightly. Soft muted music spilled out into the mild evening air.

Behind the clubhouse lay the smooth rolling lawns of the golf course. To the left green and yellow golf carts were lined up like soldiers waiting for their marching orders. Beyond, the black waters of the Hudson River reflected the lights on the opposite shore. A huge tanker, heading upriver, passed a sailboat, sails slack, moving downstream under motor power, the sound reaching them as a faint, crackling *put-put*.

The night was inky, smooth and warm, moonless but with a heady dusting of stars.

As they stepped out of the car, Brad said, as though letting her in on a little secret, "You may have noticed there isn't much doing around these parts at night."

"Leading to the current population explosion, I expect," Liz said.

He laughed. "It's either that or hit New York or Boston for a little sin and a little fun. Then again, we have the Shore Road Country Club."

"I'm impressed," Liz said. She was also glad to see that Brad had followed his own advice. He wore khaki pants, and an open-necked shirt under a navy blazer.

Still, there was something formidable and opulent about the country club, the slender women and elegant men drifting up the stairs in a slow and languid way. It was theirs. They were as familiar with it as Liz had been with her local coffee house back home.

"Something special going on tonight?" she asked. She felt she was lagging as they approached the entrance.

"I'd say so."

"Wonderful. What?"

"You. Or rather you and me."

"Oh," she groaned, "be serious."

"I'm serious, all right. You just refuse to believe me."

"There's serious and there's serious. Besides, I'm still not certain I can trust your motives."

"My motives are just what they should be," he said, opening the door and bowing her into the center hall. "Namely showing you off to the citizens of Ramsey Falls."

She looked around and recognized a few faces, although she'd have trouble attaching names to them. One thing was certain: they knew one another and appeared quite at home at the Shore Road Country Club, something she doubted she would ever feel.

There were several rooms off the center hall, each hosting a separate party, all noisy. In one she heard someone shakily singing "Happy Birthday" into a mike. From another, hilarious glee attended some arcane ceremony involving a bride and groom in the center of the dance floor. Ahead, a pair of French doors opened into a spacious, crowded dining room. They were met by the maître d', who greeted Brad with the effusive air of someone who had just had a case settled in his favor. Then his eyes slid to Liz, and his smile broadened as though she were the most enchanting creature he had ever seen.

"Your table is ready, Mr. Kent. The Red Room as you requested." He picked up two velvet-covered menu cards and led them through the restaurant to a small, romantic, candle-lit room with walnut paneling and red carpets. Liz counted half a dozen tables in the room, all occupied except for one near the window, which the maître d' led them to. The view was of the river.

"Something to drink?"

Brad raised an eyebrow at Liz. She colored slightly, aware of her innocence in the matter of wine and of country clubs and, in fact, of luxury in whatever form it took. She had lived her twenty-eight years without ever pressing her nose against the windowpane to see how the other half lived. She hadn't, quite literally, cared, or even thought about it. And now, with the maître d' respectfully waiting and Brad gazing at her as though she knew Chianti from chardonnay, all she could do was shrug. "Wine. White." She brightened. "White wine."

"A bottle of St. Emilion from my own reserve, Laurence."

Of course, Liz thought, why not? His own reserves. She held a smile on her face as if it were the most natural thing in the world. Her grandmother would be proud of her.

"Incidentally, jade looks lovely on you," he said when the maître d' had left.

"Thank you. A little Christmassy, of course, in all this red," she added, referring to the deep, warm red colors of the dining room. "But I have to admit it's one of my favorite blouses."

"Then we agree on that."

There was an awkward silence then. Two couples arrived and after greeting Brad and cursorily examining Liz, they settled at a table just vacated.

"Can't seem to get away from people you know," she remarked.

"Small town. Not exactly the place for privacy. You want to announce just what you're doing with your life, you've only to enter the Shore Road Country Club."

Liz gazed at him for a long moment. She wasn't quite certain what he meant but decided her only alternative was to ignore it.

"For instance, if I wanted to keep every eligible bachelor in town from making a pass at you," he went on, "all I have to do is take your hand and hold it, thus." He picked up her hand and drew it to his lips.

"Brad," Liz said quietly, extricating her hand from his, "I've got somebody in California. I think we've already discussed the matter. As for all the eligible men in town, I imagine you can count them on the little finger of one hand."

"Oh, considering the number of divorce cases that have come my way, I'd say there are a lot more than that. And they've all made the appropriate passes, no doubt."

She shook her head no. "Waiting for the master to tell them how, I suppose."

"Okay, you win this round," he said with a broad laugh. "I think you're a lady with a lot of experience in the matter of telling the male animal to get lost."

"You're absolutely right. I like my own space and I'm careful about who invades it."

"That why you tied yourself up with a fellow in California?"

"I should have asked him his opinion when he called tonight."

Liz was surprised at the way he took her remark. His expression froze, and it was only the arrival of the waiter that broke the silence.

"Ah, the wine," Brad said unnecessarily.

I've unnerved him, Liz thought with an unexpected frisson of pleasure. It gave her an extraordinary sense of power.

The wine bottle was wrapped in a white cloth towel. The maître d' raised the towel so Brad could see the label. When Brad nodded his approval, Laurence made a great ceremony of removing the cork and pouring a minute amount of the wine into Brad's glass. Brad waited a moment, tipped the glass, sniffed and then at last tasted the wine. He nodded his approval. Laurence filled Liz's glass, then Brad's. With a slight bow he left. There was a long, awkward moment while Brad slowly rubbed his fingers up and down the stem of the glass.

Liz picked up her glass. "I like your phony shyness about what Ramsey Falls has to offer," she told him, aware of her tone sounding unnaturally bright. She wanted the awkward moment to pass, wanted him to flirt outrageously with her, wanted the silky night to go on endlessly. "It's all very classy and Laurence could pass muster at Le Cirque in Manhattan, I'm sure."

"And you," he said, "like to pretend you're part street urchin and part guerrilla and that the good life is something to be sneered at. In reality I'd say you're about as smooth and sophisticated as they come."

Liz smiled. It was that easy, was it? Staying cool and keeping her opinions to herself. Grandmother was certainly right.

Brad raised his glass. "To the sophisticated lady in jade who's come to town to tell us what we're like and where we've gone wrong."

He took a sip and then Liz raised her glass. "To good times in the prettiest place on earth." She took a sip of the wine, watching his expectant look over the rim of the glass. The wine had a smooth and subtle taste that lingered nicely on her tongue. Yet she knew that if someone had offered her a glass of cheap house wine, she would scarcely know the difference. "Good," she said. "Bottled locally, in spite of the decidedly foreign name?"

"Bottled locally. An estate wine, meaning many grapes are grown, few are chosen."

"I wanted to do a story on some of the smaller vineyards, but Celie told me to forget it until I could dream up a new angle."

Brad examined her with interest. After a moment he said, "Can't get away from the job, can you? You've had a dreamy, distracted look on your face from the moment I picked you up tonight. And it has nothing to do with vineyards and stories Celie doesn't want you to write. Want to talk about it?"

She leveled a thoughtful gaze at him. "Are you that tuned into me? It doesn't seem possible."

"Yeah," he said, "I think I'm that tuned into you."

"Then why," she said after a moment's hesitation, "didn't you tell me Scottie was Adriana's father?"

"And Queen Elizabeth is Prince Charles's mother. Why would I talk about the obvious?"

"I found Adriana at the office, crying over that dumb police blotter report. Now I know the whole story."

"There's a story for every family in the county. Some good, some bad. Scottie will sober up for a while now, especially when I have Judge Vanderheyden ride rough-shod over him."

"When you *have*? That sounds as if you have the judge in your little pocket. But then he's your uncle, isn't he?"

"Liz." He reached across the table and put his hand over hers. "You're doing it again."

"What?" she almost screeched.

"Getting on your high horse. I know all about Adriana and I know all about the family. It's time Scottie admitted he can't take a drink and that he belongs in a program. I'm going to suggest, if you like that word better, that Hanging Judge Vanderheyden, my uncle, pull that self-indulgent rug out from under Scottie. After that, we'll see."

"If he goes to jail, it'll finish Adriana."

"Liz, mind your own business."

"I've decided that Adriana is my business."

Brad slowly took his hand off hers. For a moment they held their gaze, Brad thoughtful, Liz aware of the fire in her eyes. "John Nelson and the Vanderheydens," Brad said. "Adriana Scott and her father—you're losing your sense of proportion, Liz. You're editorializing about the very stories you should be most fair about. Is this how we're going to spend the rest of our lives, with you on one side of the fence and me on the other, arguing about methods? I'd like to warn you, Liz, I'm a dragon in the courtroom. You won't win."

But Liz scarcely heard his last words. He had said the most extraordinary thing to her. "The rest of our lives?" she asked. "Did I hear you right?"

"You heard me."

She was silent for a long while, trying to make sense of his remark. "I don't plan on spending the rest of my life in Ramsey Falls."

"You'll have to," he said with a smile. "Think of all the rearranging you have to do. You remind me, in a way, of a puppy I once adopted. I'd go for long walks with him in the woods until we hit a favorite spot of mine, a fresh growth of ash, long spindly trees, moss and leaves underfoot. There was a rock I dubbed Indian Rock because I once unearthed an arrowhead at its base. The puppy would go wild there. He'd grab a stick from one side of the forest floor, race around to the other side and drop it there. Then find another one and dash back to drop it—a mysterious game whose rules only he knew. He'd push his way through the leaves or tear around in circles as if making certain everything was to his satisfaction. I could never figure out precisely what he was doing or why, but he enjoyed himself while he was at it. In a way you remind me of that puppy. Maybe I'm wrong. Maybe you should rearrange things in Ramsey Falls. Enjoy yourself for some mysterious reasons by stirring the leaves and air, letting the rest of us worry about the debris."

"Provided I don't step a foot in your territory."

The band struck up some music in the hall next door. He grabbed her hand and said, "Come on, Liz, let's shake some of the truculence out of you."

He led her through the glass doors into the dining room and beyond to a small dance floor, which was lit softly with the low candlepower of delicate crystal chandeliers and wall sconces. The dance floor was filling up with couples. The music played was a soft, slow fifties beat. He wrapped her in his arms, and as they swayed to the music, he said, his breath warm against her ear, "You surprise me, Liz. I was afraid you'd lead."

"Bite your tongue," she said. "I was the star pupil of Mrs. Petrovski's fifth grade dance class held in the gym every Thursday afternoon, and believe me, I never missed a beat."

He whirled her around and then drew her into a deep back dip, which he held for four or five seconds.

"Way to go, Brad," someone called to him.

He drew her up, grinning, clearly pleased with himself.

"Well, well, well," Liz said when she caught her breath. "This is a side of you I'd never have believed."

"Fred Astaire on a dare when I was in my freshman year at college and my friends insisted I needed a little smoothing out. They bought me a month's lessons at the local dance studio. We're talking Hollywood moves here." He drew her around in a series of tight swirls, his long legs ranged against hers.

"If I'd known, I'd have worn chiffon and sequins instead of slacks," she told him. "And very, very, very high heels."

"Next time, Liz, we'll come prepared, me in a tux and you in silk. And, as I remember it, Ginger and Fred always ended their dances with a kiss."

"Uh-uh, they were always dancing just before or after an argument, hostilities suspended for the length of the dance, and resumed immediately thereafter. As I recall, she often walked out alone into the night."

"Ah, but he took after her with that wonderful gait of his. He never let her get very far. Then the kiss."

"Forget the kiss, Counselor."

"Right. I remember. That call from California." The music took on a very slow beat. "Cheek to cheek," he told her, gathering her close, his body touching hers at every juncture, the gentle intimacy warming through her as he laid his cheek against hers.

Liz closed her hand around his neck, and felt the new pressure of his arm and his palm against the small of her back. She wanted the music to go on forever. An ineffable joy flashed through her as everything about the room and even the music began to fade under the strange, new feeling. "We could get arrested for this, you know," she told him dreamily.

"I hope so. I can always arrange to share your cell."

"I'll bet you could."

His lips brushed hers lightly, and the kiss might have deepened right there on the crowded dance floor if they hadn't been interrupted. "Hey, Brad, X-rated behavior is against club rules. You ought to know. I heard you helped draft them."

Standing in the middle of the dance floor, his arm around a pale-skinned blond woman who was smiling at Liz with friendly bright blue eyes, was a tall, handsome man whom Liz recognized at once as Tyler Lassiter. His picture had been printed with a story she'd written about the rehabilitation of the town's waterfront.

"Ty and cousin Sarah," Brad said with distinct pleasure. The music continued and the dancers floated around them. "Come on, let's get out of here." He led them back to the Red Room, and when they were at last seated, Brad introduced Liz.

"Sarah and Ty Lassiter, Liz Grady."

"Liz Grady of the *Times Herald*?" Sarah asked. She extended a hand and shook Liz's warmly.

"Oh, decidedly that," Brad said for Liz.

"Then we've talked on the telephone," Ty said in his friendly accent, which was a mixture of Australian and British.

"You have?" Sarah turned and gave her husband a mock angry smile.

"Celie insists he's the resident genius on all matters architectural, ranging from the design of fireplugs to the new nursery school. You didn't happen to design the new restaurant-bar Willie Vanderheyden's trying to put up on I-84?"

Liz turned and saw Brad glare at her and shake his head.

"I don't need commissions that are going to desecrate the river view," he told her.

"Mind if I applaud?"

"I thought there was a zoning problem," Ty said to Brad.

"Doesn't seem to bother Will," Liz remarked. "He's already broken ground."

Ty shook his head. "I could live here forever and never get the reasons straight why some people can flout the law and others can't. We're having a devil of a time with the environmentalists over the development of Merriman's waterfront. And up the road apiece, Will decides to build a restaurant."

"Let the zoning board decide," Brad said quietly.

"Ah, let the zoning board decide," Ty said. "Familiar words to an architect."

Brad signaled the waiter and ordered another bottle of wine. "And you, my pretty cousin," he said to Sarah, "are about to extend the Crewes line into the next generation. Been meaning to call you and offer my congratulations."

"Who told you?" Sarah asked. "And it's still seven months away."

"Jemma Gardner. She seemed to think I knew. Beats me why you feel it's necessary to keep it a secret. Well, we'll have to toast the news. It isn't every day that a new baby joins the rarified atmosphere of Ramsey Falls' oldest family."

Sarah turned to Liz. "Brad puts a lot on the continuity of family. Maybe that's why I've kept the news quiet. Too many cousins I'd have to tell, and too many people offended if I forgot about distant relationships."

"The local preoccupation with history puzzles me," Liz said. "In Chicago—"

"In Chicago nothing," Brad said as the waiter brought the wine. "We'll raise a drink to the latest Crewes."

"Lassiter," Ty put in. "I believe the Lassiter line had something to do with it."

Brad grinned. "Don't let that Aussie accent fool you, Liz. Ty's roots go way back in Merriman County."

"I'm lost," Liz said, raising her glass, "but I don't mind at all. Here's to the future and to *crews* of Lassiters."

Brad threw her a grateful smile and Liz, still holding her glass up, felt a heady rush of happiness.

THE NIGHT HAD TURNED quiet and thoroughly breezeless. The newly risen moon floated in and out between fat, cottony clouds tinged with gold along their edges.

Liz, feeling content, settled back in the car as it eased out of the parking lot. "Thanks for inviting me," she said to Brad. "I really enjoyed myself. And I like Ty and Sarah."

"Good old Sarah, settling down and becoming a mother. Never thought I'd see the day. It's a little hard to discover everybody's earth mother pulling in the rug and closing the world outside."

"I'm not sure what you mean, but if she's happy, I'm happy."

"Oh, Sarah was always on the run, always handling everybody's problems one way or another, pretending her life would go on forever and she had plenty of time to settle down to the most suitable role in the world for her, wife and mother."

"I take it you're only talking about Sarah, not about every woman."

Liz didn't really expect an answer from him. She didn't even know why she made the remark. They were on the open road now. Liz gazed out at the countryside flying past, at the black trees with their baby leaves silhouetted against the night sky. They passed an occasional house, lights signaling warmth inside as though to dispel the notion that the planet was uninhabited. "Oh, scratch what I said," she remarked.

"I have already."

The world was so different in Ramsey Falls, where stars seemed brighter and closer and held out something strangely intimate, as though they were quite accessible if only she would take the time to reach for them. There were no concrete-and-steel structures jutting up angrily to hide the vast space. Perhaps it was time to reexamine her values, or to strengthen what she already knew and believed in.

When he pulled up to Mrs. Duboise's house and shut off the engine, Brad looked over at Liz. "How long do you plan on staying as a paying guest of Mrs. Duboise?"

"I've got to make certain I'll be here for a year at least. Anyway, I think Mrs. Duboise has a niece coming up north, and she's been hinting that I have the best room in the house."

"Then that's one hint you ought to take. Letting you off here makes me feel as if we've wandered into an old Andy Hardy movie."

"Andy Hardy? I thought we were Rogers and Astaire."

"Hey," he said, "I'm all for updating our relationship to something newer than either one. It's just that I'm required, while you're a paying guest of Mrs. Duboise, to kiss you good-night chastely on the cheek. After all, the woman still thinks I'm the teenage brat who got her son into all kinds of trouble."

Liz laughed. "Dead wrong. She's been telling me all about you and how you're the most eligible bachelor in Ramsey Falls."

"Has she now?" He gave her a broad grin and pulled her into his arms. "Wouldn't want to disappoint the good woman."

Liz, caught by surprise, didn't even have time to react.

"Excuse the steering wheel," he added before his lips came down on hers. "It's the best I could do on such short notice."

His lips blocked out any objections she might have made. The kiss was warm and sweet, unlike the chaste kiss of that afternoon. It was, in fact, full of wild promise. She felt his fingers tighten on her arm as he pulled her closer. His tongue gently probed at her lips until she lost all resistance and opened her mouth to him.

Her mind remained sharp and clear as she took in the newness of her feelings, the excitement that carried with it a fresh fear—fear of an explosion of desire he could send rocketing through her. But she wasn't ready—not yet. She pulled back and tried to control the breathlessness in her voice. "Brad, no, I'm not—"

"Ready?" He finished the sentence for her. "No." He didn't release her, however, but with his finger traced a line along her cheek. "There's that fellow you keep dangling on a string in California."

"I don't mean him."

An extraordinary look of satisfaction crossed his face. "You mean he doesn't count."

"Damn it, don't confuse me." She pushed hard against his chest, and he suddenly released her.

"You're something else, Liz."

His voice was husky, and Liz knew that whatever she was feeling echoed through his body, as well.

"I don't want to be soundly kissed at the moment," she told him in a sober voice. "I'm in Ramsey Falls, trying to get my act together as a reporter. I don't want to bump up against you everywhere I turn. We will, anyway, in an adversarial way. Don't make things hard for me just because you want to amuse yourself at my expense." The moment she said the words, she regretted them.

His expression was easily readable. He was surprised and annoyed, and she thought, probably insulted as well.

"Amuse myself at your expense? Liz, if that's what you think, then I'd better wish you good-night and remember that if our paths ever cross to give you as wide a berth as possible."

"Brad, it came out slightly wrong. I didn't quite mean it that way."

He unlocked his door. "Sure you did." He came around to her side and opened her door. She stepped out and stood on the sidewalk, facing him for a moment.

"Brad, look." She stopped, aware of the immobile expression on his face. "I'll see you in court on Monday, I guess. About Scottie. That's when his case comes up."

"Will you be covering it as a reporter or an interested party?" His voice was a monotone, and Liz experienced a sharp sense of disappointment with herself. She was afraid of what he had opened up in her, and the way she had chosen to hide it by playing the cool professional.

"Interested party," she said at last. She stuck out her hand. "Well, good night and thank you."

He disdained her hand. "I'll take you to the door."

"You don't have to," she said, running lightly up the stairs. He was right behind her, however, and when she turned, she bumped into him. "Brad," she said once again. And then, in one of the most spontaneous acts of her life, she threw her arms around his neck and put her lips to his. For a moment he didn't move. She felt his resistance but let her kiss deepen, and when she pulled away, he reached for her suddenly and gripped her arms.

"Liz, I think you'll always be a crazy bundle of contradictions, that you'll always surprise me, always enchant me and always drive me crazy." He cupped her face between his hands. "I'll give you plenty of space, Liz. If that's what you feel you need right now, I'd be the last person to stand in your way. If you need me, I'll be there."

He gave her a last, lingering kiss and then hurried
down the stairs. Liz stood and watched him, but he
didn't look back and didn't wave as he headed the car
back down the road.

CHAPTER SEVEN

"ALL RISE. His Honor, Judge Thadeus Vanderheyden."

There was a general shuffling of feet as conversations were cut short in midspeech and everyone in the courtroom stood. Then the walnut-paneled door to the judge's chambers opened and a tall, distinguished, silver-haired man appeared, swathed in black robes.

Liz considered him coolly. Hanging Judge Thadeus Vanderheyden, straight out of central casting, the handsome, trustworthy dispenser of justice to rich and poor alike. Recognizable, also, was the family resemblance to Brad in the arrogant tilt of his head, the look of absolute self-possession, the long, narrow, aristocratic nose.

The courtroom remained silent while Judge Vanderheyden took his seat, then pulled out a pair of tortoiseshell glasses, which he put on and spent several seconds adjusting, after which he opened a leather folder and began perusing the topmost sheet.

The early spring light, clear and bright, filtered through the high, narrow windows of the Merriman courthouse. It seemed to Liz that everything and everyone was etched in great detail, with no smudges, no shadows. Ordinarily she would have taken careful notes about sight and sound. She would have gone back to her typewriter and written a tight piece sprinkled with humor, perhaps devoid of any sense of the reality behind the story. Man shoots up neighbor's chickens, sentenced to time in coop. She'd have gone for the laughs in a dispassionate way. It might have taken up a couple of filler sentences in a big-city newspaper. But there were no laughs when a family was involved, when a youngster shed hot tears of shame and found her future blocked by a drunken father.

Brad was seated at a long wooden table with Scottie squirming next to him. Scottie was dressed a little better than the last time Liz had seen him. He wore a tweed suit that fitted him a little too loosely. She suspected that Brad had searched through his own wardrobe to come up with something appropriate for a sentencing. Scottie was also clearly sober. He moved uncomfortably in his seat, then turned around and scanned the courtroom, at last stopping to grin with embarrassment at someone sitting at the rear. Liz followed his gaze. In back of the courtroom sat a rather harried-looking woman, Mrs. Scott she supposed, with three teenagers at her side—freckle-faced twin boys with golden hair reflecting highlights of red, and a girl of about thirteen with thick black hair and Adriana's pert nose and generous mouth. Adriana was nowhere in sight.

When Liz turned back to Scottie, it was with mixed feelings. She was afraid of his receiving a too-tough sentence, thanks to Brad's determination—a sentence that would solve nothing, least of all Scottie's drinking problem. Then again she worried that nothing would ever change, that Scottie had it in him to ruin the lives of every member of his family if something drastic wasn't done.

"Robert Scott." The judge looked over at Brad, then at Scottie, his face expressionless. "Welcome back, Mr. Scott."

Of course the case would be the first on the docket, Liz realized. Brad would have seen to that.

"Yes, Your Honor." Scottie rose to his feet, kicking his chair noisily back.

"Drunk, disorderly, using a weapon with reckless disregard . . . Where have I heard that before?"

"I'm sorry, Your Honor."

"I'll bet you are. Mr. Kent?" The judge nodded at Brad, who stood beside his client. "Mr. Scott said he's sorry. Is he sorry because he's Robert Scott, or because he was drunk and disorderly and a menace to his neighbors? To say nothing," he added sarcastically, "of his neighbor's chickens."

"Your Honor, Mr. Scott would like to plead guilty with an explanation of the charges."

The judge glanced down at his papers for a moment and then murmured without looking up. "I'd like to hear his explanation."

"It was the bitch," Scottie burst out.

A long, low peal of laughter filled the courtroom.

"Quiet in the court." The bailiff glared around the room.

Judge Vanderheyden stared at Scottie for a long, icy moment, his hand on his glasses as though to steady them. "Sit down, Scottie. You have a lawyer. I think he's here to represent you."

"Yes, Your Honor." Scottie sat straight down as if his legs had buckled under him.

"He means the Brittany spaniels he raises, Your Honor." Brad explained. "It seems that real estate taxes were due on his house and Mr. Scott had to sell his prize female to pay them. This left his kennels bare of stock.''

''I don't see why paying one's taxes should lead to a drunken rampage, but go on.''

Scottie tried to get to his feet, but Brad gently pushed him back down. ''To purchase a prize female with the proper papers is financially impossible at this moment,'' he said. ''I'm afraid Mr. Scott's disappointment was released in an unfortunate manner, but I'd like to point out that he promises never to do it again.''

''A promise he intends to keep,'' the judge said dryly.

''Mr. Scott recognizes his duties as a husband and father.'' Brad remained standing, not moving a muscle, his broad shoulders taut, his hands at his sides.

He was dead serious, Liz saw with fresh admiration. She understood then that he brought the same passion to pro bono work as he would to something far greater, at least in terms of money or social consequences. She passed a hand along her brow and realized she was perspiring a little. The room was very warm, and she wished someone would open a window. There was some restless shuffling off to her right and someone whispered, ''He should throw the book at him.''

When the judge spoke again, Liz felt her heart begin to race. Throw the book at him, reason told her, but not one that would harm Adriana more than she had already been. ''Mr. Scott, will you please stand?''

Scottie cast a worried glance around the courtroom before getting noisily to his feet. He raised his right hand as though he were going to salute, then thought better of it.

''I'd say thirty days in jail might teach you something about reacting to adversity, Mr. Scott.''

Scottie staggered slightly. From behind, Liz heard a gasp and a light sob. She gazed angrily over at Brad, but he stood without moving. What Scottie needed was a detox program, and instead he was going to spend thirty days in jail.

"I'm not going to do that to your family, however," the judge went on, "but you're going to have to change your ways, Mr. Scott."

"Yes, Your Honor."

"I don't want any hollow 'yes, Your Honors,' Mr. Scott. Do you understand me?"

"Yes, Your Honor."

"Mr. Scott, if I ever see you before me again, I guarantee I won't go easy on you. I'm sentencing you to join Alcoholics Anonymous today, not tomorrow, not next week, but today. I want you to attend the program on a daily basis for ninety days, and I don't want to see you back in my courtroom ever on the same charge. Because your family needs you as head of the house, your lawyer has already promised to see that you take a job as custodian of the Ramsey Falls high school grounds. No days off, no drinking, and I'm suspending your hunting license for six months. I don't want you handling a shotgun in all that time, either, Mr. Scott. In fact, I want you to surrender any firearms you still have in your possession, as of today."

"But . . ." Scottie began.

Brad put a hand on his arm.

"Case dismissed."

Liz hurried out of the courtroom, feeling warm tears welling in her eyes. Well, it was one story she wouldn't be writing for the *Times Herald*. Justice had been served and by the last man she expected it from. And meanwhile, Adriana would be in school, trembling with fear.

She was halfway down the steps of the Merriman courthouse when she heard Brad call her name. She turned and found him coming toward her.

"Tears?" he said, looking surprised. He reached into his pocket for a handkerchief and then slowly, carefully, wiped them away, tilting her chin back with his finger.

"Allergy," she managed, feeling his faint breath against her cheek.

"Ah, allergy, that's what compassion is called these days."

"I thought you were going to have Scottie put on the rack."

"I never believed it was a rackable offence. And what do you think of my uncle, Hanging Judge Vanderheyden?"

"He has your nose."

"Has he now? Glad to hear it. I always admired the way he looked down it."

"At the Scotties of the world, I suppose?"

"I asked you what you thought of him."

"Fair," Liz admitted. "This time around. I suppose he has no stake in what Scottie does in Ramsey Falls. After all, this is Merriman, a long way from the scene of the crime. And I also think you and your uncle worked out how to handle Scottie over cocktails, spending two or three minutes on it before moving on to something else. Luckily for the jailbird it worked out to his benefit."

"Oh, cynical, cynical," Brad said. "Let me tell you how they do it in the big city, just in case you were too busy to notice. They plea-bargain in the corridors of the courthouse. Some bad guys get off easy and some good guys with lousy lawyers wind up behind bars. Families aren't considered. A man's position in his community and his capacity for change aren't either. None of it means a damn. It's a crapshoot where you come from, Lizzie, and I'm sure Scottie would rather take his licks in Merriman County than with the Windy City's idea of what to do with a drunk who goes a little wild with a shotgun.''

At that moment Scottie came out of the courtroom, surrounded by his wife and children, his daughter clinging to his arm. He hurried past Brad and Liz with an embarrassed wave. Mrs. Scott, however, stopped for a moment to shake Brad's hand.

"I can't thank you enough," she said with a quick, curious glance at Liz before turning back to Brad. "I don't know how I'll ever repay you."

"Make sure he gets on that program today and that he attends sessions religiously. That's every day for ninety days, and no time off for good or bad behavior. They're not going to put up with his antics, either. I've set up the job for him at the school. Mrs. Scott, can you see that he's there promptly at eight every morning?"

She nodded. "I'll drive him to the school myself and pick him up on the way home from my job. And take him to AA meetings, as well." She shook Brad's hand vigorously and hurried away.

Brad tucked his arm through Liz's. "I've got a one o'clock appointment here in Merriman. It's twelve now. How about lunch? I've got in mind a fish and chips joint down near the waterfront."

"I don't know," Liz said. "I'm going to do a record search at the town hall."

"Good luck. With the mess the records are in, it'll take you a decade to find anything. Cousin Sarah was in charge of straightening them out, but she abandoned ship in midstream and her replacement doesn't seem to know which end is up."

"I know all about the troubles of the county records. I've come up against them a couple of times. However, I'm here to check on the Ramsey Falls zoning board decisions for the past two years. I understand the current records are in perfect shape."

Brad frowned. "Still after Willie?"

"I hate it when you look disdainfully at me down your long, narrow, aristocratic Vanderheyden nose. I'm not *after* your beloved cousin. I'm after the truth."

"Save the truth till after lunch. You look as if you need an infusion of fish and chips."

"Okay, I'll take you up on the invitation. My treat, though. I have a small expense account, and if you have a particularly good story I could use, I can write you off as a decided expense."

"You're on. How about a profile of the judge and the way he dispenses justice?"

"Oh," she groaned, "talk me into it."

"Let's walk down to the river. Takes about ten minutes, but I'll give you a tour of the place while we're at it," Brad suggested.

"Right," she said, willingly going along. "I've been researching the restoration being undertaken by the town for a possible update on the story."

"I'm afraid the only sign you'll see of it is a general cleaning up of some of the most derelict spots, and an architect's rendering and model in the lobby of the town hall."

"The restoration will take years, I suppose."

"My recommendation, Liz, is that you buy one of the houses close to the waterfront and put in a little sweat equity. It's an investment that'll pay off."

"Sweat equity! I don't even like ironing my blouses. Besides, it's a long commute from Merriman to Ramsey Falls. Even longer to Chicago." Liz said. "No thanks. I won't be around to see the restoration, much less profit from it."

"Ah, I keep forgetting, the minute you're unhappy you're going to ride the rails out of town."

Although the downtown area of Merriman was depressed, when they reached the river, Liz once again was enchanted with the river view. "One can never grow tired of it," she said.

"Fortunately there are enough interested environmental groups in the Hudson Valley fighting to keep the view just the way it is."

"An old song," Liz commented. "Exactly what are the environmentalists fighting for?"

"A lid on overdevelopment. They don't want a circus plunked down here. They want affordable housing, small factories and plenty of recreational space, green parks and walks along the riverfront. It'll come out all right."

"Well, maybe it's time the paper did another story, if Celie doesn't tell me it's been overdone."

Barney's Fish and Chips occupied an unattractive building overlooking the waterfront. A freshly painted sign of a nondescript fish hung above the front door.

When Brad opened the door a scent of beer and deep-fried food drifted out. Inside, sawdust littered the floor.

"And which side are you on?" Liz asked once they were seated at a table near the window. "The environmentalists or unfettered progress?" They had, on their way toward the table, been stopped by half a dozen people, all of whom needed advice from Brad or wanted to see him on business that couldn't wait.

"I recommend the fish and chips," he told her without answering her question. She supposed it was a wise move. He was certain to be on the side she disapproved of. He signaled the waiter.

"Then fish and chips," Liz told the waiter. "Oh, and a bottle of white wine. The superior house quality will do." Once the waiter was gone, Liz leaned across the table and said to Brad in an exaggerated British accent, "From my private stock, don't you know."

Brad tilted his chair back and roared with laughter. "Is that how I sounded at the club on Saturday? If I did, then I deserve the house wine as penance."

"Not quite. You were infinitely more sure of yourself but not quite so British-sounding."

"Okay," he said, still laughing. "From your point of view I can see it was a little off-putting."

"Hey, I'm a reporter. It's all in a day's work, learning how the other half lives."

"Don't knock it." He reached across the table and pressed his finger against her nose. "It could all be yours one day if you play your cards right."

"I don't play cards."

"Of course not. You're a proper little critter, sitting back and making judgments on the world."

"Speaking of judgments," Liz said. "Is that the harsh sentence you said you were *having* your uncle hand down to Scottie? I thought it was hardly harsh, especially if Scottie learns nothing from it. You'll only discover if he's sticking by the rules the next time he shoots up the town."

"What did you want for him, a life sentence?"

"No, but how does this compare to his other appearances before the court?"

"He was always fined, excoriated and sent on his way. His wife and Adriana had to cough up the fine. They had to work a little harder, give up a little more and watch him fall into his old bad habits. This time he's going to attend AA meetings, or I *will* see him sent to jail. Liz, you're so afraid to agree with me, you'd see him in prison and his family's life ruined just to make a point."

"Not true," she said hotly.

The waiter came by and silently poured the wine. When he left, Liz picked up her glass and raised it in a toast. "To our agreeing on something, even if it's the taste of the wine."

He raised his glass, savored the wine and said with a grin, "A little testy around the edges." He took another sip and rolled it around his tongue. "I'd say it takes a little familiarity to get to the heart of the matter, but then it grabs you and has plenty of staying power."

"All that in a house wine. Amazing." Liz realized that while the wine was mellow enough, it didn't resemble the smooth elegance of the St. Emilio. She was beginning to feel like a kid from the backwoods lost among city slickers.

The fish and chips were served in huge baskets. "Hostilities suspended for the present, I hope," Brad remarked. "I never argue when I eat. Upbringing, I suppose. Dinners at home tend to be very formal affairs with politesse served as the main course."

"At home dinner was the noisiest part of the day," Liz told him. "Huge bowls of food in the center of the table, everybody digging in at once. We ate and weren't certain what we were eating. We were too busy politicking and trying to make ourselves heard. My brother and dad had a nightly go of it, my dad questioning him on every aspect of his life, trying to push him down the path of righteousness. And as for politics, where I come from it's taken in with mother's milk.''

"And has your brother taken the path of righteousness?'' Brad asked, clearly interested.

"He's a cop and he's going to law school.'' Then Liz added with a proud smile, "Oh, he'll be police commissioner one day. Guys with his kind of smarts rise quickly in the force.''

"The force is with him, I take it.''

She laughed and dug into her food. "We're a little competitive, my brother and I. I'm going to have to move pretty fast if I intend to keep up with him.''

"Not too fast,'' Brad said in an unexpectedly serious tone. "You don't want to miss the scenery along the way.''

For a long moment their eyes held. Liz felt a slight frisson trickle along her spine. She remembered their kiss of Saturday night and the unexpected passion she had felt. And how she had spent Sunday denying it to herself. She felt her face grow warm under his scrutiny and looked away.

"I try not to miss a trick,'' she murmured, addressing herself to her food.

He reached across the table and placed his hand on hers. "Liz, contrary to what you think, there are no tricks up my sleeves, and I don't play games unless I expect to win.''

She took in a deep, scarcely controlled breath. "I believe you,'' she said, at last looking at him. "And we agree on something there. If I roll the dice, I'm in the game for good. For the moment, I believe the dice in Ramsey Falls are loaded. I think it'll take a lot to convince me otherwise.''

He took his hand away and picked up a nicely crisp chip and popped it into his mouth. He chewed it slowly, all the time watching her. "I only ask one thing, Liz. Leave a little room for unexpected happenings."

"Like what, for instance?"

He speared another chip, but this time offered it to her. She took it into her mouth and said around it once again, "Like what, for instance?"

His answer was slow in coming as though he wanted her to be ready for it with maximum effect. "Like falling in love."

BRAD SHOVED the papers he was working on across his burled walnut desk and pushed his chair back. He muttered to himself as he leaned forward and put his head in his hands.

He had come home early from the office because suddenly the place had seemed stifling and he'd had the urge to push the walls back. Messages he had no intention of returning had kept his telephone ringing; his secretary kept poking papers under his nose for signing, and one of his partners wanted instant input on a case Brad hadn't kept up with. All in all it had been a lousy afternoon, and coming home hadn't made it any better.

There were aspects of his personal life he wasn't handling properly, and it seemed to Brad time was closing in. He lifted his head, turned in his chair and gazed out the window of the small stone dwelling that had begun life three hundred years before as an ice storage house. He could hear the sound of hammering echoing across the field to his left as work was being done on the new place. In the absolute stillness of the air he could even hear laughter and music. Someone had a radio, its volume turned up. He wondered how much his parents could hear of it in the big house that stood high on the bluff overlooking the river.

His decision to build the house had been a milestone of sorts for Brad. In fact, it had been the best decision he had made in years, even if the new house was on Kent land with Kent Hall faintly visible through a copse of trees. It represented going solo, taking himself into the present, with a contemporary establishment of his own, not the old icehouse decorated by his mother and sister with pieces of furniture heavy with family history.

It meant fresh-smelling pine floors and cabinets without a curlicue to their names. It meant contemporary furniture and wide windows and plenty of sun. It meant clearing away the clutter of the past and being his own person without reference to the way things had always been done, to the way life had always been lived.

He turned back, away from the view of the river, away from the sound of hammering and music drifting through the open window. He absentmindedly picked up an intricately carved knife that he used as a letter opener and began toying with it. It was one of the few mementos he had brought back with him from Kenya. After graduating from college and before going to law school, he had joined the Peace Corps and spent two years in East Africa. A job in his father's firm had been waiting for him and Brad had done what other Kents had before him—given some time to public service before settling down to practice law. In his case he chose to move as far away as he could from Ramsey Falls, to where he could stretch his brain and mind.

The Nyanza Plateau was one of the few regions in Kenya with adequate rainfall. The Peace Corps project was created to teach the local inhabitants to plant cash crops. It had been a mind-stretching couple of years.

Brad, in fact, was reluctant to leave when his term had come to a close. He had thought seriously of extending his stay, but his father wouldn't hear of it. There was law school to be completed and then a job waiting for him at Kent Associates in Merriman.

Brad had gone to Harvard, built a life there, fell in and out of love half a dozen times and almost made up his mind to stay in Boston upon graduation. But as graduation had come close, his father had fallen ill and it was made clear to Brad that he was expected to come home to stay. His father had recovered, but by then Brad had moved into the old icehouse on his parents' estate. He had pretended independence, convinced it all made sense—the old family ties, the forged alliances, the busy law practice, even the empty moments when he found himself asking why.

Over the years he'd met other women who inhabited his social circle or were friends of friends from law school. His cousin Sarah Crewes Lassiter, along with his mother and sister, seemed to have formed a pact to introduce him to every eligible woman in Merriman County.

Well, they could stop, he thought. He'd met Liz Grady.

The telephone sounded in the quiet little house, startling him. He reached for it, his movement more automatic than anxious. His telephone number was unlisted and he was careful about giving the number out. He thought of his mother and the fact that he hadn't seen either parent for days. Perhaps it was because of Liz. He wanted them to meet her, but Brad had a very clear notion of the kind of woman his parents expected him to marry. Introducing someone new and unexpected into their lives would curdle the cream.

He experienced a slight sense of annoyance when he heard the voice at the other end of the receiver. She had been given his telephone number the year before, and by Brad himself. At the time it had seemed like a good idea. Mimi Durant was smart enough to use the number rarely, but then Brad was rarely home to receive calls.

"Your office told me you'd be there," Mimi said. Her tone was friendly yet had a cautious edge. He hadn't called her in weeks. Her manner, in fact, was precisely the one she used for soliciting funds for her favorite charity. "Glad I caught you in. You're all right, aren't you, Brad?"

"Fine," he told her, checking his watch. It was nearly four o'clock and the hammering had stopped—the music, too. The crew had undoubtedly stopped work for the day. "Got a touch of spring fever and the backlog of work got to me. How are you, Mimi? I've been meaning to—"

"I know, you've been meaning to call," she said, as if trying to help him out of a jam. "I've been fine—busy, as you can imagine. Brad, I've just been checking my calendar and you're penciled in for Saturday."

"Penciled? Sounds erasable." He reached quickly for his calendar and found the date—a charity event at Pack College scheduled for the afternoon. Damn Victor Bosworth, he thought. There was a point where the man's propensity for good works interfered too much in his private life. Something about a show of horses involving area stud farms.

"I never know about you. Penciled is the word," Mimi said. "Victor said you volunteered to help."

"Right," he said. "Two o'clock." The notion passed through Brad's mind that he'd have to do something about Mimi and soon. She didn't deserve any bad treatment on his part. Liz Grady was an anomaly in his life. If she hadn't appeared on the scene, perhaps one day he would have married Mimi, or perhaps not.

"Fine," she told him. "How about picking me up around one?"

"I'll have to see you at the college, Mimi. I'm busy before and after, I'm afraid."

She gave a light laugh which scarcely hid her apparent anger. "You lawyers. See you there."

When Brad replaced the receiver, he sat back in his chair, arms behind his head. He was treating her badly. There was nothing wrong with Mimi Durant except the absence of magic, of that spark he had been looking for his whole life.

She came from the same kind of background as he, sat a horse well, was active in the right charities and never asked anything of him, even though they had dated on and off for almost a year. She came from a prestigious old Ramsey Falls family and was like most of the women he had dated—right in every way for the scion of the Kent line.

The relationship had actually cooled before Liz had come to Ramsey Falls, but the subtle pressure from his family and their quiet encouragement led Mimi to believe he would give in eventually. He hated the idea of hurting her. Their affair had been a pleasant enough interlude. Whether they loved each other didn't even figure in the equation. Marrying a Kent was precisely what her family expected of Mimi, and she was pliant enough to go along.

But for Brad she was wrong, although he couldn't put his finger on the exact reasons. As for Liz, she was wrong in every way that mattered to his family. She was outspoken and opinionated. She was rough around the edges, and he couldn't trust her to behave herself in company, because she didn't care about appearances. She was smart, sophisticated and funny, but the tiger that lurked beneath could spring anytime and wreak a lot of damage.

And, he thought with a smile, he had given no thought to whether Liz might return his feelings for her. Hell, he wasn't the handsomest guy around, but women always responded to him. On the other hand, she bridled at his standing in the community, at his overt sense of entitlement. He knew he could be arrogant; it came with the territory. His family was philanthropic, involved, caring. They contributed generously to charity, and he and his father donated their time to legal aid. And what in hell was he so defensive about?

He pulled himself to his feet. It was about time he made the short walk over to see his parents, stay for afternoon tea, tease his sister and find out what she was doing with her life. Franny, he thought with a certain amount of guilt, was background, too, hardly younger than Liz and unmarried. They'd get along, Franny and Liz, in spite of their differences in life-styles and even in attitudes. Hell, he thought, they'd *have* to get along.

CHAPTER EIGHT

THE SUN WAS LOW in a sky filled with cumulus clouds as Brad cut through an acre of mature mixed evergreens planted by his parents over the years. The rear of the house belied the elegant formality of the facade as seen from the road. Down a smooth green lawn lay the pool house and swimming pool designed to resemble a natural pond. Beyond that, toward the woods, lay a small maze planted by an ambitious great grandfather. It had enchanted Brad as a child but was now cropped so that even a toddler couldn't lose his way. His mother's rose garden to the right was green-leaved and thick with nascent buds. Next to it was the freshly turned earth where she had planted her prize dahlias. He went up the green slope of lawn, heading left until he hit the cutting gardens, neat patches where herbs, vegetables and flowers had been planted.

He remembered Liz's expression when she'd seen Kent Hall from his building site. She had drawn back and turned oddly silent.

She'd never admit to being impressed. The kid, who by her own admission came from the wrong side of the tracks, should have sucked in her breath, should have turned to him with fresh respect. Should have looked him over as quarry. She hadn't and, in fact, had refused to meet his sister—not from impoliteness, he'd guessed, but from a sudden attack of shyness.

Oh, she'd been impressed with Kent Hall, all right. And then been turned off.

Brad let himself into the house through the side entrance, sauntering through the mud room and the kitchen, which was empty and smelled pleasantly of baking. He supposed the family was taking tea in the small drawing room. He lifted a cup and saucer from the china cabinet and made his way into the main part of the house, peering into familiar rooms, trying to see them with Liz's eye. Old, cold and classy was how he'd describe the eighteenth-century furniture and the worn Persian carpets.

His mother was alone in the drawing room, sitting on a yellow silk damask sofa, tea cart off to her right. She was deeply engrossed in a book and didn't hear him enter. He put the teacup down, bent over the sofa and kissed her silken silver hair.

"Oh, Brad, you startled me," she said, throwing the book down and touching her heart briefly. She rose, beaming as he came around to her. "Well, welcome stranger. I was wondering when you'd remember us."

"Ouch," he said, giving her an affectionate hug and taking both her hands in his.

"Ouch is right. It isn't that you live in Timbuktu, you know."

"Been busy," he told her. "Where is everybody?"

"Your father's at work," she said, "which is where you should be." She frowned, looking him over and resting her eyes on his torn jeans. "You aren't sick, are you?"

"Do I look sick?"

"No," she said, reaching for the teapot to pour him some tea, "but you look, well, I'm not sure, a little bright around the eyes."

Brad laughed easily, wondering how Liz would view his mother. She was a pretty woman with short wavy hair carefully coiffed around her face in a style she had worn since Brad was a child. She had the Vanderheyden nose, narrow-bridged and a little supercilious. She wore only a trace of makeup, so artfully applied that the color appeared quite natural. Her clothes were the kind country women of her class always wore—expensive separates that never changed style, particularly a calf-length pleated gray skirt of soft British wool with a matching blouse and cardigan.

She was aware of his perusal and quickly, after pouring the tea, filled a plate with cookies for him. "I expect Franny any minute," she explained. "Took the dogs for a walk."

He sat opposite her and wolfed down the tea and cookies, his hunger surprising him. "Stay for dinner," his mother urged.

"Can't. Brought some work home with me."

She sighed. "Can't. Really, Brad, your father would love to have you sitting at the table with us once in a while." But since she knew better than to press him, she added, "How's the building coming along?"

"Fine," he said. "Hammering bothering you?"

"No," she told him, "but it's a fine time to ask."

"I'm thinking," he said after a moment, "that maybe the place is going to be too small after all."

"I told you that at the beginning, Brad. It's high time you gave up the idea of bachelor pads and began thinking of your plans with Mimi."

He reached over and palmed half a dozen cookies, then began to eat them quickly, not even tasting them. "It won't be Mimi," he said at last.

"What?" His mother turned sharply to him, a stricken look on her face. He had the odd notion she'd been discussing him with Mimi's parents, as though the banns only had to be read.

"I've met someone else," he said quietly.

"Brad, you fool." His mother shook her head, as though she couldn't quite understand what he was getting at.

"It doesn't add up to anything yet, but it will if I have anything to do with it."

"But Mimi."

"There's nothing between us. It's been in your head all along."

At that moment the door opened and his sister came in, followed by the dogs, an old German shepherd that was lame in one leg and a Pekingese that came bouncing over to Brad. The German shepherd, also with a burst of energy, came joyously up to him. "Hey, Lady, how you doing, baby?" He looked fondly over at his sister while fondling the animal's ears. "Fran, I was hoping to catch you."

She was a slender young woman with their father's small nose and Brad's warm blue eyes. She was far prettier than Brad was handsome, and yet she dated seldom and seemed settled into a narrow life.

"Could you do with another walk before tea?" he asked, settling a kiss on her cheek.

"Sure. Want to talk about something or someone?"

Brad glanced over at his mother She shook her head slightly in a warning. She'd lobby for Mimi, he thought, but he knew the kind of vote he'd cast, provided Liz decided to run.

LIZ LOOKED UP from her computer, yawned and caught Celie's eye through her glass partition. Celie was headed back to her office and beckoned Liz to follow. It was almost five on a Friday night, and Liz didn't want to get into any long discussion with Celie about anything. Deciding to say yes to everything her boss had to say, she rose, took her pad and pencil and followed Celie into her office.

"Put something down on your calendar for next week," Celie said immediately. "The school board is having its last meeting of the season and they're going to air some of the problems that will have to be addressed next term—like ever-lowering reading levels, impossibly low math scores and graffiti all over the handball court. Not to mention the luncheon menu, which has too much starch and not enough in the way of green vegetables, et cetera, et cetera. I'll want a short, tight article on the meeting, stating that we're going to look forward to their return with some solutions."

Liz had to stop herself from suggesting that she needn't even attend the meeting, since Celie seemed to have it down pat.

Celie handed her a slip of paper with the time and place written on it. "We want to keep them on their toes, let them know the eyes of the world are on them."

The whole world, Liz thought, tucking the paper into her jacket pocket after glancing at it. "Same day as two other meetings, one in Merriman on the new tax bite and one in Herkimer on the idea of a three-way tie between Merriman, Herkimer and Ramsey Falls on ambulance services. It'll be a squeeze to fit it all in, Celie."

"It's going to be a rough week all around," Celie said with concern. "I'll take on what I can and maybe Adriana can handle a couple of stories, although the truth is,

I don't like the way she looks lately. *Harried* is how I'd describe it."

"Don't give her any more work, Celie. I'll handle the load."

"It'll ease off now that school is out and people begin to put everything else on hold."

"I'm used to tight deadlines," Liz said. "I even think I work best that way."

There was a light knock at the door, three taps as though it were a signal. Celie brightened and pushed her tinted aviator glasses high on her head. "Come in, Victor," she called.

The door opened and Victor Bosworth peered in. "Am I disturbing you?" He cast a glance at Liz and offered her a sweet smile.

"No, no," Celie said. "Come in and wait. I won't be a minute."

Liz got to her feet immediately. Victor came over to her at once and shook her hand. "How are you, Liz?"

"Fine, Mr. Bosworth." His handshake was firm, and for a moment they remained smiling at each other, as though uncertain what to say next. His manner wasn't intimidating, yet Liz was hit with an unexpected attack of shyness. She looked entreatingly over at Celie, who was watching them, her color a little high and flushed.

"Just one more question, Liz," her boss said. "Oh, do sit down—both of you."

Liz quickly took her seat, though Victor wandered over to the window and leaned against it, arms folded across his chest.

"Anything on the zoning dispute between Nelson and Vanderheyden?"

Liz thought Celie had asked the question in too offhand a manner. "I've been slogging through zoning changes for the past year to see if I can find any conflict of interest. It's like trying to read through somebody else's glasses. How do I know a conflict of interest when I see one? Or don't see one?''

Celie turned to Victor. "Liz sees the Nelson lawsuit over Will Vanderheyden's request for a zoning change as big stuff, involving major interests.''

"Celie, I haven't made any judgment at all," Liz said in protest.

Victor, however, looked interested. "It's not up to Will. It's up to the zoning board.''

"And all I'm doing—" Liz said, but she was stopped from finishing her sentence when Celie's phone rang.

Celie picked it up. "Yes?" Then she took the receiver and handed it to Liz, frowning slightly. "Marion Nelson for you.''

Liz took the receiver after a quick look at Victor, who was watching her shrewdly. Of all the damn times and places for Marion to call, Celie's office was decidedly the last and worse. She forced herself to smile brightly. "Hi, Marion. I was just thinking about you. We ought to have lunch.''

"Uh, listen. I'm sorry. The telephone operator said you were with Mrs Decatur and put me through before I could object.''

"How about coffee, then?''

"Oh," Marion groaned, "call me back, okay? At my father's. That's where I am now.''

"Okay, honey. See you soon.''

Celie reached out to take the receiver from Liz.

"Marion?" Victor mused. "I suppose she's caught in the middle of that dispute. Her father was always a bit of a gadfly.''

"So am I," Liz said. "Maybe that's why we all get along so well." Then she added on the spur of the moment, "How's Wouldn't It Be Loverly? Taken to his new home?" She hoped Victor Bosworth would inadvertently reveal who had bought the horse.

Victor's laugh was spontaneous. "I sent the goat along with him."

"I beg your pardon."

"Horses like pets as much as humans do. The goat is his pet."

"Well," Celie said, breaking into the conversation, "my suggestion about that whole zoning business is to give it up. It's a waste of time."

"Uh-uh," Liz said as she went over to the door. "Gut instinct tells me John Nelson is getting the short end of the stick, and Will Vanderheyden has the long, golden end."

"Have a nice weekend," Celie said, dismissing her with a nod and smiling over at Victor.

Back at her cubicle, Liz found Jake Martinez sitting in her chair, his long denim-clad legs crossed on top of her desk. The caked mud on the soles of his boots had left little flecks on her desk.

He was a free-lance photographer who worked out of a small studio on Main Street next to Jemma Gardner's print shop. He had, a decade before, arrived in Ramsey Falls on a beat-up motorcycle that had brought him cross-country from Venice, California. The purpose of the trip had been to sell an apple orchard left to him by an uncle. He'd sold the orchard but had never left Ramsey Falls, although he often talked about going back to California, especially when the local roads were blocked with snow.

"Hey, what's chewing on your ear?" he asked. "You look as if you didn't get out of the ring soon enough."

"Jake, get your feet off my desk." Liz sat down on the only other chair in the room and put her own feet up on the desk. She didn't really care that Jake had made himself at home in her cubicle. She had no sense of possession, particularly about her office furniture. "I only wish I were in the ring," she told him. "That way I could see my opponent and at least know what the rules of the fight are."

"You having a hard time with Celie?" The way he shook his head told Liz she had his sympathy. He'd had his run-ins with Celie, who was fond of him but couldn't abide the way he lived and dressed. His hair was pulled back into a ponytail and tied with a leather strip. He dressed in worn, exotically embroidered jeans, and his only mode of transportation, winter and summer, was on an elaborately equipped Harley-Davidson motorcycle, known to everyone in Ramsey Falls and Merriman as belonging to Jake Martinez.

"Celie, everybody. I have to make a phone call," she said.

"Go ahead. I'll listen in without the least embarrassment."

She reached for her telephone and dialed John Nelson's number. Marion answered. "Listen, I'm sorry, Liz. I didn't want to break in on a meeting with your boss, especially since all I wanted to do was to tell you that I haven't found out who bought Wouldn't It Be Loverly, but I'm still working on it."

The name of the buyer was no longer Liz's top priority, but she was still curious. "Do you think you'll be able to come up with something soon?"

"I hope so. It's just that everybody seems to be sticking close to the office. With that big sale there's been a lot of paperwork. Still is. Anyway, don't worry. I'm still on it. Anything on my father's case?"

"I'm researching zoning board decisions for the past couple of years. Is there anything you can tell me? You know, anything that looks suspicious?"

Marion's laugh was a full, deep rumble. "Liz, everything looks suspicious to me right now. I'll call you or send you a message as soon as I learn something. I haven't forgotten."

"Great. I'm still interested."

When she put the receiver down, she turned to Jake. "What do you know about Will Vanderheyden?"

He eyed her curiously. "Something cooking with him?"

"That bar-restaurant he's planning to build on I-84."

"It's a fait accompli, as we who've been to college would put it. What do you want me to tell you about him?"

"I'm trying to understand the power structure in Ramsey Falls, that's all. How does he manage to dig the foundations for a restaurant that doesn't have zoning board approval?"

"Yet."

"Yet. That's the point, Jake, my boy."

Her telephone went off at that moment. Jake picked the receiver up and handed it to Liz. She automatically reached for her pad and pencil as she put the receiver to her ear. "Liz Grady."

"Is this the beauteous Liz Grady?"

The voice was male, unfamiliar and had an insinuating undertone that she didn't like. Jake started to get up, but Liz motioned to him to stay put. "Who's calling?" she asked in a careful voice.

"Beautiful legs, beautiful figure, beautiful eyes. Hey, the guys are all talking about beautiful Liz. You want to know what they're saying, don't you?"

Liz paled. She motioned Jake over to listen in.

"What they're saying is they'd hate to see you messed up in some unexpected accident."

Jake took the receiver away and barked into it, "Keep it up, feller, and you'll learn all about unexpected accidents." He slammed the receiver down and studied Liz. "All right, what was that about?"

"Did you recognize the voice, Jake?" She knew her own voice sounded shaky.

Jake shook his head. "Whoever it was took pains to disguise it. What story are you working on to get a call like that?"

She shrugged. "Nothing but John Nelson's real estate hassle with Will Vanderheyden."

"Will? He'll strong-arm anyone if there's a sweet deal in it for him."

"You have proof?"

"Hey, the man's my landlord," Jake said, referring to the studio on Main Street where he spent his time when not free-lancing for the *Times Herald*. "Will's been trying to get me to break my ten-year lease so that he can rent the studio to bigger fish. He tried a little arm-twisting for a while, but I wouldn't budge. He's backed off, for the moment at least."

Liz got to her feet, uncertain whether to storm into Celie's office or to talk it out with Jake. "Well, if that call was meant to scare me into backing away from the Nelson story, and if Will was behind it, he's sent me just the message I need. There's a deeper story there than I imagined.''

''You're working on the zoning board change as it affects John Nelson's property. Am I right?''

''I'm doing some research into decisions made by the board for the past couple of years. It's all in the public record.''

''Give it up,'' he said tersely.

''Wait a minute. I just heard that from Celie. I'm not giving up anything.''

''My lady,'' he told her, ''the Vanderheydens don't take kindly to people who interfere with their expressed desires. They've got the judiciary sewed up with His Honor, the judge. That's all they need. Vanderheyden justice is what they make it. Sooner or later we're all called before the judge, and he's the one person around here nobody, yours truly included, wishes to cross.''

''People are that afraid?'' Liz asked.

''Does the sun rise every morning?''

''Celie, too?''

''You mean, is she intimidated by them? Maybe not quite, but certainly cautious. She plays bridge with the judge, is friendly with his sister and would like to marry Victor Bosworth, whose main lawyer man is Bradford Kent, son of her close friend, the judge's sister. Complicated enough for you?''

She shook her head. ''I'm becoming familiar with the ins and outs of local relationships.''

''Celie's independent,'' he added with affection. ''She hired me when everyone else was hoping I'd get out of town. She and Victor saw to it that I got financial backing to open the shop.'' He hesitated, then remarked, ''If what you're doing will hurt Celie in any way, I won't back you, Liz. As it is, I'd suggest you give the sheriff a buzz and tell him about the phone call.''

"No," she said.

"Don't be a martyr, Liz.''

"What would I tell the sheriff? Someone called and flattered me with just enough oiliness in his voice to persuade me to back away?''

"So back away.''

"No," she said once again. "If I back off when I smell something, I can't call myself an investigative reporter, can I?''

He gave a short, mirthless laugh. "Investigative reporter in Ramsey Falls. Never thought I'd see the day.'' He eased himself out of the chair and went over to the door. "That's so important, calling yourself an investigative reporter?''

"Yes," she said, "it is.''

He shot a finger at her. "Check your car before you get into it, Liz. I'm not kidding.''

Not kidding. She trusted Jake's instincts, but she wanted someone else's input as well. When he was gone, she picked up the telephone receiver and dialed Brad's office, first in Merriman and then in Ramsey Falls. He'd gone home, she was informed and his telephone number wasn't listed. She shivered, although the office was warm. *Beauteous Liz Grady. The guys are all talking about beautiful Liz.* Liz hurried out of her office to catch Celie before she left with Victor, but Celie was already gone. Anyway, Liz thought, it was Brad she wanted to see, Brad she had to talk to.

LIZ PAUSED outside the *Times Herald* building. It was dusk and the sky was cloudy. A chilly breeze swept in off the river, making it feel more like autumn than spring.

She looked back up at the restored newspaper building, its four stories making it the tallest structure in Ramsey Falls. All the windows in the building were lit, including the large drugstore that occupied the ground floor. The street was quiet, with few cars and no pedestrians.

From where Liz stood she could see Whiting Printing, which looked shut up tight. Jemma Gardner had obviously taken her own advice and left at six o'clock. Liz went down Decatur to the parking area behind the building.

Jake had suggested that she check her car thoroughly before getting into it. She stood for a moment and wondered. She had covered tough stories in Chicago and had even received angry phone calls that passed as threats. Never bodily threats, however. Curses had rained upon her and her parents and her bosses and lawsuits had been broadly hinted at, but she'd always been careful about stirring up the waters and had had a strong paper to back her. Here, in Ramsey Falls, she was being equally careful, but she had no idea where Celie would draw the line at helping her.

The advertising manager came into the parking lot and Liz, who was holding her car key in her hand, greeted him.

"Think it might rain?" he asked.

"Clouds are a little too high," she said.

"You're right. Could use some rain, though. Night, Liz."

"Night," she returned as he got into his car and drove slowly out of the lot. She'd had a chance to ask his help but hadn't.

Liz slipped her key into the door lock and turned quickly, not giving herself a chance to change her mind. She pulled the car door open, aware of holding her breath. Nothing happened. She climbed in. No, they wouldn't rig a car with a bomb, not in Ramsey Falls. A phone call maybe, but they wouldn't blow up a car, not in the lot behind the Decatur Building, not while it was still light out. This was real life, not a television movie. She put her key in the ignition. The car started in its usual way.

She didn't stop until she reached the tall fieldstone plinths that marked the entrance to Kent Hall. The property was completely surrounded by a fieldstone wall. The wrought-iron entrance gates were open, although there was a sign that warned trespassers away. At the end of a circular paved driveway lined with artfully pruned trees and bushes was the baronial, intimidating manor house. Somewhere on the property was the small stone house that Brad occupied.

"Service entrance," she said out loud. "That would be it." She turned right and continued driving parallel to the stone wall until she discovered a closed double gate in the wall, with a small sign indicating that it was indeed the service entrance. She got out of her car and found the gate secured with a hook. After she pushed the gate open, she got back into her car and drove through. There were half a dozen buildings on the property, all of stone and all very ancient, ranging from a great barn built in Dutch Colonial style to small outbuildings of no discernible use.

The icehouse was a low, narrow stone building with curtains in the window and a front door painted red. She drew up, stepped out and walked smartly to the front door, summoning the same kind of courage that she used for difficult interviews. There was no bell, so she rapped three times and waited, then rapped again. Through the trees she could see the lights of the main house. That was when her courage failed her. He wasn't home, and she had come charging to him for some obscure reason that she couldn't properly name.

"Liz?"

She whipped around at the sound of his voice. He came toward her in the early dusk, and she felt a curious quickening of her heart when she saw him. Wearing jeans and a denim shirt, both molded to his body, he walked with an easy, athletic stride.

"What are you doing here?" He seemed glad to see her, but a little confused, as though he had found her in the wrong place at the wrong time. He took her arms in a strong grip and kissed her cheek. "Is anything wrong?"

"I don't know," she said, flustered. "I think so. Maybe."

"Come on inside. How'd you find me? Why didn't you call? No, you couldn't. You don't have my number. We'll have to fix that, won't we? Anyway, I was over at the main house. Lord, am I glad to see you."

He opened the door to the cottage, still holding her arm. There was a small entryway blazing with light, and somehow the sight of it made her realize her vulnerability. No, she didn't want to confront him on his territory. She pulled away.

"No, I don't think it's a good idea. Look," she said, "I'm a little confused but maybe we can go for a drive."

His expression was serious and a little worried. "If that's what you want."

"My car," she said with determination.

"Mine," he said with equal determination, gripping her arm. "You look a little pale and tired."

It was when they were clear of the estate and well out on the highway heading toward the mountains that Liz spoke for the first time. "Well, I guess you can congratulate me," she said. "I received my first threatening phone call today."

There was a long moment of silence before Brad spoke, his voice tight. "Go on."

"Some joker told me that I was a dish and that a lot of guys around Ramsey Falls thought so, too. He let me know, not in so many words, that if I wanted to remain a dish, I should step away from the zoning dispute story. Jake Martinez listened in, then told my caller not to try that sort of thing again. The call was a decided threat as far as I'm concerned."

"Did you go to the police?"

"No. What do I have to tell them, that somebody in an obviously phony voice called me to flatter me on behalf of every male in Ramsey Falls?"

"You're sure that's not what happened?"

"Oh, Brad, for God's sake, stop being a lawyer. I've received enough phone calls from strangers to know an out-and-out threat when I hear one."

"Liz, you're not making sense. Look, there's a small park about a quarter mile down. I'll pull off. Then I want you to look me straight in the eye and tell me what in hell's going on."

She was silent, sorry she had come, sorry she had told him anything. His lawyer's mind was already at work. He'd have her convinced the call was from a masher and to let it go until another one came in.

Brad parked the car beneath a grove of trees that sat at the edge of a small lake. There were a couple of other cars, unoccupied, and on the opposite side of the lake she saw a picnic table lit with candles. Half a dozen people sat around it, enjoying their outdoor meals. A barbecue had been set up, and she saw the glow of charcoal.

"I'm working on only one project that could raise anyone's hackles," she told him. She stepped out of the car and made her way to the lakeshore. The moon, glimpsed above high, fast-moving clouds, was three-quarters full. There was a ring around it, portending rain the next day.

Brad came over and joined her. "What are you working on that could have prompted such a phone call?"

"The only one I can think of is the zoning dispute between John Nelson and Will Vanderheyden."

He laughed. "You'd better come up with something more ominous than that. The monthly meetings of the zoning board are open to the public. It's the state law. John Nelson will have his day, the zoning board will vote democratically—"

"And Will's restaurant will go up as ordained."

"Then you don't have to worry about threatening phone calls on Will's account, do you?"

"I know what I heard. The only other project is—" She stopped, remembering Marion Nelson's promise to find the name of the person who had purchased Wouldn't It Be Loverly. But then Marion hadn't come through and was obviously being very cautious.

He reached over and straightened her shirt collar. "The only other project is what?"

"Nothing, as a matter of fact. Brad, I came running to you because I thought maybe, in some odd way, you'd be on my side."

"I am, Liz. Will is my cousin. He may be arrogant and selfish, but that's because the judge has always let him get away with murder."

"Murder?" She shook her head and gave him a half smile. "Clever of you to use that word."

"What do you want me to do?"

She shook her head slowly. Perhaps take her in his arms and tell her everything would be okay. "I don't know."

"Scared?"

"I shouldn't be. I'm tough as nails."

"But you came running to me."

"Tell your cousin Willie to back away. I'm only doing my job. If he's got nothing to hide, I'll be the first one to sing his praises."

"Nobody sings praises to Willie. I'll talk to him, but believe me, there's only a little piece of land at stake."

"With a spectacular view," she threw in.

"With a spectacular view. But Willie doesn't win them all, contrary to what you believe."

"Oh, I'll find that out, as soon as I work my way through the zoning board decisions."

"Waste of time, Liz. The zoning board consists of five citizens of varying degrees of prosperity, but they're not stitched together. They vote by conscience."

"How do they get their jobs?" Liz asked, genuinely curious.

"The mayor selects them for a two-year term."

"The mayor selects them. Ah, of course. Is the mayor related to Will, or to you, for that matter?"

"You know what, Liz?" Brad took her hand in his. "I'm not going to answer that question." He opened her palm and put his lips against it. "I'll talk to Will if that's what you want me to do," he said. He took her chin in his hand. "I like the part about your coming to me for help. I like that part a lot."

"Brad, you know the kind of help I mean."

"I do know, Liz," he said softly.

She had asked for it, she thought, as he pulled her into his arms. It was inevitable, as inevitable as the moon's flight around the earth, as inevitable as the stars' pilgrimage through the galaxy. Just before Liz closed her eyes, she saw the stars tumble from the sky and their glow light the lake. She had asked for it, and it all belonged to something wonderful close at hand, right at her fingertips, as close as the air she breathed. His mouth came down on hers, hard and insistent.

She touched his shirt collar, the warm skin at his neck. His hands slid across her back, curving downward over her hips to press her into his body, then stroking slowly along her spine. His lips were firm but no longer hard. They teased and aroused rather than plundered. His tongue took moisture from their mouths and soothed and bathed her tingling lips.

Liz moaned. The sound startled her. She had trouble opening her eyes. Her lids were heavy and seemed to have a will of their own. Then his hand lifted and she felt his fingers trace a line from her waist to her breast. He enclosed her softly and she felt his intake of breath.

"Come home with me now," he whispered close to her mouth.

"Home?" The question came out in a scarcely whispered sound. She pulled back, frowning in disbelief, putting both hands against his chest. He was smiling at her, and for a moment she felt disoriented. But then the stars were back in the sky and her head cleared.

"I came to you asking for help," she said.

"I don't think you'd take my help," he said.

"Do I look that easy?"

"No," he said with a deadly serious expression, turning and heading back to the car, "you're not easy, not easy at all. Oh, baby, how I wish you were."

CHAPTER NINE

WITH A FRUSTRATION that was new to him, Brad watched Liz run up the steps of the Duboise house. He'd tried to talk to her on the ride back, had apologized a dozen different ways for his clumsy pass, but she wouldn't listen.

Then, when he'd stopped the car to let her out, Liz had turned to him. "I don't know why I came running to you for help, Brad. It seemed like the right thing at the time, as if you were the most mature person in the world, the most responsible, the one I could truly count on. I was frightened. I figured you'd make the bogeyman go away." She'd shaken her head as he'd reached for her, touched by her words, her trust.

"No, please," she'd said. "Oh, maybe you helped, after all. I just realized suddenly that I'm not worried about the phone call. I told you what happened. You didn't grab your white horse and go charging after him. Instead, you just...just made a little pass at me." She'd laughed, although it came out with an apologetic sound like a hiccup. "I believe," she'd continued after a moment of thought, "that you care about what happens to me. That's why I think if the caller were anyone more than your basic everyday masher, you'd tear up the town looking for him."

"I think I would, too," he'd said quietly.

"Not believing it," she'd gone on in an even voice, letting him know he wasn't off the hook, "you took the opportunity to do a bit of mashing of your own. How do I know you aren't the voice behind the call?"

He'd looked at her, shaking his head slowly. "You've just made a pretty deep cut, Liz. The trouble is, I kissed you, which any red-blooded male would do given the circumstances."

"What circumstances?" she'd asked in a rough, insulted voice.

"Looking vulnerable and terrific. And coming to me for help."

"Brad, you kissed me. I kissed you back. It felt good. It felt terrific. It also didn't call for an invitation to spend the night with you."

"Can you blame me for trying?"

"Yes," she'd said, reaching for the door handle. "It was out of line, considering my vulnerability." And with that, she'd left him and run up the stairs before he could stop her.

Of course, suggesting she come back to his cottage had been a stupid, clumsy move on his part. The feel of her, the smell of her, had simply dissolved his usual caution. He hadn't given a thought to what she must have been feeling. A tide of sensual pleasure had swept through his body as she'd pressed against him. All he had felt were the sweet heat of her breath and the softness of her lips as she'd responded to him. He'd been excited farther by the way her mouth had opened to him, by the way her heartbeat had quickened when he'd pulled her close. It had been a revelation—the sudden and frightening knowledge that he wanted Liz more than he had ever wanted anyone in his life.

And so he had thrown caution to the wind and mindlessly suggested they spend the night together. Foolish move. Brad stayed in the car and looked up at the old stone house. A light went on in a second-floor window—hers he supposed. He could still feel the need for her. He had to clear his head, had to know her, know what she was feeling.

He wanted her to come to the window, to gaze down at him, to see he wouldn't abandon her, that he'd made a mistake and would do anything to correct it. After a while the light went out. He had botched things up. It was a feeling he wasn't used to having.

No, he hadn't thought the telephone call was merely one of the games played by the locals. He cast his mind about, wondering which of the town's looser characters could have made the call. And why.

Running around Ramsey Falls with a notebook in hand, wearing jeans and a loose shirt, or the likes of Henry David Thoreau, her hair usually wind-tossed, her lipstick possibly chewed down, certainly didn't qualify Liz Grady for a sex goddess. The trouble could be traced directly to his cousin Will's door. A discreet word to one of his cronies, and if Celie didn't warn off Liz from the story, maybe a nasty phone call would do it. The trouble was no one would talk. Will knew who his friends were, and in Ramsey Falls memories were long and debts were always paid up.

Brad tightened his seat belt, gazed one more time at Liz's window and started the car. Once on the dark and lonely road, he watched the speedometer register seventy and then eighty miles per hour.

LIZ OPENED HER EYES, suddenly wide awake. The digital clock read 3:00 a.m. Hours before, she had thrown herself down on the bed, holding back her breath as if that would make the whole sordid episode disappear. And then, when she hadn't heard his car start up, she'd turned out the light. Only then did he leave. She'd fallen asleep instantly, not even bothering to undress, wanting only the sweet amnesia of total withdrawal.

It was a habit of hers since childhood. When faced with trying times or monumental decisions, she climbed into bed, pulled the covers over her head and fell asleep at once. Of course such actions solved nothing. Usually she found herself awake in the early-morning hours with the problem unsolved. Tonight was no different.

Loneliness, she told herself, had made her respond so strongly to his touch. Loneliness pure and simple. With maybe a little desire for sex thrown in. She could still feel Brad's hard readiness as he'd held her, his hand caressing her breast. She still heard the soft longing in his words, except they were the wrong words. *Let's go back to my place.*

The truth was she shouldn't have expected anything less. She had gone to him for help, and maybe with his kiss he had given it to her. He had kissed her out there in the silence of the night, with a party going on across the lake. No one had seen them, of course.

Still, somehow everyone would know what was going on if she stepped into an affair with Brad Kent. He might not care; perhaps the town expected that of him. And she was only Liz Grady, late of the crowded mean streets of the big city, a temporary aberration and a troublesome one at that. What better way to compromise her integrity than involve her in an affair with the local counselor. With his willing collusion of course. If she lost her reputation for fairness, honesty and distance, it would render her useless as a confidante to Marion and

John Nelson and to Adriana and anyone else in town who might have a stake in the way she covered the news.

And Celie Decatur would have a fit.

Good Lord, she was cloaked in middle-of-the-night paranoia, the deep, dark craziness that fed every neurotic nerve in her body. Why didn't she face up to the truth? Brad wanted to make love to her and she wanted him to. It was as simple as that. What had frightened her was the unexpected and nearly desperate yearning she had felt for him.

He wasn't even the kind of man she was ordinarily attracted to. He was close-minded, opinionated, patrician, imperious—oh, the list was a long one.

There was no use in pretending she was going to go back to sleep. She sat up in bed and reached for the light, a small lamp that cast the room in a warm, protective, rosy hue. She lay back for a while, listening to the old house creak and moan, as though it too suffered from some deep night craziness. Liz struggled off the bed and only then looked down at her clothes. Her stockings were twisted, her clothes wrinkled. Served her right for tumbling into bed without even undressing.

She knew that if she turned on the bath, the noise would announce to the entire house that she was up and washing away the evening. What would Mrs. Duboise make of that?

There was a full-length standing mirror near the closet, and without knowing why, Liz watched herself undress. It was only when she was naked that she allowed herself to wonder. What would Brad have thought of her? She placed her fingers on her breast exactly where his had been, and in that instant brought back the intensity and confusion of her feelings for him.

No, she thought, turning away from her reflection, it was an impossible situation. She had said no to Brad and it had been a wise and necessary decision. No hanky-panky with the scion of the Kent fortune, the nephew of the judge and the cousin of the defendant. Bad news all around.

She slipped on a flannel gown and settled once again into bed. She was wrong about not falling asleep. She didn't stir again until the sun forced its way through the curtains and lit the room with the challenge of a new day.

Liz sat bolt upright. It took her a moment to remember it was Saturday and that she could sleep all day if she wished. Then she remembered the insinuating voice over the telephone and how she had gone running to Brad. The weekend ahead suddenly looked long and bleak. She wanted it to be Monday when she could run over to Merriman and continue her search through the zoning records. There was the laundry to be done and then a phone call home. She hadn't spoken to her mother all week, and now she needed to touch base.

One thing was certain: she wasn't going to stay around, waiting for the telephone to ring. She didn't want to hear from Brad and she didn't want to be tempted to call him. She would do her laundry, call her mother, then climb into her car and drive down to New York City for the weekend. She had several addresses of friends who'd invited her to visit. Done.

She climbed out of bed with her usual energy. Liz Grady was never one to do things in half measures.

"YOU AGAIN?" the receptionist at Merriman's town hall groaned, giving Liz an exasperated smile.

Refreshed from a weekend in New York where her friends had taken her to several head-clearing cultural events, Liz was ready to take on anyone. "Here to see the zoning board files again," she said politely.

"You know where they are. Go right back. Oh, listen," the receptionist said, giving her a sudden broad grin, "I've got a brother who's an artist, and a pretty good one. Watercolors. He's going to have an exhibition. How about giving him a write-up in the *Times Herald*."

"Sure," Liz said, "if it passes muster with my editor. Where's the exhibition going to be?"

"Barney's Fish and Chips. They're giving him wall space at the back of the restaurant."

"Be my pleasure to attend the opening," Liz said. "Tell him to send me an invitation."

"Right," the receptionist told her, beaming. "Great. It's going to be quite an opening. A vernissage he calls it. *Très* French. He'll send the invitation to the newspaper."

To Liz's surprise, the clerk behind the desk in the records department wasn't quite as friendly as the receptionist, nor as she had been the week before. She was, in fact, cold and reluctant, frowning at Liz through her thick-lensed glasses. "Okay, what is it this time?"

"July through December of last year, January through May of this year," Liz said.

A deep sigh was dredged up. "July through December, January through May of *what*?"

"Zoning board decisions," Liz said, leaning across the desk and saying the words in a loud whisper. "For Ramsey Falls, part of Merriman County and the greater township of Merriman."

"Why didn't you say so in the first place?"

Because I've been here three times before on exactly the same errand, Liz remarked to herself. Something was

going on, and it had to do with the threatening telephone call she had received. Somebody had passed the
word: *Watch every move Liz Grady makes. Block her,
tackle her, do whatever you have to, but make sure she
falls down.*

The woman reluctantly dragged herself back to the
files and emerged with them after twenty minutes had
elapsed, during which time she fielded three long, loud
telephone conversations, most of which seemed to have
something to do with missed hairdressing appoint-
ments. After the last call, she quite obviously made fresh
coffee, the scent drifting out to the front of the office.

"Here," the woman said irritably, slamming the files
down on the desk.

"Thanks a million. You're an angel," Liz said, picking the files up as though she had been handed something precious.

"Not to be taken out of this department," the clerk
said.

"Yes, of course, certainly. I understand perfectly. I'll
be using them right over there," Liz said, pointing to an
oak library table beneath the window, the one she had
used before. "I'll bring them all back as soon as I've
finished with them." When she sat down, however, and
checked over the tabs, she found November of the previous year missing.

She went back to the clerk, who was now speaking
with another staff member about something inconse-
quential involving a lot of "he saids" and "she saids."
Liz waited, tapping her fingers on top of the desk. When
at last she got the clerk's attention, she said, "Excuse
me. You didn't give me November of last year."

The woman stared at her.

"November of last year," Liz repeated patiently. "The file. It isn't here." For a moment she thought the woman was going to accuse her of stealing it.

"I know. The file's missing."

"Missing? You mean somebody else has it."

"It's missing. There's no checkout mark in the file. It's missing."

"Missing." Liz tapped her fingers on the counter a few more times and tried to stare the woman down. There was something about the wide, unblinking, hostile eyes made huge by thick-lensed glasses that defeated Liz. "Missing," she said once again, and turned away. Someone had removed the file. Someone had been talking to the clerk. Someone desperately didn't want her nosing around zoning board decisions.

THE DOOR TO CELIE'S office was open and Liz stuck her head in. "Aha!" she said in a triumphant voice.

"Aha what?"

"Aha, there's dirty business afoot and I've got the proof. Would you like to hear it?"

"Can I stop you?"

Liz came into the office and snapped her fingers. "Not when I'm on a roll. Vanderheyden dirty business, and they've obviously got the clerk at the Merriman town hall on their payroll."

Celie cleared her throat and looked past Liz. For the first time Liz realized they weren't alone. She whipped around and discovered Brad standing on the other side of the open door, hands stuffed into his pockets. He gave her a crooked grin and bent his head in greeting.

Liz backed away, feeling her face redden. "Oh, I'm sorry," she said to Celie. "I...I thought you were alone, open door and all that." She had an uncanny sensation of having been the subject of their discussion.

"Sit down, Liz, and reasonably and calmly, without editorializing, tell me what you've found."

Brad made a halfhearted effort to leave. "Brad, stay," Celie told him. "And both of you, for heaven's sake, sit down."

Brad, however, went over to Celie's desk, bent over and kissed her on the cheek. "I'll see you later, Celie." He turned to Liz and, still smiling, said, "Watch what you say about the Vanderheydens. They're a litigious bunch." He left, closing the door behind him.

Liz pushed her chair up at Celie's desk. "I'm sorry," she said. "But really, it's all beginning to look a little hairy. In the first place the normally friendly clerk at the town hall really gave me the cold shoulder when I asked to see the zoning board decisions. Then she told me November of last year was missing—unchecked out, but missing."

"Which puts her in the pay of the Vanderheydens."

"Okay, I exaggerated a bit," Liz said.

"Try not to exaggerate from now on, please."

"I've found out a couple of interesting things, anyway," Liz said. "Arbitrary zoning board decisions, for one. Example, residential property purchased by Will and rezoned for commercial use in Merriman down at the waterfront. Purchased, by the way, *before* the decision to develop was made final. Then there was a fortuitous business of the Ryerson farm near the Merriman airport. Soon after Will took possession, talk surfaced that the airport was being expanded and the land was rezoned for commercial use. Will seems to be on the cutting edge of rezoning, doesn't he? There's lots more, besides."

All during her recital Celie had been shaking her head. "You know, Liz, when I started out in this business I couldn't wait to nail something to the wall that I thought everyone else had overlooked. Only now I'm boss and I know the price a newspaper pays with allegations that can't be proven. Will Vanderheyden is in the real estate business. If he can't read the pulse of what's happening in the area, then he's in the wrong business. Missing files and a clerk in a bad mood do not an accusation make."

Liz stood, and on an impulse went around the desk and placed a kiss on Celie's cheek in the approximate spot touched by Brad's kiss. "Got your point, although I also believe in operating on gut instinct."

"I agree that instinct is an effective weapon in following a lead, but proof positive is what we need. Now get out of here. I've work to do. Incidentally, I've got a notice here that they're convening a meeting of the zoning board to discuss Will's request for a variance."

Liz's eyes widened in surprise. "That wasn't scheduled for another month."

Celie rummaged through the papers on her desk and found the notice. "I'll concede this much," she said, handing the notice to Liz. "The meeting is for tomorrow night. Scheduled a little too quickly, as if they're hoping to catch John Nelson and his lawyer off guard."

Liz felt her heart sink as she looked over the notice. Brad would be there representing Will Vanderheyden. She had a feeling the deck was being stacked against John Nelson and she had no idea how to help.

"About the missing November file," Celie said as Liz headed for the door. "Check our files for that time. After all, we do print zoning board decisions. They're already on microfiche, and I can't imagine—" She frowned, motioned to Liz to wait, picked up the telephone receiver and punched in the extension of the newspaper archives. "November of last year," she told the librarian. "Pull those files. Liz Grady is coming in for them."

"Right," Liz said as she went out the door.

"Liz!"

Liz turned and Celie said, "If even a page is missing, I want to know about it."

In the archives however, which was a cavernous room on the third floor filled with packed bookshelves and filing cabinets, the librarian pointed to a desk on which one of the microfiche viewers sat. Brad was using it. "Just before Mrs. Decatur called, Mr. Kent came in and asked for them," she told Liz. "What's in those files, anyway? The secrets to the atom bomb?"

"Could be." Liz turned and looked over at Brad, who was staring through the viewer with dogged interest. Liz screwed up her determination and went quickly over to him.

Brad smiled at her with what she thought was some embarrassment. "Looking for me?"

"Yes, as a matter of fact."

"You knew I'd be here?"

"I heard your name whispered in the corridors. Just followed all the deep feminine sighs." Brad was wearing a dark blue, well-cut suit, a white shirt and a conservative tie, and he looked, she thought, with a sudden little catch of her heart, very handsome. She wondered then how she could ever have thought of him otherwise.

"Something you wanted to talk to me about?" he asked. "It seems to me the last time you wanted advice—"

"I thought you might take me out to lunch," she threw in quickly, not even stopping to think. "Right now. I'm starved."

His look brightened. It was as if Liz had offered him a present he'd been dreaming about. The knowledge was unsettling, and for a moment she wavered. It was still possible to change her mind, to run away, but when he glanced quickly at the files sitting on the desk, she said, "I forgot to have breakfast this morning."

"Mustn't let a lady starve," he told her, getting to his feet and gathering the microfiche files together. He brought them over to the desk and said to the librarian, "Hold these for me. I'll be back for them."

When they were halfway out the door, Liz stopped and said to Brad, "Oh, wait, I just wanted to ask the librarian about something." She went back to the desk. "Those mircofiches Mr. Kent just gave you."

The librarian shook her head. "I'm holding them for him."

Liz glanced back at Brad, who stood at the door watching her. "Are they all there?"

The librarian went through them quickly. "Seem to be."

"Send them up to Mrs. Decatur, then, with a note asking her to keep them for me and that I'll be back after lunch for them."

"But Mr. Kent—"

"Forget Mr. Kent."

She went swiftly back to Brad. "I've taken command of the microfiches," she said, heading out into the hall. "I hope you don't mind."

He laughed out loud. "You little sneak."

"Hungry little sneak. Come on."

"I ought to haul you before court on a charge of bamboozling an honest man. Haddie's suit you?"

"Suits me fine," she told him. "I'll take my car and meet you there. I'll need it for afterward," she added as he started to object. "I have an appointment at two." While it was the truth, Liz realized she didn't dare to be alone with him more than she had to. She was afraid he'd ask questions to which she had no answers.

When they arrived at Haddie's, they discovered Jemma Gardner and her second husband, Hunt, sitting at a big corner table with Jemma's young son, Seth Whiting. Liz was relieved to see them. She didn't want to be alone with Brad, not when there was so much to be said that was best left unsaid. She hurried over and greeted the Gardners like long-lost friends.

"Join us," Jemma said. She signaled the waitress for another chair.

"Great," Liz said with alacrity. Hunt, who taught education at Pack College, was an expert on educational teaching techniques in primitive societies. "Planning any trips abroad?" she asked him.

"Not this year."

"Nor the next, if I can help it," Jemma said.

Brad sat down next to Seth, immediately engaging the six-year-old in conversation. Liz decided that perhaps he, too, felt a moratorium was due. They'd get through lunch, Liz thought, with no problems, no questions and no answers. Then she'd escape and head back to the paper for a look at the microfiches for November of the previous year.

An hour and a half later she pulled into the parking lot behind the newspaper. With a wave of her hand she had left Brad behind at the table, still talking to the Gard-

ners. He had smiled, and she thought, but couldn't be
certain, that he had mouthed the words, "I'll call you."

There were half a dozen cars in the *Times Herald* lot,
and as Liz headed for the Decatur Building, she passed
a dark blue Chevy. A window was rolled down and she
heard her name whispered.

"Who's that?" She bent down and peered in the window. She found Marion Nelson looking worriedly at her.

"I've been waiting for you," Marion said. She
glanced nervously around. "I don't think I should even
be here."

"Why not? We haven't made any secret of knowing
each other."

Marion shrugged. "I know, but if they ever found
out . . ."

"They? Found out what? Do you have something for
me?"

"Look, Liz, it's the best I could do and it's not much.
If anything ever happened. If they found out I was being
nosy . . ." She left the sentence unfinished, reached into
her bag and immediately drew out a piece of paper,
which she handed over. "Listen, I'd better go."

Liz opened the slip and read two words on it. "Gambling Man? What does that mean?"

"It's too complicated, Liz. I'm sorry I started the
whole thing." She turned the key in the ignition, then
said in a low voice, barely concealing her disappointment, "I promised you something if you helped my father. So far I don't see any action whatsoever. They
moved the zoning board meeting up for tomorrow evening. They're giving my father the bum's rush, and nobody's interested in what's happening to him because
there hasn't been any publicity about it."

"Look, I think I'm onto something," Liz said. "I need a little more time. Tomorrow's only an airing of grievances. They won't make a decision."

"Time," Marion said angrily, hitting the gas pedal and moving out of the lot, "is something we haven't got."

"One thing doesn't have to do with another," Liz said, walking alongside the car as it edged slowly toward the exit. "Which has gotten you frightened? Is it about Wouldn't It Be Loverly? Are you afraid of Victor Bosworth? And what does Gambling Man mean, anyway?"

"That's it," Marion said. "I've kept my promise as best I could. Which is more than you did."

"What's wrong with people in this town?" Liz asked. "What are you afraid of? All I wanted was the name of the man or syndicate who purchased Wouldn't It Be Loverly."

"Sorry," Marion threw out at her. "I can't say anything more. I don't know anything." She rolled up her window, paused at the exit and then turned left.

Liz watched her tear up the street. Gambling Man. She frowned. Marion seemed downright scared. Perhaps she had been warned away by Victor Bosworth. And then, of course, Liz had promised to do a story on her father and it was languishing.

She sighed and made her way up to Celie's office to retrieve the microfiches. "Gambling man," she said to Celie on her way out. "Does that sound familiar to you?"

"I don't get it."

"Title of a song, a book, a horse."

"A horse," Celie said matter-of-factly. "Victor had a horse named Gamblin' Man. Sold it sometime ago. What's this all about?"

"Thanks," Liz said. "I'll get back to you as soon as I find out."

Back in the archives, Liz scanned only for a story concerning zoning board decisions for November of the previous year. There had been eight editions of the newspaper that month, and no zoning board decisions were recorded. She shut the viewer off and sat for a long time, thinking.

Then she turned on the viewer again and began to go through the issues slowly, looking for a longer article that might concern the Ramsey Falls zoning board. She found it on page one of a weekend edition. She'd been so busy checking for a story hidden on the back pages, that she had skimmed right over it. Even then Liz didn't think it amounted to anything.

The story concerned a dispute between the boundaries of two pieces of land, one owned by someone named Bees Johnson, the other owned by Ramsey Lumber. The initial charge had been made by Bees Johnson that the lumber company was felling trees on his property. The lumber company insisted the land was part of its domain. A first decision went to the lumber company, but in an interesting twist Johnson appealed to the planning board, which refused to overturn the judge's decision. It landed in the state court where the decision was reversed. The original judge was one Thadeus Vanderheyden.

Cut and dried, Liz decided, and in the public record. She wondered if this was what Brad had been looking for. Cut and dried. He wouldn't have stolen the microfiche to hide such information. She filed the story in her memory.

There was one other item that she had missed the first time around—a photograph. An article about Will Vanderheyden's real estate activities also revealed his interest in horses and racing. A photograph accompanying the article showed a beaming, attractive Will— which was why Jake had selected it, she supposed. She'd have to talk to Jake about it. But again the story was in the public record, and there didn't seem to be anything sinister about it.

She studied the photograph. A good-looking man stood with his arm around Will's shoulders, identified, she saw, as Patrick Lucas. The name meant nothing to her. According to the caption, they were snapped in front of a gambling casino in Atlantic City. Well, she thought, Will had friends in Atlantic City, but that wasn't a crime and had nothing to do with the zoning board. Once again she shut off the viewer and left. The November zoning board file was missing, but maybe it was just *missing*, with nothing mysterious about it.

CHAPTER TEN

RAMSEY FALLS' TOWN HALL, sitting amid an acre of fir trees, was a small, friendly white clapboard building off Main Street. An open porch that ran around three sides, with wicker furniture on it painted a bright pink. Although the official pronouncement of summer was still a week away, the day had been warm and sunny. Some of the warmth still lingered into the evening. The lights shining through open windows of the town hall seemed to beckon out into the dark. However, as she climbed the steps to the porch, Liz felt as if she were going to an execution.

She was surprised to find the meeting room crowded and noisy. Seated at the trestle table up front were the five members of the zoning board—three men and two women. There were two tables facing them. At one sat Will Vanderheyden, a woman she presumed was his wife and two teenagers. Brad wasn't there. But it wasn't a trial, and the parties involved were expected to speak for themselves, not through an attorney. At the other table she found John Nelson, his daughter, Marion, and a young man in his late twenties whom she presumed to be their lawyer.

The building was leased for auctions when not in use by the town, and several large pieces of furniture were stacked up on either side of the room. American and state flags stood in the corner, with a large yellowing surveyor's map behind glass on the right wall.

Well, let's hope for a little justice, Liz thought, standing to one side where she had a good view of both parties to the complaint. She made a cursory count of the crowd and came up with eighty-seven, including Mrs. Randall and several of Nelson's other neighbors. Perhaps he'd have some luck after all.

She had attended meetings of the zoning board before, but without a vested interest in the proceedings. She knew the members by sight and wrote their names down, making a note to check on their relationships to one another and to the Vanderheydens. Zeke Peterson, who ran the meetings, rapped his gavel and the noise subsided at once.

"Okay," he said, "we're having a town meeting on a requested variance for a parcel of land running along I-84." He read out the exact acreage involved and its lines along the road frontage, beginning with an iron rod and running so many hundred feet north by northwest to an iron rod bordering the Nelson property. "Let's see, we've got Willie, William Vanderheyden, requesting a zoning change to commercial. We've got John Nelson asking us to turn down the request. Willie, suppose you explain why you want the zoning changed."

Will, dressed in a business suit, got to his feet slowly after glancing around the room with a half a smile. Then he turned back to the zoning board members. It was evident from his body language alone that he knew all the board members well and that they deferred to him. The hall was silent while he spoke. "Change is what it's all about," he said, turning to John Nelson and offering him a warm, friendly smile. "Ramsey Falls has to move with the times. You know that, John, as well as I. Re-zone the road frontage and your house will be worth ten times what it is now."

John Nelson refused to smile; in fact, he remained very still during the recital.

Will continued. "The significance of this particular regulation is the jump in revenue it'll bring the town. Hell, it's not just the restaurant. It's all the other businesses that'll spring to life." He talked on in that vein for a while, ending with a subtle reminder of how the Vanderheydens had the good of the town in mind, as they always had. "Progress," he added before sitting down, "is going to come sooner or later, John, and there isn't anything you can do to prevent it."

Smooth, Liz thought. There was a smattering of applause when he sat down.

Zeke Peterson pounded his gavel again. "That's enough," he said sharply. Then he turned to John Nelson. "All right, Mr. Nelson, I understand your attorney is with you, but this isn't a court of law and we'd appreciate it if you'd talk on your own behalf."

There was a bit of laughter in the room and a quick rap of the gavel. John Nelson took his time getting to his feet. Then he turned and surveyed the audience with raised eyebrows.

"I see a number of my good neighbors here," he said. His voice, which was a pleasant one, could be heard easily at the back of the room. "And a few faces I recognize and a number I don't. Never thought I'd see a turnout of this size, but it does my heart good."

"Perhaps you ought to come to zoning board meetings more often," Will said from his seat. There was general laughter at his remark.

"No doubt you've been to enough of them," Nelson said, "considering how many zoning ordinances you've had overturned in your benefit."

It was then that Liz noticed the chattering and moving of feet that had begun at the back of the room and seemed to be making its way slowly toward the front.

"Okay," Zeke Peterson said, raising his gavel as though to make a point, "let's get on with your grievance."

"If you call a grievance a request to keep the status quo," Nelson said. "Be that as it may, I've plenty of arguments for keeping the status quo. And my neighbors agree with me."

"Do you have petitions signed to that effect?" Peterson asked.

"No," Nelson admitted. "The Vanderheydens saw to that."

Will jumped to his feet. "Are you accusing me of forcing your neighbors to sign my petition?"

Nelson's lawyer touched John on the arm and shook his head slightly. Nelson frowned, then continued.

"I'd also like to mention the fact that building the restaurant will damage my sewer system. It has already." His last words were almost lost, however, in the sudden din of loud talk and laughter that swept through the room.

Zeke Peterson rapped his gavel ineffectually on the table, but the din continued. John Nelson tried to shout above the noise but couldn't be heard.

"Hey, John," someone boomed out. "Speak up. We can't hear you."

"Yeah." The audience applauded. "Speak up, speak up, speak up." There was a general stamping of feet.

Nelson's face turned an angry red. His daughter reached up and put her hand on his arm. Liz examined the members of the zoning board. They had already made up their minds, or had had their minds made up for them. It didn't matter what Nelson had to say or even whether they heard him. They didn't even know there were two sides to the story. Ramsey Falls was a closed, contained little world, open only to members, and John Nelson wasn't a member. Even as he spoke she could see the resigned look on the man's face.

"No justice at all," Liz said quietly to herself, then was aware of some movement next to her. She turned to find herself facing Brad.

"What the devil's going on?" he asked. She realized he had come in with someone—a tall gray-haired man.

"Your cousin Will," she said in a tight voice. "He's rigged the meeting."

"Has he now?"

Liz thought, with a sharp intake of breath, that she had never seen him with a look so controlled yet so full of fury.

"Dad, I'll be right back," he said, turning to the gentleman at his side. "Stay put and don't say a word."

"Wait a minute, son. Hold on. I don't want you interfering."

"Somebody should."

Brad threw a glance at Liz, and with a rapid stride went up the aisle. Nelson continued to talk, but the noise, unabated, drowned out his words. Brad stood for a long moment in front of Will, then reached out and grabbed him by the collar. The noise in the room subsided, then dropped away entirely. Nelson, who hadn't stopped talking all that while, continued on for a moment.

"And dozens of cars parked in my front yard. It's inevitable..." Then, aware of what was happening, he, too, stopped.

But Brad spoke in a tone so low that only the hiss of his anger could be heard. It took him no time at all to release his cousin and to walk back up the aisle.

Nelson picked up where he'd left off. Only now the silence in the room was complete. Brad came back and smiled grimly at his father. "Well, did I embarrass you?" he asked. "Oh, incidentally, Dad, this is Liz Grady."

"Will always had a way about him," Mr. Kent said to Liz, shaking her hand vigorously and smiling with a certain amount of pride over his son. "Pleased to meet you, my dear."

"Pleased to meet you, Mr. Kent." She turned to Nelson, who had just finished his presentation and had sat down.

"Anybody else have something to say about this?" Zeke Peterson looked around at the audience, which was already rising and filing out of the room.

Liz tucked her notebook into her bag, telling herself it wasn't over until it was over. Someone had buttonholed Brad and his father, so she slipped past them and followed the crowd out of the building.

As she was backing out of her parking spot, however, she discovered Brad coming toward her, waving at her to stop. She put her foot on the brake and waited until he came alongside.

"Well, you did your knight-on-the-white-charger bit," she said. "Very noble of you, indeed. Except you know it's a lost cause for Mr. Nelson and you didn't want me to write about the rowdies who appeared at the meeting and didn't let him speak. Clever, Brad. I suppose Will is going to take it out of your hide later."

"Stop jumping to conclusions," he told her in an irritated tone. "The board isn't making its decision tonight. Since Nelson is planning on taking his case to court if it goes against him, Will is a long way from building his restaurant."

"Really? Does the operator of the backhoe who's cutting up the property know that?"

"You really have the most damn suspicious nature. This isn't the Wild West where gunslingers shoot you and then burn down your barn. Those people in there are responsible, respectable citizens and you're accusing them of violating the public trust."

"Fancy words, Counselor, but I saw how Will rigged the meeting with his pals, or were they brought in from out of town and paid to make a ruckus?"

"Boyish enthusiasm, Liz. You've got it all wrong. Those were men who'll make money on the construction job or in the restaurant itself. They consider John Nelson a nuisance, that's all."

"A nuisance who's stuck with Will's sewer problems. I'd be curious to know what you told Will to get him to call his rowdies off."

Brad gave her a boyish grin. "Figured you'd get around to that sooner or later. I told him not to try to imitate how they do things in Chicago, that's all."

"You don't know the first thing about life in the city," she said, "and I'll bet you're afraid of it."

He laughed. "You're right, I don't."

"Don't what?" His father had come up behind him and clapped a hand on his shoulder. "Ready?"

"Better go without me," Brad said. "I'm trying to convince Liz to have dinner with me."

"You don't have to convince her of anything," Mr. Kent said. "Bring her back with us. Your mother always likes extra company."

Brad opened the door to Liz's car. "I'll go with her," he said, "just to make certain she arrives. You take my car."

"See you there." Mr. Kent smiled at Liz with a bit more curiosity than she liked.

"I've got an odd feeling I've been snookered," Liz said, backing out of her parking spot and getting behind the line of cars heading for the highway.

"About being invited for dinner? Don't blame me. Blame my old man. Incidentally, I owe you an apology."

She turned. "Just one?"

"About the other night."

"Ah. And to think I'd almost forgotten."

"I can't apologize for wanting to finish what we started. I can only apologize for thinking it was what you wanted as well."

"You're really a lawyer, aren't you? You're trying to back me up against the wall again, to make me admit it was what I wanted, too, but that I got all flustered and maidenly and wanted to run away and to blame my embarrassment on you."

She paused for a moment and saw the smile he was trying to hide. He obviously knew he'd made his point.

"My father likes you," he finally said. "I think you're going to impress my mother, as well."

"I've had dinner, sort of," she said, remembering the slice of toast spread with apricot jam and the cup of coffee in Mrs. Duboise's kitchen. She wasn't anxious to meet Brad's mother and didn't want to impress her, either.

"You'll have to pretend, I'm afraid."

"And look at the way I'm dressed."

"Black pants, red plaid jacket. I believe I read in the *New York Times* the other day that it's the most respectable way to dress for casual invitations to dinner."

"But . . ."

"Turn left at the next light, left at the hardware store, then down Old Country Road toward the river."

"I think I know the way," she said in a dry tone of voice.

"Yes, you're right. I suppose you do."

Two miles out of town the country road wound past a dairy farm. "Hey, wait a second," Liz said in a moment of inspiration, pulling over to the side of the road. "Be right back," she told Brad, hopping out of the car.

A clump of white daisies, looking silvery in the moonlight, grew by the side of the road, and with the aid of a small pair of scissors that she carried in her bag and a rubber band, Liz succeeded in making a small bouquet to bring with her. She shook them carefully free of bugs and marched triumphantly back to the car.

"I suppose your mother has orchids in her garden, but there's nothing friendlier than a bunch of daisies," she said, climbing back into the driver's seat.

"She's going to love you for that," he said.

"Really?" She saw the smile on his face and wondered. "Maybe it's a mistake. Of course I shook all the bugs out—I hope."

He laughed, leaned across the seat and deposited a kiss on her cheek. "Darling Liz, you're a treasure, and so's your bouquet."

"I know," she said, automatically raising her hand and touching the spot he had kissed, "your mother's going to be impressed. Brad, the truth is, this is one visit

I could do without. I don't know why I let your father talk me into it."

"I slipped him ten dollars and promised him more if you came along."

"Oh," she groaned, "you're incorrigible."

When they arrived at Kent Hall, Liz sailed through the wrought-iron gates and down the drive to the imposing entrance of the main house. Even before she drew to a stop, the front door opened and a man came hurrying down the steps, evidently expecting them. He opened the car door for Liz and gave her a brief smile. She grabbed the bouquet of daisies and stepped out, parting her lips, although she had no idea whether the result emerged as a smile or the nervous twitch it really was.

"My father home?" Brad asked.

"Yes, Mr. Kent. He just came in."

Brad came around and took Liz's arm while the butler ran up the stairs ahead of them and opened the front door.

Liz, ushered in by Brad, took in her surroundings: the marble floor of the central hall, the silk brocade wall covering, the paintings of dour-faced ancestors, the bronze sculptures at either end of the hall, the Aubusson rug carefully centered and, centered upon that, a carved mahogany table holding a great urn of flamboyant flowers artfully arranged. She clutched her bouquet of daisies tighter.

Liz had, of course, been in similar houses as a reporter in Chicago, but never as a guest. Yet *guest* was the wrong word when it came to Kent Hall, as well. Guests were expected and treated as welcome visitors. Brad had brought her home in an effort to open his life to her, to show her that everything about him was as ordinary as apple pie. It wasn't working. *Tartes des pommes* perhaps, but not apple pie. There was nothing ordinary about living in a marble mansion.

She dragged her feet a bit, remembering the four-room apartment in a housing development where her father greeted her friends in his favorite worn T-shirt with Chicago Gas and Electric printed on the front.

"Hey, wake up."

She turned and looked at Brad, then realized she had stopped cold in front of the center hall table.

"You were a million miles away," he said. "What's going on in that head of yours? Never mind." He took her hand in a firm grip and brought her into a high-ceilinged room of immense proportions that dwarfed several groups of comfortable sofas and chairs. There were imposing vases of hothouse flowers everywhere.

Seated in a wing chair, holding a large unfinished needlepoint, sat an attractive silver-haired woman with a narrow, haughty nose—the Vanderheyden nose. Clearly this was Brad's mother. She brightened when she saw Brad and put the needlepoint down. A Pekingese pup that had been curled up on the Persian carpet sprang to life and, with a joyous bark, came over to sniff at Liz.

"Beijing, behave yourself." Mrs. Kent said, coming toward them.

Brad picked up the dog. "Liz, I guess he's the first member of the family you're going to meet, and the newest, incidentally. Beijing, this is Liz Grady. Liz, this is Beijing."

Liz, still clutching the bouquet, put her hand out and solemnly shook the dog's paw. "Pleased to meet you, Beijing."

"There's also a large, friendly old German shepherd named Lady who's been in the family for decades."

"Brad, decades?" His mother directed a smile at Liz. "He exaggerates. The dog is scarcely twelve."

"Where is Lady, anyway?"

"In your room where she always is. She keeps expecting you to come home to stay."

"So do you," Brad said with a laugh. "Well, I'm here for dinner and I've brought Liz. Did Dad tell you?"

"Yes, he did. How are you, my dear?"

"Mrs. Kent," Liz said quietly, offering her hand and noting the cool, appraising glance she was given. "Oh, these are for you," she added, thrusting the flowers out.

"Well, how wonderful, fresh daisies." Mrs. Kent took the bouquet and put her nose to it as though the daisies were possessed of an extraordinary fragrance when, in fact, they had none. "You know, I often think of putting in an English cottage garden just so I could have my fill of wildflowers and homespun perennials. And daisies. You can always count on them."

Practiced charm, Liz thought, and hated herself for her cynicism. Still, that there was a faint undercurrent of hostility, she had no doubt, although it was clear Brad had no knowledge of it.

"Don't let her get started on gardening," Mr. Kent said, coming into the room. He took Liz's hand in his. "I just realized who you are. You're the reporter Celie Decatur took on. Been hearing things about you."

Liz looked closely into navy blue eyes that were exactly like Brad's, and warmed up to him immediately. "Dare I ask what things people are saying?"

"As far as I can remember, all Celia said was, 'She's a damn fine reporter.'"

Liz colored slightly. She could see Brad taking in the scene with a serious expression on his face. It had never occurred to her that she might be the object of conversation out of earshot. "Celie said that?" she remarked to Mr. Kent.

"Afraid she did, my dear. Now, what can I offer you to drink?"

"White wine," Brad said for her. "Incidentally, my dad is Bradford the third, always called Bradford. I'm Bradford the fourth, always called Brad. Bradford's one and two are hanging on the wall near the staircase."

"I'll just put these daisies in water," his mother said, "and see to one more place for dinner. Brad, would you like to come with me? We haven't talked in ages."

"Haven't we, old bean?" Brad put his arm around his mother. "I could've sworn I was here the other day." The dog ran out with them. "Where's Franny?" he asked as they went out the door.

"Oh, off to one of her meetings. You know Franny."

Left alone with Mr. Kent, Liz felt decidedly uncomfortable while he went over to a portable bar and proceeded to pour her wine. She stood her ground and gazed at a large oil painting over a huge mahogany credenza.

Hudson River School of painting, she had decided when Mr. Kent came over to her and handed her a crystal wineglass.

"That painting's by George Inness," he told her, "and the wine's local."

"I like the local wine," she said.

"Particularly recommend this variety," he mumbled. "Kents have an interest in a local winery."

"Don't tell me. Lotus Vineyards."

"Precisely."

Precisely, she thought, wondering how she could be so clever. "I'm becoming a bit of a connoisseur myself," she remarked, taking a sip. "Considering how my favorite drink before I came to Ramsey Falls was diet soda.''

Kent laughed. "Diet soda? So that's the favorite drink of Chicagoans.''

"Chicago," Mrs. Kent said, coming back into the room. "I have the most affectionate memories of that city. Wonderful art museum, of course. And so beautiful around the lake. And the people one knows. I love their accents. Such pure speech. Yours, too, Liz. I can tell that you're beautifully educated. What school did you attend?''

"The University of Chicago.''

Mrs. Kent hesitated a beat, almost unwilling to show how impressed she was. She went over to the portable bar and poured a glass of sherry for herself. "Do you know the Gregorys, my dear? Aldo Gregory? Cattle, mining, real estate? His wife was my roommate at college.''

Brad came into the room, followed by an old, plodding dog, a German shepherd with an arthritic front paw. Brad clearly caught his mother's question and mugged a smile at Liz, as though trying to tell her to agree with his mother at all costs.

Gregory was a name Liz knew well. "As a matter of fact, I've met Aldo Gregory on at least two occasions,'' she said, wondering if it were wise to mention that both times concerned a story she'd been working on. The portrait she'd painted hadn't been a very flattering one. A telephone call from the politically connected Gregory had landed both Liz and her editor in hot water with the publisher. They had been told to drop the story, and Liz had had no choice but to go along. She had made a promise that she would go back to it one day, but had never found the time. "I interviewed him for the newspaper I worked at, actually," Liz added.

"How lovely."

"I'm afraid Mr. Gregory rather objected to it."

"Well, I'm sure I don't know what you mean," Mrs. Kent said, looking vaguely offended.

Brad, however, tilted his head back and roared. "Darling," he said to his mother, "Liz is what they call a muckraker. Given half a chance, she'll dig up your ancestors' bones and use them for boomerangs."

"They have a daughter about your age," Mrs. Kent went on, glancing at her son, but not missing a beat. "Her coming-out party was a great, rather fantastic event. Remember, Bradford? We flew out in that raging storm. Then when we arrived in Chicago there was the most dramatic rainbow."

"The rainbow courtesy of the Chicago board of public works," Brad threw in, going over to Liz and smiling at her.

"Damn waste of money, the whole business," her husband said to Liz. "Is that what you did the story on?"

"No," she said. "It was on something a lot more serious."

"Waste of money?" Mrs. Kent shook her head in exasperation. "For heaven's sake, Bradford, it's tradition. And how else is a young woman introduced into society?"

"She takes a job," Brad threw in. "That's how it's done in this day and age." Lady came in close to him, and he bent down to ruffle her ears.

"And you, Liz," his mother said, ignoring his remark, "Where was your party?"

Liz gazed over at Brad, but he was still engaged in petting his dog. "I'm afraid we don't have that sort of thing in the section of Chicago I come from, Mrs. Kent."

Brad stirred. The Pekingese dashed into the room and tried to jump into his arms. "Beijing, down." His tone sounded unexpectedly sharp.

"But what section are you talking about?" Mrs. Kent brightened, as though Liz were about to tell her she came from some enlightened zone near the university where society was correct if a little oddball. Brad glanced over at her then, and Liz caught the most extraordinary look in his eye, a look telling her to fudge for once, for his sake, that the time for candor would come later.

He stood and placed an arm once again around his mother's shoulders. "I'm starved," he told her. "When's dinner?"

"Good heavens, I must be getting old. I came in to gather you all up. Come along, come along," she said, hurrying them out. "And, Brad, over dinner I want to learn just how you and Liz met."

"THAT WAS A LOW-DOWN dirty trick," Liz said two hours later to Brad. They were outside of Kent Hall, standing in front of Liz's car. "You just left me there on center stage while you sat on the sidelines mugging at me when to talk or when to smile and let the moment pass."

"What was low-down about it?"

"Everything. Insisting I come along, to begin with."

"Blame my father. He's the one who fell in love with you."

"I had the odd feeling your mother was measuring me against somebody."

"She knows better than that," Brad said a little sharply.

"Well, I'm going," Liz said, opening the car door. She thrust her hand out. "I've had, well, an *interesting* time."

Brad took her hand, but then didn't release it. "Look, I can't say I like your inherent snobbism and the way it colors everything you say and do."

"That's ridiculous," Liz snapped. "It was your mother who asked me all those fascinating questions. 'When did you have your coming-out party?' 'Oh, I did, Mrs. Kent. It was held at union headquarters with paper streamers and cheap silver balloons, and we served lasagna in the shape of a swan for the main course. Everyone dressed in jeans and T-shirts with white ties, even the young ladies.'"

"Those are her values, Liz. She thinks they're important. Don't take them so personally."

"I felt as if I were under a microscope and she wanted to put on rubber gloves before touching the slide."

"You must have taken a degree in overreacting," he said.

"Perhaps I did. But I don't want to have to apologize because I grew up in the Stone Street Housing Projects."

He climbed into her car behind the wheel. "Get in."

"I can drive myself home."

"That's not where we're going," he told her.

"Then where?"

"You know damn well," he said, turning the key in the ignition and hitting the accelerator.

CHAPTER ELEVEN

BRAD OPENED THE DOOR to his cottage, and after hesitating a moment, Liz threw him a glance, set her shoulders straight and marched briskly inside.

"Interior decoration by Mrs. Bradford Kent III and Frances Kent the original," Brad said, closing the door behind him. "Objects culled from the vast Bradford holdings, mostly moldy nineteenth-century castoffs that had been stashed in the barn before coming to rest here. If they date from the eighteenth century, they're no longer considered castoffs and they've been moved to the big house. All I know is I couldn't stop my mother and sister once they made up their minds to see me domesticated."

"The big house?" Liz asked. "You make Kent Hall sound like a prison."

His laugh was brief, but he bent his head in acknowledgment of what he clearly thought was an astute remark. "Maybe it is for the current crop."

In spite of the decorating contributions of his mother and sister, the house had a distinctly masculine air. The large room they stood in was furnished with rosewood and mahogany pieces, sofas and chairs upholstered in heavy fabrics. A massive fieldstone fireplace took up half of the left-hand wall. The pine floors were covered with Persian carpets. At the back was a newly constructed loft, and from where she stood Liz could see that it held a bed and dresser. Below, a small kitchen had been installed.

"I moved out of my family quarters as soon as I could," Liz remarked. "My brother, who'd been sleeping in an alcove off the entrance, pounced on my old room. He's still there, incidentally," she added with a good-natured smile, "sponging off the folks."

"They must like it, being sponged on."

"Of course he isn't around much, what with work, school and swinging in his spare time."

"Swingin' bachelor. I suppose Chicago is the place for it."

"Right. We're a little short of elegant country clubs in the middle of town." They were just talking. Liz realized that. Brad couldn't be in the least interested in her family or in what passed for swinging in Chicago. And he didn't care a thing about showing her the way he lived. In fact, the air in spite of the chill she had first felt upon entering the house was slowly heating up between them.

"Can't I get you something to drink?" he asked.

She shook her head. "I ought to be getting home."

"Ought to?" He smiled and took a step toward her.

There were some decisions you marched into, knowing they'd change your life forever, and others to be slipped into without realizing something monumental is about to happen. It was no contest about how she had come there and why. If she let Brad make love to her, and she wanted him to, there would no longer be any room in her life for Doug, or anyone else for that matter.

For a long moment she waited, as though Brad had just entered her dreams. Her bones felt soft, unable to support her weight. If she let him touch her, she'd be saying goodbye to her past and to Doug. But she no longer had any choice. Since the first moment they'd met, Liz had felt Brad would be something special in her life, although when he reached for her, a sudden chill covered her skin, as if telling her *special* didn't necessarily mean good.

When he took her in his arms it was with a determination she couldn't mistake. He'd have her in bed in no time at all. Her objection stuck in her throat. She drew her arms around his neck, damning the mischievous demons lurking in corners, because she was where she wanted to be.

Liz opened her mouth and his tongue darted in, dueling with hers for a moment, then pulling back to wet her lips. His breath had quickened, and she could feel the hard response of his body. In another instant there would be no turning back. No turning back at all. She'd be his, and the look and the need would be written all over her like a scarlet letter to be seen by everyone in Ramsey Falls. And she was thinking too much even as she took in his kisses and returned them eagerly. Thinking too much as his kisses rained over her, as her body weakened and seemed to meld into his.

Thinking too much. He murmured her name, his breath hot against her cheek. "Liz, we both want this, and damn it, I can hear your mind going a mile a minute."

"It's all wrong," she said.

His mouth ranged over her cheek, her hair, her neck. "This isn't wrong. It's about as right as anything will ever be."

"No, don't try to sell me on anything, Brad. I won't have it. I can't." She pulled out of his arms, her eyes blazing defiantly. She was aware of how flushed she was

and how cool and yet angry he looked. "I'm not starting a cheap affair with you because it's *what we want*."

"Is that what you think? That my wanting to make
love to you constitutes a cheap affair?"

She shook her head, aware of the shallow breaths she
was having trouble taking. "You're not listening to me."

"Liz, I'm listening to my heart and my body and I'm
listening to the words whirling around in your head. Is
it your friend in California?"

"It's Ramsey Falls. It's you. It's that house, that big
pile of stone and your mother asking me about where I
made my debut. *Debut!* Her smile as we left tonight
seemed to say, 'Liz will go to bed with him, but then after all, it's about all we can expect, isn't it?'"

"Liz, you're going off half-cocked."

Perhaps she was, but she couldn't stop the rush of
words. They flowed out, a veritable waterfall of why she
couldn't let him kiss her or make love to her. "Oh, Lord,
it's Celie and the paper and everything, my whole *life*.
It isn't just whether you or I hit the sack tonight to satisfy an urge. It's...it's everything else around Ramsey
Falls, the lack of bloody privacy. The whole town seems
to have an invisible fence around it. And there's this
undercurrent I can't quite put my finger on, and it scares
me. Oh," she said, reaching for her bag, which she had
tossed on the sofa, "call me some time and maybe we
can sort it all out."

Liz whipped around and ran to the door, but he
reached it at the same time and slipped his hand over
hers when she grabbed the doorknob. "You want me,
but you don't want me," he said quietly.

"I don't want the fallout."

"You're sure there'll be a fallout."

"Brad, I don't want to test the theory. I shouldn't have come back with you. I led you on. That's not very lady-like of me, is it?"

He reached for her and took her in his arms. "Lady, I like you no matter what you do." He kissed her slowly and thoroughly but with a certain amount of chasteness behind it. "Do you know what else?" he said in a voice as gentle as though he were about to explain something to a small, endearing child. "I believe you came with me because you wanted to finish the evening in my arms. I don't believe you led me on. I think, however," he added, combing his fingers slowly through her hair, "that you're every bit as interested in who you are and how you're perceived by the locals as the most patrician among us, and you know what else?"

She slowly shook her head.

"You're a snob, Lizzie. But added to all the other qualities that make up your charming, funny, clever personality, I'd say you're as unique a snob as ever existed."

"Oh, thanks," she said. "That's a compliment I could do without."

"I'll take you home now," he said.

"It's my car," she said, reaching for the door. "I'll drive myself."

He followed her out to the car. When she turned to say good-night, he took her head between his hands. "You're going to turn bitter and old if you don't let loose once in a while. I mean with me—no one else." He placed his lips against hers, and once again she felt their soft warmth and knew she was close to tears. He drew away, still holding her, and gazed for a long moment into her eyes. "Maybe you never should have come to Ramsey Falls," he said. "I thought my life was on an even keel at last until you showed up." He kissed her once more. "I'll call you tomorrow."

She stepped into her car and didn't answer him, although her smile as she drove away was wobbly.

"A SUDDEN, UNEXPECTED MELEE took place at Tuesday's zoning board meeting," Liz wrote, then erased the sentence from her word processor. It wasn't a melee. It was a bunch of rowdies paid to keep John Nelson from saying his piece. She began again. "Emotions ran high at the zoning board meeting on Tuesday night over the variance requested by Will Vanderheyden for a piece of residential property on I-84." Better. She pulled her chair closer to the desk. "A sudden outbreak of near violence, however, was averted with a few words from lawyer Brad Kent."

"Oh, no," she groaned out loud. "Am I mad?"

Perhaps she was. She hadn't had much sleep after arriving home the night before. The memory of Brad's words, Brad's kisses, Brad's touch, Brad's forgiveness had kept her awake most of the night, and now she was paying the price for it.

"Disturbing you?" Jake Martinez asked, peering around the door to her cubicle, and without waiting for an answer, slid in and sat down. His camera dangled from his neck along with a string of film cartridges. "Just saw Adriana with a long face. Thought maybe Scottie was acting up again, but I figured it wasn't my place to ask her."

Liz shook her head. "No, I have the impression the judge knocked some sense into him."

"I think he's more afraid of his lawyer than the judge."

"Brad Kent, you mean?"

"Brad Kent, I mean. He gets it into his head to save someone's soul, he'll do it."

"I wish he'd think about saving John Nelson's soul," she said.

"Hey, that's something else. Big bucks at stake. Scottie represents a cheap cure for the soul. John Nelson means a real estate deal didn't go through."

"Anyway, Adriana's just worried about her scholarship," Liz said, anxious to change the subject. "There's a time limit on it. She knows she won't be able to go but keeps hoping for a miracle, which means she hasn't given it up yet."

"Can't we take up a collection?" Jake asked. "She deserves a change to get out of this burg before her old man ruins her life."

"This burg? I thought you chose this burg over California."

"This burg chose me," he said with a grin.

"I think I'll talk to Celie about Adriana," Liz said. "She's the lady with all the right connections. As far as I'm concerned, Scottie's pulling everybody's chain. He's holding out for a payoff."

Jake gave her a disbelieving look. "Payoff? Blackmail? I think people go to jail for that kind of thing."

"He keeps saying he can't support his family on a custodian's pay."

"He should be given a raise for creative thinking, considering his wife is the main support of the family and it's the first steady job he's held in years."

"He needs a good spanking," Liz said.

"How about following him around for a while and doing a story on him? He'll enjoy being the center of attention. Might keep his mind exercised."

"Boring, Jake. You'd better stick to photography. Everybody in town knows Scottie's peccadillos. The only thing they'd want to read about him is his going to jail."

"You're right. I was just shooting my mouth off."

"Better than a shotgun. Look, he's overwhelmed by his new job and with having to give up the fiery demon. I'll talk to Celie. The reason people fail even when they're supposed to act in their best interests is when the rest of us lose interest."

"And speaking of interest," Jake said, "any more threatening phone calls?"

"None," Liz said with a laugh. "It must have come as a shock when he heard your voice at the other end of the receiver. But then again, I haven't come up with anything incriminating yet. Whoever called me probably thinks I'm scared, since no story has appeared. However," she said, pointing at her screen, "I'm piecing together a report on last night's zoning board meeting. I can always start the ball rolling just by mentioning facts such as the meeting unexpectedly convening a month early and the place being seeded with Will Vanderheyden's pals."

"You know that for a fact?"

"Read the story in the weekend edition."

"Liz, back up everything you say with facts."

She grinned. "Would Celie let me get away with anything less?"

THE RECEPTIONIST at the Kent law offices in Merriman buzzed Brad's line. "Mr. Kent, Mr. Will Vanderheyden is on his way back. I asked him to wait until I called you, but he walked right past me."

"Well, now that the horse has escaped we'll have to see about putting a lock on the front door. Thanks anyway, Janie."

By the time Brad had replaced the receiver, the door to his office burst open and Will came storming in. Brad's secretary was right behind him looking worried and apologetic.

"It's all right, Mrs. Keeler," he assured her.

Will slammed the door behind him and marched across the office and around the desk to where Brad sat.

"Sit down, Will, why don't you?"

"Don't ever try that again," Will said, his mouth twisted in anger.

"Inviting you to sit down? That's an odd request, but if it's what you want . . ."

"For two cents, I'd—"

"You'd what, Will?" Brad slowly uncurled and got to his feet. His cousin was pugnacious—he'd been a boxer in college—but Brad towered over Will and for that Brad was sorry. Punching him out would feel so good.

"You made a fool out of me in front of my friends last night. That variance means too much to me. Otherwise I'd have taken you on then and there. As it was, a couple of the boys offered to do a little number on you, but I said no, told them to let me handle you myself."

"I was beginning to wonder about those boys," Brad said. "I'd no idea you had so many friends willing to show up for you. Tell me, did you have a rehearsal beforehand, about how you'd drown out John Nelson? 'Speak up, John. We can't hear you.' Gave a touch of drama to the proceedings that must have gone down well with the zoning board. Gave them a taste of what life would be like if they failed to come through for you."

"Why you..." Will, his face a deep red, lunged for Brad, throwing out a wild punch.

All Brad did was shake his head and laugh, and then in another swift move, he grabbed Will by his starched white collar as he had the night before. "What's your game, Will? You might as well tell me, because if I don't find out one way, I'll find out another."

"I don't know what you're talking about, but if you interfere..."

"You don't know nothing, but if I interfere. Clever, Will. What's the game? Why did you bring your gang with you last night to disrupt the meeting? Why did you have one of your pals call up Liz Grady and threaten her off the story?"

There was a sudden gleam of light in Will's eyes, but all he said was, "Liz Grady. I didn't know you were so friendly with...I don't know what you're talking about. And take your hands off me."

"Sure." Brad released him and stepped back. "I wasn't aware that I had my hands on you. And if you don't have anything to tell me, I'll wish you good day."

"I won't forget this," Will said in a low, threatening voice. He stormed across the room and pulled the door open.

"Keep away from Liz Grady, or I'll take great pleasure in pulling you apart limb from limb."

"And you're fired as my attorney," Will threw back before he slammed the door behind him.

Brad resisted the temptation to laugh long and hard after his cousin had departed. Instead he returned to his desk with a sober, thoughtful expression on his face. He'd been a passive observer of his cousin's shenanigans far too long. Brad's motto was a very simple one:

Don't worry about what they do as long as they do it in the street and don't frighten the horses.

He picked up his phone and called his law clerk. "Andy, when you have a chance I want you to check through the zoning board decisions for the past three or four years and cull out anything to do with Will Vanderheyden." He knew the ground had already been covered by Liz, but he wanted to find out for himself. Maybe Liz was right about his family riding roughshod over the community. There was one thing he did know: she was a breath of fresh air in his life, and he couldn't afford to lose her, not for some act of stupidity on his part.

All morning long he'd been itching to call Liz just to hear her voice. But he'd held back. He'd made a play for her without considering the consequences and how deeply enmeshed he'd be if they had spent the night together.

She wasn't just another woman; he'd known that from the beginning. She'd never fit into the life his parents wanted for him. Even though he'd fought unsuccessfully against their managing his life, they hadn't quite given up the notion that he'd marry a woman from what they considered a suitable class.

And he supposed he might have come around after a while except that Liz had happened to him, and after meeting her it was no contest. However, in the end it wasn't his mother who was the problem; it was Liz. She was as skittish and high-strung as a racehorse, and she didn't need any prompting from his mother to turn her against his family. She had enough prejudices of her own to carry her through the rest of her life. Well, he thought, picking up the telephone and dialing her number at the paper, the object was to proceed slowly and firmly. He knew what he wanted, and sooner or later Liz—and his parents—would have to know it, too.

"I said I'd call," he said the moment he heard her voice at the other end.

"And you always keep your promises."

His heart lifted at her voice with its warm tones and rough edges. "Thought you'd like to know that cousin Will has fired me on account of my rough handling of him in front of his friends."

"Oh, I feel so bad. Welcome to the right side of the law."

"I said he fired me because I embarrassed him, not because I can't do my job. And knowing Will, he'll worm, and I mean worm, his way into my good offices again. I give him a couple of days at most. And, furthermore, I'm not certain which side of the fence I'm on at the moment. Liz, after that first threatening phone call, have you received any others?"

"No."

"You don't think it was some local Lothario?"

"Brad, I know why I received that call. And I'm not off the story, if that's what you're getting at."

"Found anything?" he asked carefully.

"Wouldn't tell you if I did."

He suspected she knew just about as much as he did, which was nothing. Knowing he had a lot more access to town files than she did, Brad went on to why he had really made the phone call. "Liz, about last night."

"Let's not discuss it," she said. "We both made mistakes."

"I'd like to see you again."

There was a long moment of silence from the other end. "For lunch in a very crowded restaurant," she said at last. "We arrive and leave in separate cars. Hand-shakes allowed at ten paces."

"I'm talking about Saturday night at Kent Hall. Formal attire not necessary but also not frowned upon."

"Oh, no, not again. I'm afraid you'll have to count me out."

"The invitation comes directly from the mistress of the house."

"You called her and twisted her arm."

"Liz, stop putting words in my mouth. I'll pick you up at eight. I promise you a passel of people you know. Sarah and Ty, for instance, and Jemma and Hunt, and Celie and Victor as well."

"I like your sales pitch. I accept," she said with an alacrity that didn't surprise Brad at all.

"Leave your notebook at home," he said. "It's a dinner party."

"It's okay," she told him, laughing. "I've got the kind of memory that makes notebooks obsolete. Is this evening anything special?"

"Nothing much to do in these parts except give dinner parties or ride horses."

"Oh, there's plenty to do, Brad—church dinners, penny socials. Good heavens, I never want for entertainment!"

"Snob, I'll see you Saturday."

"Saturday it is, then. Thanks for asking me. Bye."

"Liz, wait. Don't hang up."

"I'm here," she said in a suddenly quiet tone.

"Be careful."

There was a beat of a couple of seconds, then she asked, "Are you talking about your cousin and what he can do?"

"I'm talking about threatening telephone calls."

"Jake told me to check my car before I step into it. If I'm going to be paranoid about what I'm doing, then it's a business I ought not to be in."

"I wish to hell you weren't," he said, and angrily put the receiver down. He was sorry almost at once. His own behavior over Liz was becoming paranoid.

Will, who was a bully, didn't like having the tables turned on him. That was all. He'd been a spoiled brat when he was young and he was a spoiled brat now. There was nothing sinister about erecting a restaurant next door to John Nelson's house. The only thing involved was expedience. No crime was being committed, and the zoning board's decision could always be challenged before the town board.

Ramsey Falls was a small community, and the worst thing to have happened there in recent memory was a tricentennial celebrated a year too soon. Judge Thadeus Vanderneyden's son, Will, was used to having his own way, but then he wasn't the only one.

Brad got restlessly out of his chair and stood for a while at the window, gazing down at Merriman's busy main street. We're all equal, he thought. Only the Kents, the Vanderheydens, the Decaturs, the Bosworths, without spelling it out, felt they were more equal than others. And the trouble was, until Liz Grady had come along, no one had bothered questioning the system.

Will's words came back to him: *You're no longer my attorney.* Brad's laughter at the notion was so hearty that his secretary stuck her head in the doorway and asked him if anything was the matter.

LIZ HATED IT. The dress was awful. Its mauve color was all wrong, and suddenly the soft silk fabric seemed to have a funny drape to it. And there was a silly bow that was slightly askew at the hips. How had she ever stood in front of a dressing room mirror in Marshall Fields in Chicago and allowed a saleslady to talk her into parting with a week's salary for the pleasure of owning it? And how could she have worn it to an awards dinner and a wedding reception without the least embarrassment?

She thought of the way Celie dressed—in exquisite, tasteful clothes. She thought of her T-shirt with Thoreau's face on it and Brad's grin when he'd met her. She stepped into the dress and pulled up the zipper. Then, without checking herself in the mirror, she rummaged through her meager collection of jewelry to find her grandmother's rhinestone brooch, which she placed in the center of the bow. Then she went over to the mirror and examined herself. The mirror was old with some of the silvering gone from the back. Her reflection was a bit fuzzy, but it was enough to tell her that the dress fitted, the silk swing skirt draped the way it was supposed to and mauve suited her coloring exactly.

She twirled in the dress and then stopped and stared at herself. She wondered just how expensive the dress really looked. She had bought it on sale, and yet it was still the most costly purchase she had ever made.

Liz knew exactly what was going on in her head. She was measuring herself against every other woman who would be at Kent Hall that night—all, no doubt, in designer originals. And it wouldn't be rhinestones that twinkled from their bosoms; it would be the real thing. She touched the brooch, almost undoing it. No, the little Art Deco design with a center rectangle of black onyx was one of the few Grady heirlooms, and it meant more to her than any diamond would. Pride was another Grady heirloom—one she possessed in spades. It wouldn't fail her now.

She had applied a touch of mauve shadow to her upper eyelids and wore a deep but subdued lip color. Her hair, which was thick and wavy, was worn in the thirties style, parted at the side and loose. Liz Grady at her fanciest. Even the antique mirror seemed to wink its approval.

At precisely eight o'clock, Liz heard the sound of a car engine below, glanced out the window and saw Brad pull up to the curb. She grabbed her bag and stole, flew down the stairs and was at the front door to greet him before he knocked.

He greeted her with some surprise, his appreciation of the way she looked evident in his smile. "I was afraid you'd escaped out of town."

"And give up the chance to meet the town's movers and shakers on a social level? You have me all wrong, Brad."

"Did I mention that you look wonderful?"

"Mind if I give you a similar compliment?"

"Not at all. My ego can stand all the soothing it can get."

"Brad, you look wonderful."

He was dressed elegantly in a deep blue tuxedo with a red cummerbund, and for a magic instant Liz felt as if he had stepped out of her deepest fantasy. The wind had tousled his hair, and she longed to reach over and pat it down.

He bent and spontaneously placed a kiss on the tip of her nose. "Come on, killer, I think I want to show you off tonight."

A half hour later they were having cocktails with a dozen other guests in the main salon of Kent Hall. It was a high-ceilinged room of great elegance, with a crystal chandelier whose lights were reflected back by tall, narrow mirrors in rococo frames. Brad proudly introduced Liz to Fran, his sister. She had his eyes and shook Liz's hand shyly, looking at her brother as if for guidance on how to act.

"I always thought I'd like to be a reporter," she said to Liz.

"The *Times Herald* is going daily," Liz said. "Celie will be looking for people to come on board."

Brad put a brotherly arm around Fran and squeezed her. "She writes like a dream," he said. "But you can't sell her on the idea."

"You'll have to show me something you've done," Liz said. Fran blushed and Liz was prevented from continuing the conversation by the arrival of Judge Vanderheyden and Will with their wives. Fran seemed to take the opportunity to fade to the other side of the room. The Vanderheydens' entrance was followed by a couple introduced as the Durants. With them was a tall, beautiful woman whom Mrs. Kent brought directly over to Brad and Liz.

"Here's Mimi," she announced in a pointed manner. Brad, who was sitting with Liz on a love seat, jumped to his feet immediately and kissed Mimi on both cheeks.

"I've wanted you two to meet," he said. "Liz Grady, Mimi Durant."

Liz stood, and with an unexpected sense of foreboding, extended a hand. "How are you?"

"You're Celie's new reporter." The woman examined her curiously. "Is it true Celie's going daily?"

"Yes it is, but you'll have to ask Celie, I'm afraid. She's over there with Victor Bosworth," Liz said, nodding at the double set of couches that flanked the fireplace. The Gardners and Lassiters seemed to be having a serious conversation with both Celie and Victor Bosworth.

"Oh, well, knowing Celie," Mimi said, "when the time comes she'll send out a town crier to announce it. And, Brad, you've been an absolute stranger," she said, turning away from Liz. She tucked her arm through Brad's and dragged him over to her parents. "Come and tell me everything."

In a moment Liz had the whole picture. Both Mr. and Mrs. Durant beamed at their daughter and at Brad, the mother bending forward for what seemed a cool ritual kiss on each cheek. Mimi and Brad were a pair, an item, a couple.

The butler came in and announced dinner, and Liz found her arm taken by Will Vanderheyden. "I peeked at the table arrangement," he told her, drawing her steadily and firmly on. "You're my companion. Wonderful. I've been wanting to talk to you."

"Really, I thought you said everything you had to when I was in your office." She saw Brad and Mimi ahead of them, Mimi's hand clamped firmly onto Brad's arm. Mrs. Kent had obviously seen to everything. All Liz knew was that she wanted to cut and run—run so far away and so fast that she'd eventually end up in Chicago. Or California.

The dining room, painted a soft beige-pink, was lit solely by candlelight. Crystal and silver gleamed on a pink damask tablecloth. When they were seated at the long, romantically set table, Liz found Will on her right and Judge Vanderheyden on her left. She had no heart for entering into conversation with either one, although she knew she'd regret it later.

For now, all she saw was Brad sitting opposite with Mimi on one side and Sarah on the other.

"Now when do you suppose they're going to get married," Will asked, as though Liz could supply the answer.

"They, who?" she asked.

They were interrupted by the arrival of the food. A clear consommé was served with a small leaf of parsley floating on it. Liz picked up her spoon and took a sip or two before putting the spoon down. She had no appetite. She caught Brad's eye, but he was laughing at something at the same time and turned back to Mimi almost at once.

"Mimi and Brad," Will finally replied. "Did Brad ever tell you about the practical jokes I used to play on him as a kid?"

"Why would he tell me anything?" she asked, turning to Will and discovering a look of scarcely disguised fury on his face. He hates Brad, she realized. He's jealous of him and at the same time he's furious about the incident at the zoning board hearing. It was an unforgiving anger, and for a moment she felt a cold chill rocket unrestrainedly through her.

During the main course, Liz managed a desultory conversation with the judge about Chicago weather, but that was all. Close up, he was an attractive and charming man with, she suspected, an eye for the ladies.

It was later, when dessert was served, that the talk at the table became general. From the far end she heard Mr. Durant's voice. "As for the development of Merriman's waterfront, I'll fight tooth and nail to see no public housing is put up nearby," he was saying.

Liz waited for a moment during the general approving silence that followed. Then she caught Ty Lassiter's eye. He was sitting at an angle to her, and she could see that he was holding himself in. As the architect in charge of the development, he had to walk a fine line, but there was no reason why Liz had to hold her tongue. She saw Sarah Lassiter reach carefully for a breadstick and, with a little snap, break it in two as if to sever the tension, as well.

Sarah wasn't going to defend the project, either, Liz realized. It was an unwritten law to keep things civilized over dinner, she supposed. Still, she couldn't resist asking a simple question.

"I'm sorry," she said in a clear, loud voice. "I don't think I understand. Why can't you build public housing near the river?" she asked. "The view certainly isn't exclusive."

"Liz." It was Celie, shaking her head imperceptibly.

"We're spending a pretty hefty sum to upgrade the area for business," Mr. Durant said. "If we allow just anyone in, well, it's not good for business."

"What Mr. Durant means," Brad cut in, "is that the area is being renovated for mixed use, but public housing opens up a whole can of worms."

"Worms, apt term," Liz said.

"It would mean building schools, playgrounds, sewage that could conceivably ruin the river. It would change the atmosphere of the area. Public housing—"

"Would bring in the wrong kind of people," Liz finished for him.

"What's all the fuss?" Mimi asked. "They probably wouldn't want to live there, anyway. They'd rather be with their own kind down at the south end of Merriman."

"Their own kind," Liz echoed. "In other words the development is mixed use as long as it's the right kind of mix."

"Liz, you've got a heart as big as the moon," Celie said. "But you can't have a perfect society in which everyone gets what he wants or deserves, no matter how democratic we try to be."

At that moment the butler came into the room and bent over Celie. She stood and said apologetically to her hosts, "I'm sorry. I have a phone call. I'll take it in the library, Olivia, if that's all right with you."

She returned after a few moments and came over to Liz. "There's a fire in the high school basement. Jake just called me. He's on his way to cover it. They think they've contained it—"

"It's Scottie," Will Vanderheyden said at her side. "I'd make book on it."

"Damn," Judge Vanderheyden whispered.

"Where's Scottie?" Brad asked. "Do you know?"

Celie shrugged. "Why would he be at the school at this time of night, and on a weekend?"

"Riffraff," Mrs. Durant snapped. "Sleeping there, no doubt. Wife probably threw him out."

The air was suddenly charged, and Liz pushed her chair back. "I'll go over to the school, Celie, and cover the story with Jake." She smiled down the table at Mrs. Kent. "If you'll excuse me, Mrs. Kent."

"Of course, my dear." Mrs. Kent gave her a smile that nonetheless held something of impatience in it.

Liz gave a blanket apology to the others at the table, though she avoided Brad's eyes. Then, with a deep sigh of relief, she hurried out of the dining room. It was only when she was in the center hall that Liz realized she was without transportation. Brad came walking quickly after her.

"You little coward," he said, spinning her around. "You couldn't wait until you got out of there, and everybody knew it, felt it."

"And it couldn't be fast enough," she said. "I don't belong here and I don't want to be here. It's a good thing the phone call came in. Five more minutes and I would have had everyone down for the count. Public housing, riffraff—poor Scottie, who's probably home in bed."

"You love this little act you put on, don't you? Champion of the poor and downtrodden."

"Where's the telephone?" she asked him sharply. "I need to call a taxi."

"I'm taking you," he said, gripping her arm. "You came with me and you're leaving with me."

She thought of Mimi Durant and what was certainly his parents' expectations.

"A taxi," she told him firmly. "Please, Brad. I've got work to do and you don't figure in it in any way."

He propelled her toward the door, his expression purposeful. It was only when they were in his car that he turned to her and said, "Don't ever use those words with me again. There isn't anything you're ever going to do in your life that won't have me in it some way or other."

CHAPTER TWELVE

THE REVOLVING RED LIGHTS of fire engines illuminating the night sky could be seen a quarter mile away. As Brad and Liz drew closer to the school, they could detect the acrid smell of smoke in the air, though no visible sign of fire.

"I guess they contained it," Liz said.

"I hope no one was hurt," Brad put in grimly, "and that Scottie isn't the culprit."

"Don't keep saying that, Brad. There's no reason for Scottie to be at the school on a Saturday night. Yet you're all so busy condemning him. If I ever had you for a lawyer, I'd throw myself on the mercy of the court."

"I think I know Scottie a little better than you do."

Bright pink flares lined the road, and there were a dozen people standing nearby, talking excitedly among themselves. Brad pulled up before the police barricade, and as they bolted from the car, Liz felt a welcome shot of adrenaline rush through her, which meant she was operating at peak condition.

"Hey!" The deputy sheriff raised a hand to stop them, then waved them on when he recognized Brad.

As they dashed into the school yard, Liz saw that fire departments from Ramsey Falls, Merriman and a small town to the southwest had responded. The paramedic ambulance was standing idle as the firemen began hauling in the hoses.

"Andy, anyone hurt?" Brad asked the Ramsey Falls fire chief as he came out into the school yard with a couple of his men.

"No. Happened in the custodian's office, but they caught it before any real damage was done."

"Scottie around?"

"Scottie?"

"The custodian."

The fire chief shrugged. "Oh, right, Scottie." He shook his head. "No one was down there, Brad. Not a soul."

"How'd it happen?" Liz asked.

"Can't tell yet. The important thing is we responded quickly and contained it."

At that moment Liz spied Adriana Scott wandering around as if lost. That was all the confirmation she needed about Scottie being somewhere on the premises, and if ever Scottie didn't need Bradford Kent, it was now. She cast a glance at Brad, but he was still engaged in conversation with the fire chief. She went quickly over to Adriana, took her by the arm and led her behind one of the huge fire trucks. "I want to talk to you," she said, "and frankly not where Mr. Kent can see us. Where's your father?"

Adriana shook her head. "That's what I'm worried about, Liz. I think he's around here somewhere. Reg, that's my boyfriend, is a volunteer fireman. He was with me when the call came in about this fire. I've been looking all over for my dad."

"The fire was contained before it could cause any trouble," Liz said. "They found no one injured, Adriana. Why would your father be on the school grounds, anyway?"

"That's the trouble. He had this big row with my mother and said he was coming here to spend the night."

"Did they argue about his drinking?"

"Yeah, sort of. My mom met his AA sponsor this afternoon on Main Street, and he said Scottie hadn't attended any meetings this past week. She came home fit to be tied. All my dad said was he hadn't been drinking, that he was just too tired to attend."

"I thought she was supposed to deliver Scottie to the meetings and pick him up after."

"She did. She drops him off and picks him up. I guess the only thing she didn't do was walk him into the hall and make sure he attended the meetings."

"Has Reg been in the school?"

"He said my dad wasn't in the basement, but they found a six-pack of beer in the custodian's office."

"Damn. Have you looked around the school interior for him?"

Adriana shook her head. "I didn't dare go in there. Liz, what should I do? I don't want him in trouble with Judge Vanderheyden. Do you think Mr. Kent—"

"Forget Mr. Kent for the time being. He's ready to tie your dad up in knots if he steps out of line even an inch. Is it possible your father is sleeping it off in one of the classrooms?"

"It's possible," Adriana said. "He can sleep anywhere anytime."

"Come on," Liz said, "let's have a peek."

Adriana, however, held back. "Can we do that?"

"We're reporters for the *Times Herald*, and we're going to do a little reconnoitering of the damage done by the fire."

As they headed for the side entrance, Liz kept an eye out for Brad, but he wasn't anywhere in sight. They found Jake Martinez, however, on his way out, camera in hand. He raised his eyebrows when he saw Liz. "Nice," he said, referring to her dress. "I like it. Better than jeans and a T-shirt for this kind of work."

"You haven't seen Scottie, have you?" Liz asked him.

"No. Listen, don't even bother covering the story. I took a couple of pictures, but it definitely wasn't the Chicago Fire."

"Jake, we have to find Scottie. Come with us upstairs. Perhaps he's asleep in one of the classrooms."

Jake glanced over at Adriana, and the look on her face seemed to convince him. "Sure. Come on." He led them into the building. "Considering that business with the judge throwing the book at him if he's ever caught drinking again," he remarked to Adriana, "I gather you want your father home quietly in bed when the gendarmes come to call."

"I guess so," Adriana responded, with what seemed to be a supreme effort.

Jake shook his head at Liz. "That's not the way to solve his particular problem, Liz. You know that."

"Let's not condemn him, Jake. We don't know if he started the fire."

"We know Nero fiddled while Rome burned, but who actually did the burning?"

"Let's reserve the history lesson for later." Liz raced through the double set of doors leading to the ground-floor classrooms. She suggested that Adriana stay put as a lookout. "I'll take the right-hand rooms and Jake the left."

Adriana nodded and slumped against the wall. Liz began opening and closing classroom doors. Halfway down the corridor, she discovered Scottie asleep in the art room. "Here," she called out to Jake and Adriana.

She was shaking Scottie awake when his daughter came into the room. "What am I doing here?" he asked, looking around sleepily and yawning.

"That's what we'd like to know," Liz said. "It's Saturday and you're supposed to be home in bed."

"Isn't this bed?"

"Scottie, you're in the art room at the high school."

He opened his eyes wide, and with a sheepish smile, said, "Oh, so that's it. Thought the wife had redecorated."

"Dad, you've been drinking," Adriana said in an anguished tone. "How could you?"

"Was I drinking? I don't remember."

"Come on home," Adriana urged, reaching for his arm. "You're in enough trouble. Mom's going to be furious. There's been a fire, and they're going to blame you and put you in jail."

"Huh?" Scottie didn't seem to understand what his daughter was saying.

"Here, let me. This is no time for lectures." Jake pulled Scottie to his feet and hauled him unceremoniously from the room. "Let's get out of here," he said to Liz. "I'll take Scottie home in my car."

"I'll follow," Adriana said, looking relieved, as though Jake's presence would calm things down in her household. "What about you, Liz?"

Whatever Brad might be doing about Scottie, Liz decided it was as good a time as any to cut out. She certainly didn't want to go back to Kent Hall. "If you won't mind a slight detour," she told Adriana, "just drop me off at home."

"Sure." For the first time Adriana seemed to realize Liz was dressed as if for a party. "You look really beautiful, Liz. Were you at a party? Don't you want to go back?"

Liz shook her head. "No thanks. I've had about all the partying I can take."

"Gosh," Adriana said after a moment, "you've been terrific. I don't know how to—"

"Don't, then," Liz said. She drew her stole around her as Adriana drove out of the school yard. She didn't dare look around for Brad.

THE NEXT MORNING, Sunday, Adriana came bouncing into Liz's room at Mrs. Duboise's and handed her a bunch of flowers. Then she gave Liz a peck on the cheek.

"Thanks," Liz said with surprise. "What's all that for?"

"Mr. Kent was on the phone last night, looking for Dad. Mom said he was in bed, but she'd wake him up if necessary. That was the God's honest truth. Mr. Kent said not to bother, that that's just where he expected my father to be. And he hung up. That's all, thanks to you and Jake. What can I get Jake as a present?"

"I imagine a kiss on the cheek might do. How's your dad this morning?"

"Shaved and showered and looking sheepish. Going to church with Mom. Liz, when he heard that maybe he could've set the school on fire, he really got depressed."

"Does he remember what happened?"

Adriana shrugged. "He can't really remember, and I believe him. He thinks he was smoking. He figured he tossed the cigarette into the wastebasket. The trouble is, he isn't sure whether he called the fire department or not. He doesn't remember even going upstairs to the art room and falling asleep."

"Well, we found him in the art room, and there's no proof that he was ever in the custodian's room or that he started the fire. After I interview the fire chief, I'll write a covering story, leaving out your father's rescue. Jake was great in spiriting him away, but we can't keep mounting rescue operations, Adriana. Your father has to help himself. No one else can."

"I know. Today he's got a terrific headache, but he's really behaving himself. I wish it could last."

"What's his excuse for not attending the AA meetings?"

"Liz, he just didn't think he needed help. But now he's changed his mind. Or at least," Adriana added, "that's what he says. Anyway, today for the first time ever he admitted he's addicted, and that's one of the very first steps you have to take toward rehabilitation. Listen, I have to go now, but the flowers and the kiss are from my mom and me."

Liz went over to her window and looked up at the sunny spring sky. "Well, maybe that's one rescue operation we mounted that was worth the risk," she told Adriana.

"It was. Oh, it was. See you tomorrow at work."

Liz smiled. It was also a rescue operation that saved her from finishing the evening back at Kent Hall. She owed Brad and his parents an apology, but didn't have the heart for it.

Still, when the telephone went off in the hall downstairs, Liz was on her way to make her apologies to the Kent family.

"For you," Mrs. Duboise said, handing her the receiver. Liz took it, hoping it might be Brad, but it wasn't.

"Liz, is that you?"

"Doug?" She felt sudden remorse and guilt. She hadn't written him in a couple of weeks, and worse, he was the last person she wanted to deal with just then.

"Hey, you remembered. Hallelujah. How are you, babe?"

"Busy. Busy, busy, busy. I know, I *know*. I owe you a letter. I owe you a couple of letters. I feel terrible about it, Doug."

"Hey, Liz, calm down. It's okay. I figured as much. I know you—get your nose into a story and the rest of us cease to exist."

"Right, Doug. I hate it when you're so damn forgiving," she said with a laugh that was more a nervous release than real mirth.

"Liz," he said, "I'm thinking of coming east in a couple of weeks."

"Here?" She held her breath for a moment. "Ramsey Falls?"

"I haven't figured that part out yet. I think there are things we have to discuss."

"Yes," she said, looking up at the portrait of an ancient Duboise ancestor as she had once before while talking to Brad. "I suppose it's time. How are you doing, anyway? You sound good," she added, realizing his voice held a bubble of happiness she hadn't heard before.

"Thanks, I feel great. Listen, I'll let you know what my plans are as soon as I can. Just wanted to touch base for now. Good to talk to you, Liz."

She was a little surprised at how quickly he hung up. But if he hadn't, Liz knew she still wouldn't have spoken her mind. She was a coward. She was confused and couldn't get Brad out of her mind.

She was distracted by the ring of the telephone and found Celie at the other end, wondering why Liz hadn't come back to Kent Hall with Brad.

Liz was tired of fudging the truth, but it seemed to her that life in Ramsey Falls sometimes required it. "Oh, I managed a lift home," she said, "and decided I was too tired to go back to the party. Was Brad angry?"

"He didn't look it. Well, we missed you and your confrontational presence," Celie said.

"Oh, Celie, I'm sorry. You know me, the windy mouth from the Windy City. Did I embarrass you?"

"No, but then I'm used to your shenanigans."

"Ouch. I guess I ought to call his mother and apologize."

"I don't think you should, Liz. You can't apologize for being the liveliest thing around. Incidentally, Brad said the fire last night was confined to the custodian's office and that Scottie was safely home in bed. Think there's anything mysterious in it?"

"Thought I'd interview the fire chief today," Liz said. "By the way, Jake took some pictures of the offending receptacle."

"It's possible vandals broke into the school," Celie said. "It seems they found a six-pack of beer in the office. Scottie drink beer?"

"Celie, you'll have to ask Scottie that question."

"If the chief can't come up with anything, we'll handle it as a blurb," Celie said in a businesslike tone, as though she found nothing wrong with the answer Liz had given.

"Right." Liz wasn't anxious to continue the conversation. This was one case where knowing the whole story was the last thing she wanted.

The fire chief had yet another surprise for Liz when she interviewed him later at the fire house. "Faulty wiring in the wall," he told her.

"What?" And so Scottie was exonerated after all. She recovered her senses sufficiently to ask the next logical question. "And who's responsible for the wiring?"

"Now don't get your hopes up that there's a big story, Liz. School's old and it's possible an animal chewed on the wire."

"Wonder if they can issue an arrest warrant for an offending animal."

When she returned home, Mrs. Duboise told her that she'd received half a dozen phone calls while she was gone.

Liz brightened. She'd been toying with the idea of calling Brad but couldn't quite make up her mind. She hadn't been able to work out a suitable apology and felt one was due for running out on him "Any messages?" she asked hopefully.

"Well, one was from your mother, but all the rest, no."

"Are you telling me that five people called and didn't leave any messages? Men or women or both?"

"Well, that's the funny thing," Mrs. Duboise remarked. "Both, but they all said the same thing. I said, 'She's not here. Any message?' And each and every one answered, 'She'll get the message.' Is it some sort of joke?"

"I'll get the message," Liz mused out loud. "I'm afraid I don't get it. Maybe it is a joke."

"I don't like the sound of it, then," Mrs. Duboise said.

Neither do I, thought Liz, but all she did was assure her landlady that it was the kind of thing reporters have happen to them when they work on unpopular stories.

"And you like what you do," Mrs. Duboise remarked, frowning at her.

"Love it."

Back in her room Liz toyed once again with the idea of calling Brad. They were at an impasse, and she decided to wait a day or two before calling him. The evening at Kent Hall had been a disaster, but then she'd been spoiling for trouble. She found it impossible to separate Brad from his family, his commitments, his lifestyle. She had come to the dinner party with clenched fists, ready to swing at the first glass jaw in sight. *I'm not one of you,* she'd wanted to scream, *and I'm glad of it.* And the best thing to do about Brad was consign him to history. It wouldn't be easy, but Liz was an old hand at certain kinds of discipline.

Doug's call, however, preyed on her mind. She even considered calling him back. He didn't need a trip east to break with her. They could accomplish the same thing with a civilized telephone call or a letter. She decided to think long and seriously about how to handle breaking up with Doug, but a half hour later Liz got up from her desk with a letter in hand. In it she said that it wasn't necessary for Doug to come east to tell her what was evident in his voice. She ended the letter in as sweet and kindly a manner as she could. She slipped the sheets into an envelope, addressed it, put a stamp on it and then posted it before she had a chance to change her mind.

ON MONDAY Liz began the morning with her usual rounds of the police station, the fire house, the various churches and the town hall. She came away with enough material for half a dozen stories. When she arrived at the *Times Herald* offices, she grabbed a copy of the weekend edition from the receptionist and a batch of telephone messages. "Oh," the receptionist said, "you also got a bunch of other calls, but whoever it was hung up."

Liz's heart froze. This was one time she couldn't go running to Brad for help. "Men or women?"

"Both, and strangely enough they all said the same thing."

"Which was?"

"'She'll get the message.' You in some kind of trouble, Liz?"

"Not that I know of."

On the way back to her desk, Liz sifted through her other calls. None from Brad, but there were two from the Nelsons, one from John and one from Marion, both thanking her for the article on the zoning board meeting that had appeared in the weekend edition.

In her office Liz opened the *Times Herald* and found the zoning board article at the bottom of page one. It was an evenhanded story listing John Nelson's grievances and Will Vanderheyden's reasons for wanting a variance on his property. Pro and con, dispassionate and detached. Just the facts, ma'am. No hearsay, no suspicions, no guts. Except for the last paragraph, which Celie had let go without blue-penciling. It referred vaguely to the imbroglio at the meeting. No blame was attached, but perhaps it was enough to set local tongues wagging. And tongues wagging were the last thing Will needed. Obviously he had called in reinforcements.

She picked up the phone and dialed Marion Nelson at Bosworth Stud.

"Thanks for the story," Marion said at once. "It was really fair. I appreciate it."

"I didn't want to write it until I had something concrete," Liz said. "That's why nothing appeared before now. I'm glad my boss left in the business about the noisy audience."

"Well, it's up to the gods now," Marion said.

"Marion, I was wondering if—"

"I know what you're going to ask," Marion told her, "but please don't. If I can help, I promise I will."

"Right," Liz said. "And tell your dad I appreciate his call. I'll keep working on the story in case anything turns up that can help him."

"Thanks again," Marion said, clearly not wanting to continue the conversation.

"You're welcome," Liz said, hanging up. She'd write finis to the story about Wouldn't It Be Loverly. Without help from Marion, Liz decided, she'd just have to file the foggy clue about Gambling Man. Maybe she'd get back to it after her story on the zoning board was finished. A moment after she hung up, Liz's phone rang.

"Miss Grady?" The voice at the other end was low and raspy.

Liz was immediately on her guard, although she didn't recognize the voice. "The zoning board story you wrote, Miss Grady. Nelson isn't going to win that one, not unless he has a trigger-happy finger and is mad enough to keep pushing."

"Who is this?"

"Never mind. Just check Bees Johnson versus Ramsey Lumber." The phone clicked in her ear.

Bees Johnson. Ramsey Lumber. Something else clicked besides the telephone receiver. She'd come across the names before. She was about to reach for her notebook when another call came in. A woman who refused to identify herself suggested that Liz look into a real estate deal dating from two years before that involved Will Vanderheyden. She said it had the same sound as the one with John Nelson.

"Bees Johnson?" Liz asked.

The call was disconnected. There was yet another call about a boundary dispute and water rights, then several more followed. Each was from an anonymous caller who had either come up against the local zoning board or knew someone who had. Her last telephone call came late in the day. The voice was muffled. Like the others, it was unrecognizable, but his message was clear. "This is a nice, quiet town, Miss Grady. We want to keep it that way."

"Well, so do I," she said in a falsely cheerful voice. "Just who is this, anyway? I like to know the names of the people calling me." Still holding the receiver to her ear, Liz went around to her office door to look for Jake, but he wasn't in sight. The only person she could see was the advertising manager, who was on the telephone and facing away from her.

"Miss Grady," the voice went on, "why don't you just stick to what you do best?"

"Well, that's pretty sound advice. If you tell me your name, maybe I'll be able to thank you in person," she said. At that moment Celie came out of her office. Liz waved frantically at her, but Celie, heading for the advertising manager's desk, didn't see her.

"And obviously what you do best has nothing to do with writing."

Liz resisted slamming the receiver down. "Go ahead," she said carefully. "Spell out just what you mean."

"This is a nice, quiet town. We don't need muckrakers. Clear enough, Miss Grady? It had better be, or you might lose more than your job." The phone went dead.

She put her receiver down and realized how rapidly her heart was beating. If Will was trying to scare her, he was succeeding extremely well. But she wasn't about to back down, not by a long shot.

Celie turned, saw Liz and came over to her. "I didn't know you were still here," she said, smiling as though nothing in the world were wrong. "At the risk of seeming too curious, can I ask you something?" Celie went on, standing at the door to Liz's cubicle and peering in at her. "Brad brought you to Kent Hall on Saturday night. He returned home from the fire at the school without you, looking absolutely furious, and when the dinner was over he took Mimi Durant home. Is there anything you want to talk to me about?"

"No," Liz said. Of all the times to discuss Brad, she thought, this wasn't it. "Listen, Celie," she began.

But Celie interrupted her. "You know his mother has been trying for a long time to sell him on the idea of Mimi as a fit and proper wife."

"His mother is a fit and proper pain in the neck. But that's neither here nor there..."

Celie laughed. "Brad's the catch of the century."

"I've heard the same thing about Hunt Gardner, Tyler Lassiter and Victor Bosworth."

"I'm not blind, Liz, and from the way Brad has been looking at you from day one, I'd say you have a chance with him."

"No, I don't," Liz said. "Not with his harridan of a mother."

"You wouldn't be marrying his mother."

"Marriage? You must think I've been considering Brad as husband material, and I haven't. I just came up against his mother and that *house* and I think they're both made of the same stone. Forget it, Celie. There's nothing between Brad and me. I wish him good luck with Mimi Durant. I'm sure they deserve each other.''

"Oooh," Celie said, advancing into the office, "you're protesting too much." She gave Liz a girlish, intimate smile, as though she'd like nothing more than a good, friendly session discussing the men in their lives.

"Celie, I've got a lot more on my mind than Brad Kent and Mimi Durant."

"You look awfully pale," Celie said suddenly, looking closely at her. "What's wrong, then?"

"The telephone call I just received. Look, Celie, sit down," Liz said, waving to a chair. "I've got a lot to tell you, and now is as good a time as any. But first, we aren't calling the sheriff and you can't pull me off the story. Those are givens."

Celie sat down and listened as Liz talked. It took no more than ten minutes. Liz finished with a carefully worded summation. "People seem to feel their grievances don't get a fair hearing. All it should take is research into how some of these past zoning variances were allowed. See if there's a pattern. See who seems to benefit most. No one says we have to dive into the pool until we're sure it's filled with water."

Celie didn't answer at once. Liz waited quietly, knowing that Celie often required time before making important decisions.

"I don't think there's any set pattern to how things are done around Ramsey Falls," Celie said. "We're too small a community. People are respectful of one another. They live here out of choice. It's a garden spot— a small, beautiful, homogeneous community. Besides," she added, "I'd have heard something before this."

"Celie, until now maybe you've thought there's nothing wrong with the way power is used in Ramsey Falls."

Celie blanched, and then with a long, drawn-out sigh said, "Okay, maybe I deserve that. I don't know. You'll still have to prove it."

"I'm going to."

"Okay, go for it," Celie said. "I've got me a hotshot big-city reporter, and it's about time I put her to good use." Then she added with an earnest smile, "Be careful, Liz. I want the *Times Herald* to go daily, so we'd better begin to take the initiative, but if something happened—"

"Nothing will happen," Liz assured her. "I have eyes in the back of my head. Oh, another thing," Liz added, pulling out her notebook and flipping through the pages, "Bees Johnson versus Ramsey Lumber. Was there anything outstanding about that dispute? I had a call on it and it has a familiar sound."

"Bees Johnson. He's a loner who lives in the backwoods off Mountain Road. He and Ramsey Lumber had a set-to a couple of years ago about a boundary line. He won the case, Liz. A mere citizen up against the corporate world and he won it."

"Okay, okay," Liz said. "He's probably the exception that proves the rule. I'll go see him."

Celie got slowly to her feet. "See him. You may even find justice was served in Merriman County. Anyway, I want to know everything you're doing. I don't want to be caught off guard."

"I know, and check my car before getting into it."

Celie was on her way out when she turned back for an instant. "Don't even joke about it."

Liz sat quietly at her desk after Celie left. Her mind was a blank. Then after a while she reached for her telephone and punched in Brad's office number in Ramsey Falls. She almost hung up before his secretary got on the line.

"Is Mr. Kent there?" she asked.

"Sorry. Mr. Kent's gone out of town. Who shall I say is calling?"

"Out of town?" Liz asked the question dully.

"Who's calling, please?"

"Miss Grady."

"Miss Grady, I'll tell him you called."

"When do you expect him back?"

"Well, it was a little unexpected, the whole thing. He flew to Florida on business but said he was going to make a vacation of it. Two weeks, I think."

Gone. Without a call. Liz replaced the receiver and rested her head in her hands. She didn't care. There was a division between them wide enough to sink Kent Hall and all the land around it. She had come to Ramsey Falls to find herself, and she had. The street urchin hadn't changed and never would and the Kents be damned, all of them.

There was work to be done. And if Brad was involved, it was better that he was out of sight and out of mind.

Bees Johnson was apparently the man who fought back and won. She picked up the receiver again. There was nothing she'd like better than to meet the man who'd beaten the system.

THE HOUSE WAS SET back in the woods on a roaring stream that hadn't been affected by the early summer drought. It wasn't the ramshackle place Liz expected but a sturdy log cabin with a wide front porch that held several inviting Adirondack chairs.

Bees Johnson was sitting on the porch, waiting for Liz, when she pulled up in her car early the next morning.

"Beautiful place back here," she called, heading for the porch. "I'm Liz Grady."

"Been wanting to meet you," he said, gesturing to her to join him. "I've been following your coverage of the Nelson-Vanderheyden business." Bees was a barrel-chested man in his late fifties with a crop of wild hair floating around his head. The jeans he wore, held up by suspenders, should have been thrown out long before. Liz mounted the stairs to the porch. Two huge dogs at his feet didn't even bother to check her out.

"Come on indoors," he said. "I've got a pitcher of cold lemonade, unless you want something stronger." He led Liz into a room with a huge fieldstone fireplace at one end and a bookshelf filled with hunting trophies at the other. The furniture was homely, old and comfortable. She wished she had Jake Martinez with her to photograph both the man and the way he lived. In black and white or sepia-toned, it could win a prize.

"Lemonade will do fine," Liz said when they were settled in the kitchen.

"You want to know about that hassle I had with Ramsey Lumber, don't you?" he remarked as he poured the lemonade for her out of a cracked pitcher.

"You're one of the rare people who challenged a request for variance and won."

"That's 'cause I'm one of the few people ain't scared of what passes for the law around here, or the fancy lawyers who try to scare the devil out of you while they're at it. You dredging it up for the paper?" Bees threw some ice into the glass and handed it to her.

"No, I'm doing a general story on zoning board decisions. What happened exactly in your case?" The lemonade was tart and good and clearly homemade.

Bees appeared eager to talk. "Plain and simple and crooked as an unwound snake. Ramsey sneaked around in the middle of the night and moved an iron post in about twenty feet."

"I don't get it."

"You a city girl?"

"Yes."

"Thought so. The reason you move posts is to blur the exact boundary between two parcels of land. Then they started chopping down the trees on my land, claiming the land was theirs."

"What about surveying maps?"

"Surveyors start surveying from iron posts. Ramsey figured I wouldn't ante up the money for a new survey and that I wouldn't pay a lawyer to fight. Only they were dead wrong."

"And you lost the first go-around before Judge Vanderheyden."

He gave her a grim smile. "I expected to, seeing that his son is part owner of Ramsey Lumber."

"What?" The question came out as a near squeal. Liz hadn't had time to check into the ownership of Ramsey Lumber. "Couldn't you have asked for a change of venue, knowing that Judge Vanderheyden would try the case?"

"I was going one step at a time. I don't like anybody taking what's mine, and I figured I might as well get the judge out of my way early."

"I heard you're related to the judge."

He shrugged. "Way back. Anyway, that's one thing a man can't help—his relations. Dig deep enough into the town's past and you'll find we all had the same ten times great grandpappy."

"Did anyone threaten you at any time?"

He looked at his hunting trophies and then turned back to her with a smile. "I can give and take as good as I get."

"Yes," Liz said. "I suppose you can."

"I got a fairer shake in Merriman. Ramsey had to move the iron post back and pay me for damages. Had to ante up the profits for the trees they took down and for my lawyer, as well."

"I suppose there's no real compensation for trees that take fifty or seventy-five years to reach their full growth."

"That was my point."

"Well, Will's doing it again on some property he owns on I-84. Some beautiful old trees went under the axe." Liz finished off the last of the lemonade and stood, ready to leave. "I like to hear an occasional success story around here. I wonder why more people don't take them on."

"Money. I'd have mortgaged the old place to beat 'em. Oh, and there's something else. That lumber company was started with an unsecured loan from a local bank."

"I suppose that happens in a small town where everybody knows everybody."

"You ever try to get money from a bank without giving them your left arm as collateral?"

"Okay," Liz conceded. "What should I be looking for?"

"Well, the land belonged to the Kents, and Will's part of the family. You might start with Victor Bosworth. Along with the Kents, he backed the loan and wanted it kept quiet."

Liz stared long and hard at Bees Johnson. "You know all this for a fact?"

"Brad Kent IV isn't the only lawyer around with connections," he told her. "My lawyer won for me because he was armed with the facts, and that's one of the facts. And I might add, it was a pleasure to see Brad against the wall. Nice guy in a lot of ways, but he's one of them and he can't see the woods for the trees."

"But if Victor Bosworth backed the loan," Liz said, "the bank considered it secured."

"The owners of Ramsey Lumber are a pack of thieves. Victor Bosworth traveling with thieves?" Bees shook his head in mock wonder. "Odd doings for a man not on the board of Ramsey Lumber. Odd doings for a man who has the reputation in town that Victor Bosworth has."

"Are you including the Kents in your definition of thieves?"

He shook his head once again. "No. Opportunists, maybe, but not thieves. Will's the bad apple and his old man Thadeus lets him get away with it."

"Know anyone else on the board of Ramsey Lumber?"

"Well, that was a couple of years ago. I think things have changed there. I'm not sure. Got them out of my hair. That's all I cared about. Patrick Lucas," he added suddenly.

She shook her head. "Patrick Lucas? Name isn't familiar."

"He was one of those named in the suit."

"From around here?"

"Out of town. Can't help you more than that."

The missing November file. Liz supposed it was all in there. Missing and why? She stuck out her hand. "Thanks for your help, Bees."

"I know what John Nelson's going through," he said, grasping her hand in a large paw. "He's a good man."

Liz left, but all the way back to town she had the feeling she had stepped into a maze and that something lay at the center that was too awful to contemplate. It struck her that if she followed the story to its logical conclusion, she'd destroy Brad, and for the first time she understood the power of loyalty and love and how easy it would be to let matters slide.

An interview with the director of Ramsey Lumber proved of little value. The original owner had died the year before. His widow ran the company now and professed to have little knowledge of the lawsuit. She knew nothing about the original loan and said there were no partners, limited or otherwise.

When Liz left, she made a note to check into the probated will in Merriman.

After that, Liz set out a pattern for herself. She went into the office every morning at eight and worked at her daily assignments until one. Then she grabbed a light lunch and headed for Merriman and its town hall. The clerk handed her the files each time with a sober face, her manner of someone greatly put upon. Liz accepted the files as graciously as she could, forcing a smile. The missing November file never did turn up.

A look at the probated will of the late owner of Ramsey Lumber showed it to be a solely owned corporation inherited by his wife. There were no liens against it and the loan had been fully repaid. Perhaps Will and his partners had decided the lawsuit was bad publicity and had stepped away. Bees Johnson versus Ramsey Lumber seemed to be a dead end, and in a way Liz was glad. It was one less incident involving Brad Kent that she had to worry about.

And every day she awoke with Brad's face imprinted on her memory. Every day at least once she thought seriously of packing it in and returning to Chicago. Then after her first cup of coffee she'd come to her senses. She was going to nail Will Vanderheyden first and prove to Brad that she knew what she was doing. She'd prove that small towns weren't all apple pie and honey. If Brad were part of it, she'd have to nail him, too.

The yellow and mauve flowers of spring had given way to the bright colors of summer. Trees were garbed in their deep, lush green leaves. The grass grew tall and then was mowed, freeing its sweet scent on the summer air. Crows and blue jays seemed to rise earlier and earlier, waking Liz with their raucous cries, reminding her of another day to be faced.

And then one afternoon, sitting in Merriman's town hall with the summer sun beckoning from an open window and a fly buzzing lazily around the room, Liz threw her pencil down and sat daydreaming. Except for Bees Johnson and his successful fight, taking on the establishment in the town seemed an exercise in futility.

Just then there was a slight rustle behind her. Someone had come up close. Her spine stiffened and she waited, realizing for the past two weeks she'd been on the edge, waiting for something to happen, waiting for the unexpected.

"Liz."

The voice was soft and welcoming and set her heart beating rapidly. She turned to find Brad gazing down at her out of his deep, unfathomable eyes.

CHAPTER THIRTEEN

"I SAW YOU from across the room," Brad said, "and didn't want to go away without talking to you."

Liz quickly scraped her chair back and stood without quite knowing what she was doing. "Welcome home," she said with a catch in her voice.

"You knew I was away, then?"

"I think they announced it in lights over Main Street."

"But not that I'd come back."

"I haven't been checking the lights over Main Street lately."

"Out of sight, out of mind." His smile was wistful.

Oh, Lord, she thought, she was doing it again, being tough and smart when all she wanted to do was feel his arms around her. "I called the day you left." She wondered why the words were so hard to say, but plowed bravely on. "I wanted to apologize for my behavior the night before."

"Let's get out of here, Lizzie. It's been too long."

Those were the words she wanted to hear. She picked up her notebook and tucked it into her bag. Then, reaching for the folder, she went ahead of him to the reception desk where she handed it in. Bees Johnson versus Ramsey Lumber—she couldn't care less. Then, as they stepped into the bright sunlight of late afternoon, Brad said, "I wanted to call you before I left but decided against it. I thought, no, let the lady get herself out of this one all by herself.''

''Because of what happened at Kent Hall?'' she said dully. ''My dreadful reaction to your parents' friends?''

''No, you've got it all wrong. Because I saw Jake Martinez haul Scottie out of the school building that night and saw you and Adriana exit a couple of minutes later. Because you thought so little of me that you didn't tell me you'd found him and that he was drunk.''

''You'd have thrown him in jail. Maybe he deserved it, but Adriana didn't. And by the way, thanks to our rescue efforts, the man's on the wagon.''

''And he was home in bed when I called. In fact, I called so I could tell the judge that's where all good custodians were on a Saturday night. Liz, the subject is finished. Scottie is toeing the mark. The fire was started by faulty wiring. And Scottie escaped by the skin of his teeth. I just wanted to have some of your trust, that's all.''

''I was a little mixed up to say the least,'' she conceded, ''but I was worried about my not very lady-like behavior at Kent Hall. You didn't deserve it, and neither did your parents. I owe all of you an apology.''

''You told them what they should have learned a long time ago, Liz. And you enabled me to see a couple of my peers in a new light.''

''Like Mimi Durant and her parents, for instance.''

''Liz, don't change. Don't ever change.''

Liz gazed at him and thought with a lift of her heart that he was the handsomest man she had ever known and that she'd fight Mimi Durant tooth and nail for him.

''Why the gleam in your eye?'' he asked.

On the steps of the town hall she threw her arms around his neck and planted a kiss on his narrow, aristocratic nose. "Because I'm very happy to see you."

"Hey, Brad, looks as if you won a case," someone coming up the stairs called out to him. Brad ignored the remark by putting his mouth against hers. "I missed you, damn it," he said.

"Come on, let me buy you a drink," she told him, feeling the warmth suffuse her cheeks. "I know just the place."

"I know a better place."

"Uh-uh, out in public where you'll have to behave yourself."

HORGAN'S WAS a dark little corner pub near the town hall that catered to civil service employees, lawyers and their clients and to reporters from the Merriman newspaper and the local radio stations as well. The sawdust on the floor was shaken up every now and then by a waiter wielding a straw broom, and beer was served in oversize mugs. Liz and Jake occasionally spent time there.

"I see you've discovered the best watering hole in town," Brad commented once they were seated together in a back booth.

"You keep forgetting I'm a restaurant critic. I gave this place five stars—four for the beer and one for atmosphere."

"Hey, don't knock the atmosphere. Something very friendly about it. I like dark back corners and booths where two can cuddle."

"You've done a lot of that, I suppose, back here."

He laughed as the waiter came along and took their order after swiping at the table with a damp cloth. Once he was gone, Brad leaned over and kissed Liz on the cheek. "I tried not to think about you," he said. "It worked for about a minute and a half."

"But nothing's changed. I'm the same old Liz, the one you invite home and who embarrasses you with her tart tongue and self-righteousness."

"Tell me something I haven't thought about. I'm a sucker for a tart tongue and a self-righteous muck-raker."

"I have a habit of getting mixed up in things that could shake the town wide open, create a schism, with you on one side and me on the other."

"I know what you can do, Liz. We've got Scottie as a good example of how to defy authority. Drop the whole subject, Liz. That's not what I want to talk about."

"But the differences between us are precisely what we should talk about," she said evenly. "Because you're a good kisser doesn't mean I'll stop what I'm doing."

He gazed at her for a long moment. "What precisely were you after at the town hall?"

"Discovering things, such as the case of Johnson against Ramsey Lumber—Bradford Kent the fourth representing Ramsey Lumber."

"I lost that one," he said with a smile bordering on the nostalgic. "Happens sometimes. A case of an iron stake pulled up and a surveyor's mistake, that's all."

"Your uncle originally found for the lumber company. His son was on the board. Why didn't the good judge take himself off the case and save Johnson the expense of going to a higher court?"

"If the judge took himself off every case involving Vanderheydens and their relations, he'd have to move to a new county. Incidentally, Johnson is also stained with the Vanderheyden genes going back a century or two."

"I'm not impressed with a case of watered-down genes. Obviously Johnson had a good argument."

"Liz, there's no black and white in most cases that come before the court. Judgments often teeter on a fine edge. Perhaps my uncle has made poor calls in certain cases. I'll concede that much. He should have asked for the Johnson-Ramsey case to be heard in another court."

"Well," she said, offering him a smile of surprise. "Well, well, well, am I hearing correctly? Are you admitting the judge should step down, that he had his hand in the cookie jar?"

"I'm only saying that a word to the wise should be sufficient. Let me handle the judge, Liz. I promise you the problem won't be swept under the rug."

Liz shook her head. "There's still the matter of John Nelson, who believes he's being unfairly treated. I'm not trying to bargain for Mr. Nelson. I'm just trying to get to the bottom of the way justice is meted out around Ramsey Falls."

"Liz—" he reached over and took her hand in his "—you're doing it again."

"Doing what again?"

"Baiting me."

He was right, of course. Dual emotions seemed to fight for control inside her. She was daring him to love her no matter who she was, how she acted or what she did that might hurt him. And yet she couldn't be any other way. She waited, knowing that whatever his attitude would be, it would decide whether or not they would see each other again.

He looked past her as the waiter placed their beer mugs on the table. Brad lifted his and said, "To the most stubborn, bullheaded woman I've ever met." Then he grinned and added, "And to tomorrow."

Liz relaxed visibly. She raised her glass and touched his, the clink sealing an unspoken bargain. He was daring her, too, to find something. Perhaps he was adept at covering tracks, but she was just as adept at uncovering them.

"Know what?" he asked.

She shook her head. "What?"

"I'd like to take you in my arms and kiss you thoroughly. But not here. And don't give me any of your lip. I mean, not that way." He reached for his wallet and drew out a bill.

"I was buying," Liz said.

"The woman must argue," he said, raising his eyes to the ceiling. "Next time." He took her arm. Once they were outside, he said, "Come on, my car's parked in the back lot of my office building."

"My car," Liz insisted. "End of discussion."

He gave her a crooked grin. "Your car, Grady. I'll drive. Absolute end of discussion."

An absolute end to the discussion, she thought, because otherwise she'd have to ask where they were going and why, and she knew and didn't want to feel obliged to object. She settled herself into the passenger seat and kept her eye on the road. It was all there ahead of her, and she could think of nothing she wanted as much as his arms around her.

When they arrived at Brad's cottage, they carried a couple of containers of fragrant, spicy Chinese food bought at a restaurant en route. But even as Liz stepped into the entryway of the cottage, she knew their hunger was of a far different kind.

Brad put the containers of food on a hall table and then took her bag and placed it on a chair. Liz watched him as he performed what seemed to be a preordained ritual. Then he turned and stood very still, studying her with a gentle, teasing smile.

She felt a little shock, as though the meeting at the town hall had been planned, as though he had known all along exactly what he would do and how she'd react. "Is that the look you have in front of a jury when you're certain of a verdict in your favor?"

The smile turned into a crooked grin. "You've hit the nail on the head."

"You planned all this. I suppose it's written down on your daily calendar. 'Bring Liz and a couple of cartons of Chinese food out to cottage. She'll be absolute soy sauce in your hands.'"

"Oh, not soy sauce, Liz. I did consult a fortune cookie, however. The future looks quite good from where I stand."

"You're absolutely insufferable, arrogant, smug and self-satisfied." Liz kicked her shoes off and came slowly toward him. "You're bossy, narrow-minded and ruthless. Sexy, seductive..." Her arms went around his neck and her lips collided with his. She had never felt this way, never had an urge to taste, touch, feel—own—the way she did now.

He lifted his head. "Good girl," he whispered. "I knew if I waited long enough, I'd get some kind words out of you."

They were facing the moment of truth. She'd gone through every argument against loving him. By every measurement of what made a relationship work, theirs would fail, but her signals were being short-circuited. Apart from knowing exactly what she wanted of him at that precise moment, her mind was a blank. His lips brushed hers, and then in another moment the kiss deepened, full of unasked questions and savage electricity. Liz gave up any thoughts that might conflict with the rapture she was experiencing. It was new and startling. She had never felt this way before, not with Doug, not with anyone.

Brad ran his hands along her back, tightening his grip. She felt his hesitation and then growing certainty as he slowly inched toward her breast and curled his fingers around the soft, impatient flesh. She heard a moan and had no idea who had uttered the sound.

A wave of pure sensation, tumultuous and overwhelming, roiled through her. Her body yearned for something just out of reach, and she began to tremble, knowing she was lost. Whatever he wanted, she was ready for it. She could feel her body reaching, opening, when surprisingly he pulled back and gripped her shoulders as he fought to keep his breath steady.

"From the moment I met you, I couldn't think of anything but making love to you. It was stupid to tell myself I could bring you here for any other reason. And you wouldn't have come without knowing it." His eyes, laser beams of blue, shot bolts of charged power through her.

"You've got a fire in you, Liz. I've never known anyone who could make me feel so alive." Then, in one swift movement, he swept her into his arms and carried her up the stairway to his loft. He put her down on his bed in a room of unsparing whiteness, and then was over her, his body pressing her down, his eyes blazing with heat and longing.

He placed tiny kisses on her mouth, her nose, her cheeks, her eyes. His tongue played lightly with her lashes and then moved in a slow line down her nose. When his mouth claimed hers, it was with a stunning, fierce strength that left her powerless.

In another moment he lifted her gently and, with strokes and caresses, removed her barrier of cotton, silk and lace. She realized through half-opened lids that he was regarding her naked body with such tenderness and open love that any sense of shyness was swept away.

"You're beautiful," he said, "so beautiful." He leaned over her, kissing her with provocative slowness, coaxing a response. She reached for him, but he lifted himself and with swift movements removed his own clothes, letting them fall to the floor over hers.

She took in a deep, ragged breath. He was magnificent, his body strong, firm and ready. The savage expression in his eyes made her feel wanted and irresistible. He eased himself on her, bending to her breasts and brushing his lips methodically back and forth across the tips, teasing and tugging gently with his teeth. Her body was awash with strange sensations, and an unfamiliar heat swept along her flesh. She thought, grasping him, that she couldn't seem to get close enough. His mouth was wild, hungry, with a basic need that was on the edge of flaring out of control. A mindless little whimper of delight escaped her throat, her body catching fire. She was beyond rational thought as her hands stroked his back and muscular shoulders, savoring his silken skin.

"Sweet Liz. I knew it would be like this."

His closeness was intoxicating, and she slid her hand lower to gently caress him, everything blocked out but the certainty of the fulfillment she was ready for. Within moments he had kissed and licked and nipped at every part of her. Liz was certain she was burning with a strange fever. His fingers at the core of her being, stroked and probed the soft, sweet dampness with a passion that was new to her. His touch was a message that he could be tender but that he would claim what was his.

She touched his face, whispering she was ready, the moment was now. Brad held her hips and moved to take her, his breathing rapid as his face pressed to hers. Their lips connected in a long, drawn-out kiss as she arched and opened to him. He held her tight, and with excruciating slowness he began to move. Liz wrapped her legs around him, securing him close as she stirred and shifted beneath him. At last he plunged more deeply into her, and in one violent instant—an instant that would be seared into her memory forever—she crashed through a barricade she hadn't even known was there. Lightning soared through her body, binding her to him in a blinding flash.

AFTERWARD, having lost all sense of time and even of place, Liz realized that neither of them had spoken. The power of their lovemaking had taken Liz totally by surprise, and her body still tingled from the heat and flame. It was all too new. She slept lightly and then awakened with a little start.

"Liz?" The word was said dreamily. Brad lay with his head against her breast. "Do you realize that the food is as cold as a Swedish smorgasbord?"

"I can't believe it," Liz said, "but I'm starved." She drew her fingers through his hair and then bent and kissed the top of his head.

"Yeah, I do that to women. I unlock their appetites."

"I forgot to have lunch. And dinner, as I recall, was a sip of beer."

"Why didn't you tell me before?"

"I was hungry for something else before."

He lifted himself over her and gazed into her eyes. She found herself reveling in his weight and the sweet male smell of his body. Studying every centimeter of her skin, he asked, "Do you do that often? Forget to eat?"

"Are you worried I'll waste away to nothing?"

"You won't if I have anything to do with it." He ran his fingers gently down her face. "Come on, time for a celebration."

"The tricentennial isn't until later this month."

"Odd, I thought the fireworks had already begun." He kissed her lips. "Stay right here," he said. "I'll be back in five minutes with the microwaved works."

"Mmm, great idea." As she settled among the pillows, she thought that she hadn't felt so warm and co-cooned in years. His touch was soft and had a sweet tenderness that let her know she had found something new and wonderful. She closed her eyes and fell into a soft, dreamless sleep almost before he was out the door.

"Damn it, you've got to help me."

She was in the middle of a dream and Brad was brushing her away.

"I said I don't want to talk about it now."

Liz opened her eyes abruptly and sat up. It was no dream. Brad was arguing with someone below, and she realized almost at once that the other voice belonged to Will Vanderheyden.

"All right, Brad. I admit I'm in the hole for a bundle, but you'd think after all I've done for him, he'd give me a little time. I dug into company funds to cover my bets. Hell, I was going along great, beating the house . . . and then it all came crashing down."

Liz grabbed the blanket and wrapped it around herself. She stepped softly out of bed and went over to the landing, protected from view by a partition.

She heard the restrained care with which Brad answered his cousin. "Patrick Lucas knew what he was getting into when he took you for a partner, Will. Get down on your knees to him and tell him you're sorry, that you'll be a good little boy."

Patrick Lucas. The name sounded familiar to Liz. Then she remembered. Lucas had surfaced when she was researching Ramsey Lumber versus Bees Johnson. He was a principal in Ramsey Lumber.

"You being sarcastic?" Will asked. "You're not being paid to tell me what I don't want to hear."

"You're perfectly right. I seem to recall you fired me sometime back. The front door is straight ahead. Try not to slam it when you leave."

"Hey, hey, wait a minute. Hold everything. You know me, Brad. I get ticked off and then I forget about it. I'm not about to hire another lawyer. You know too much. You've been in on too many deals."

"Will, never mind what I know and don't know, or even how many deals I've watched you and Lucas make a killing over. I respect lawyer-client confidentiality. I'm no longer your lawyer, but I'll continue to respect confidentiality because it's the way things have always been done in Ramsey Falls, isn't it?"

"That's right, and they'll continue that way if you just get Lucas off my back."

"I warned you a long time ago that your gambling was getting out of hand. Pay the piper, Will. Then step back. Sell some of your real estate, like the piece on I-84. It's possible John Nelson might have the money to swing a deal."

"I've reached the end of my rope as far as Lucas is concerned. I told you I can't sell anything without his permission. Just call him. Talk to him. You know, tell him I'm good for the money. Remind him how much the old man has. He's in Florida at Glenhollow Stud. Call him, Brad. Come on, call him now. Sweet-talk him.''

"So long, Will. You want an appointment, call me at my office. I'll try to fit you in.''

"You'll fit me in. You always have. Out of respect for the judge, and your parents, you'll handle it. Man, for a minute you had me worried there.''

Liz heard footsteps move along the floor. She heard the doorknob turn and then Will spoke, his voice suddenly filled with repressed laughter. "Oh-ho! I understand. Right. You've got company. Right. I won't even ask who, but I can guess. It's that muckraker you've been playing around with. But maybe it's not a bad idea. At least you know her moves as well as I do, and maybe a lot I don't.''

"You son of a—''

"Hold it! No rough stuff, Brad. I'm talking for your own good. You've been out of town, but I can tell you this much. She's been at the town hall in Merriman, checking through the zoning files. And while I'm here, let me pass on a little warning to your lady friend.'' His voice rose so that Liz could hear every syllable. "I don't think it's wise to stir up trouble where there isn't any. People get into all kinds of trouble when they shove their noses into other people's business. Good night, Brad. I'll see you in the morning. I figure you'll make that phone call for me now.'' She heard the door slam behind him.

"Damn!'' She heard Brad growl as he strode across the floor.

Liz flew into the bathroom and turned the shower on full blast. She had to think. Quite suddenly her relationship with Brad fell into focus. She was out of her league. She knew that now. Brad was part of a world that used other people, relationships and influence as if they were rights handed down with the old estates and the pictures of ancestors. Brad understood what was going on in Ramsey Falls and hadn't raised a finger to change the way things were—because of a misplaced sense of entitlement. It wasn't the way she did business, however.

As she let the water pound her skin, the words kept coming at her. Patrick Lucas of Glenhollow Stud—a perfect stranger who was able to control zoning board decisions from Florida because Will Vanderheyden was indebted to him. She had come to Ramsey Falls to get away from the big-city hustle. She was the worst sort of fool, she thought, breathing deeply.

She turned off the shower and was toweling herself dry when Brad knocked at the bathroom door. "Dinner ready in five minutes, Liz."

"Perfect," she said in as bright a tone as she could muster. "I'm starved."

"I am, too," he called out, "but maybe not for food."

She waited until she heard him retreat downstairs, then dressed quickly. Brad was standing in the kitchen, staring at the microwave when she came quietly down the stairs. She had to think. She had no heart for confrontation, so she strode silently across the wooden floor to the front door. She was in her car, backing out of the driveway, when the door to the cottage opened. Brad rushed toward her, but she shook her head and drove on.

CHAPTER FOURTEEN

THERE WAS an hour's time difference between New York and Chicago. That would make it somewhere around nine o'clock. Liz dialed a well-remembered number once she was back at Mrs. Duboise's and was rewarded with a screech of delight before she could finish announcing her name.

"Lizzie, you're back! Incredible! I've missed you. Where are you? Don't say another word. I'm coming to see you."

"Annette, calm down. I'm not in Chicago. I'm calling from Ramsey Falls and I've got a favor to ask."

Annette Deems still worked at the night desk on the paper Liz had abandoned for the *Ramsey Falls Times Herald.* "Oh," she said with a false groan. "I should know you by now. Workaholic Liz Grady, we used to call you. You sound serious. What's up?"

"I was wondering if you could do a bit of nosing around for me. I need to know something about a stud farm in Florida called Glenhollow Stud, possibly run by someone called Patrick Lucas. Even at this time of night, you can run that by your sports department connections, can't you?"

There was a moment of dead silence at the other end. Then Annette said, "That's it? You're calling me from New York State at nine o'clock at night to find out the name of a stud farm in Florida?"

"Libraries are closed, and our local newspaper office might not contain a compendium of horse farms throughout the United States. And I don't want anyone to know at the moment that I'm doing a little research."

"Can't this wait until tomorrow?"

"I'm thinking of waking up in Florida tomorrow."

"Dare I ask what's happening?"

"Nothing, probably, but I have to get away for a while, get my head together and follow up something to my satisfaction."

"Okay. Patrick Lucas, Glenhollow Stud, Florida."

Liz thought of something else, although she had no notion why it had suddenly come to mind. "I've been vaguely following up what happened to a horse sold at auction here. I can't get a line on where he is, but I wonder if there isn't some kind of registry available that keeps tabs on where thirteen-million-dollar horses end up."

"What's the horse's name?"

"Wouldn't It Be Loverly."

"It would. Name of horse, please."

"This sounds like a comedy routine. That's his name and he was sold a short time ago at an auction here at Bosworth Stud."

"You'll hear from me, Liz. You'd be surprised at the depth of research information we have around here at the touch of a button."

"I wouldn't be amazed at all. I worked there once, remember?"

Annette laughed. "Give me an hour, okay?"

"I'll be packing."

"Listen, if there's something in it for me—"

"You'll get a Chicago exclusive."

When the telephone rang just before midnight, Liz called an apology to Mrs. Duboise and picked up the receiver.

"Liz? What the devil are you working on?" Annette's voice seemed to have dropped an octave.

"Why?"

"Okay, Glenhollow Stud is halfway between Tampa and Ocala, but I'm more interested in talking about Patrick Lucas. He belongs to the Lucas clan, and the Lucases certainly have an outpost here in Chicago, which is why we have a file on him. When it comes to the Mob, it's a small world."

"Go on."

"The family is low-profile, but you name the game and they have something to do with it. But most of all they have a lot to do with money-laundering. Is this interesting to you, or am I getting too far afield?"

"Keep going." Money-laundering was the way the Mob made its illegally gained cash disappear—usually by funneling the money into legitimate businesses or into banks abroad. Their methods of laundering money and making it seem legitimate were as varied as lottery numbers, and it often appeared to be a game the government would never win.

"Tell me more about Patrick Lucas," Liz said.

"Now that's an interesting story," Annette replied eagerly. "He's part of the first generation of the family to be born in America. Went to Harvard, then to Wharton, then into the family business. He's the American dream come true," she added with a bitter laugh. "He's the one who set up tax shelters for the Lucas clan, took in 'laundry,' made it nice and clean by investing it in real estate, hotels, restaurants, stud farms—you name it—all very respectable stuff."

"Know anything about him personally?" Liz asked.

"Wife in Santa Fe he rarely sees, one boy, one girl, both very young. Lives an upright life, makes donations to charity, and he's seen at all the right events. He travels the country, checking up on the family investments, but his heart is in raising Thoroughbreds. Glenhollow Stud is held in high esteem, apparently."

"And Lucas apparently owns a lumber company in Ramsey Falls," Liz said.

"Want to run that by me again?"

"Just that he gets around. It's a long way from Chicago to Tampa to upper New York State. Is there more, Annette?"

"Just think of ways the Mob earns money and you should come up with what keeps a man like Lucas busy. Now, as for Wouldn't It Be Loverly, he was bought at auction by a company operating under the name of White Horse Farms."

"Know who the owner is?"

"Does the sun know whether to rise in the east or not? Owner is William Vanderheyden, a name totally unfamiliar to me. If you want me to do further research..."

Liz sucked in a surprised breath. "Will Vanderheyden? But that's impossible. No, nothing's impossible. Did you say White Horse Farms? Where's that?"

"No address. The colt, however, is boarding at Bosworth Stud."

"But he's not!" Liz exclaimed. "Marion would've told me. Curiouser and curiouser. Okay, I'm stunned, but I'm going to have to let that ride for the time being."

"Anything else you want me to do?" Annette asked. "When are you coming back? Haven't you had enough of the backwoods?"

"I'll let you know as soon as I return from Florida."

"Florida! Wait a minute. You're not planning to meet Lucas, are you? You won't get a word out of him."

"I don't suppose I will, but the last time I let a story get by me it won a Pulitzer Prize. This time I'm tracking my leads to the source."

"Okay, Liz, but watch your rear at all times. Oh, incidentally, our worthy senior editor told me to tell you you're welcome back anytime."

THE AIRPORT AT TAMPA was a whole new experience for Liz. She had never been to the South before and expected things to be slow-moving and laid-back. The next time she headed for a big city, she'd remember to do a little research ahead of time. Tampa wasn't a sleepy backwater at all, but a busy, bustling brand-new city of skyscrapers.

And next time, she might give her plans a little more thought. The nearer she came to her destination, the more her flight from Ramsey Falls that morning before dawn looked hasty and foolish. At the time her decision to go to Tampa had seemed to make sense. She'd wanted to escape Brad. She'd wanted to find out about Patrick Lucas. And she'd wanted to discover why Patrick Lucas was pulling Will's strings all the way from Florida.

But it might all be quite harmless, she'd realized, and if she went, she might make a fool of herself in the bargain.

Liz had left a note for Mrs. Duboise, stating that she had decided to fly to Tampa and would return in a day or two. Then she'd packed a bag, climbed into her car and headed downstate for the airport. She'd figured she'd phone Celie from the hotel in Tampa, knowing that she'd as good as quit her job, anyway.

When she stepped out of the limousine at her hotel, it was into a still, hot morning. The hotel, in contrast, was ice-cold. Her room on the twelfth floor had a view of the bay. Liz, however, didn't stop to admire the view. She had to find Patrick Lucas. Reaching him on the telephone was far easier than she had expected.

"I'm a free-lance writer," she explained when he came on the phone, "and I've been preparing a book for a major publisher on horse breeding. I was told that when I came down to Florida I shouldn't miss Glenhollow Stud." She took in a deep breath. Being a reporter called for a tough hide, but for the first time Liz realized she had come a long way without knowing whether Lucas would meet her or not. And she had no idea what she'd learn, anyway. "I'm staying at the Sheraton in downtown Tampa," she added. "I wondered if I might come by and talk to you."

"It would be a pleasure," he said in an affable voice. "How about this afternoon? I can give you a half hour, say four to four-thirty."

"Thanks so much, Mr. Lucas."

He gave her directions for Glenhollow Stud, located on the highway to Ocala. That gave her a couple of hours to do some research down at the *Tampa Times*. She ordered a rental car, and forty minutes later arrived at the newspaper's offices, where she was given access to the morgue without any trouble at all.

The Tampa papers seemed to be full of articles about Patrick Lucas. She found half a dozen recent stories about Glenhollow, all favorable. It was a prestigious breeding farm, home to famous breeding mares and stallions.

But what took her breath away was the photograph of Patrick Lucas. She remembered now where she had first learned his name. She had been looking through old newspaper articles in Ramsey Falls and had come across a picture of Will Vanderheyden taken in Atlantic City. The man who had his arm around Will's shoulders was Patrick Lucas.

She got heavily to her feet, suddenly aware of how far she had come and how fast she was running in pursuit of—*what*? The story had begun in Ramsey Falls, with a zoning dispute. Now she was investigating Will Vanderheyden's ties to a businessman who was really a mobster. Was she so bent on the truth that she would poke around where angels might fear to tread and even risk losing the man she loved? What if she found him in collusion with the Mob? Would she kill the story, or publish, consequences be damned.

As she left the newspaper office, Liz knew she had no answers. Perhaps she'd find them at Glenhollow Stud. Perhaps she wouldn't.

The route out to the farm was flat, the scenery nondescript. But as she approached her destination, the land broke up into neat grids of pasture defined by white wooden fencing. Mares and foals grazed on still-dewy grass.

The driveway to Glenhollow led in a long, straight line directly to the main house a quarter mile away. The sides of the road were shaded with southern pin oak, and beyond that were pristine white fences enclosing paddocks. A small sign pointed to the offices at the back. There, in the rear parking grounds, she found about a dozen cars. Off in the distance, on a rolling green slope shaded by tall trees, several horses were being led around by grooms. There was no reception area in the long, low building that served as Glenhollow's office, just a list of names in the front hall enclosed in a glass case with room numbers next to them. Mr. Lucas could be found in room 3.

Quite informal, Liz thought as she went down the carpeted hallway. The door to number three was open. Liz tapped lightly and then stepped inside to find herself in a simply furnished office. No one was there. She glanced at her watch. She was on time.

There were several diplomas on the wall attesting to Lucas's graduation from both Harvard and the Wharton School of Business. On a shelf below were some silver trophies and pictures of horses and their jockeys in the winner's circle. The room had a broad view of the grounds and stables through a wide, curtainless window. Another open door led to an adjoining room.

"Mr. Lucas?" she called out softly.

"Be with you in a minute," he called out from the other room. The voice had a warm timbre. It was deep and possibly trained. Intuition told Liz that Lucas was perfectly aware of who she was and that somehow he was studying her. The thought was unnerving, and for an instant Liz thought of running away from what could turn out to be a reckless journey.

Patrick Lucas came into the room, wiping his hands on a towel. "Well, Miss Grady." He threw the towel unceremoniously onto a chair before he reached for her hand.

"Sorry," he said, holding her hand in a strong grip. "I was out at the stables, and that always requires a general cleanup." Liz was taken totally by surprise. Although she had studied his picture at the newspaper morgue, she wasn't at all prepared for the Patrick Lucas who stood before her. His smile was dazzling, and she could see a hint of appreciative interest in his eyes as he gazed at her.

He was tall, in his late thirties, with white teeth in a deeply tanned face. His hair was dark and thick, and his eyes, fringed by black lashes, were a deep green. It was certain that when he set out to charm a lady, which Liz guessed was more often than not, most ladies would be thoroughly and completely smitten.

He still held her hand as he guided her to a chair. "It was good of you to see me on such short notice," Liz said, sitting down.

"It would please me greatly to have Glenhollow included in a work on stud farms. That's what you're planning, isn't it?"

Liz held her breath for a moment and then smiled up at him. His eyes held hers for an instant before he went over to a small oak cabinet.

"What can I get you to drink?"

"Perrier with lime, please."

"What do you think of our weather, Miss Grady?"

"I'm afraid it's the kind you have to think about all the time. A little too hot."

"You should be here around racing season." He handed her a tall glass bearing the initials of the breeding farm. "Where did you say you were from?"

She hesitated, then said, "Ramsey Falls. That's a small town in upstate New York."

"Ramsey Falls." He studied her for a full ten seconds. "Home to one of the great stud farms. I suppose you know it—Bosworth."

"Yes, of course," Liz said, looking enthusiastic. "Actually, that's how I got the idea for the book. Do you know Victor?" she said as though she and Victor Bosworth were on very friendly terms.

"I've bought a couple of breeding horses from Bosworth Stud," he said.

"Yes. Yes, he told me."

"He's a very obliging fellow." He filled a tall glass with ice and poured a Perrier for himself, then went behind his desk and sat down, his back to the window. "Incidentally," he told her, "we're over the formalities. I'm Pat to my friends."

"And I'm Liz, to friends and enemies alike."

He laughed. "You're much too pretty to have enemies."

She moved uncomfortably in her chair. She had a half hour in which to learn what Lucas had to do with Will, and he was taking the conversation down byways that had nothing to do with why she was in Tampa. "I'd love to see the layout of Glenhollow."

"Will you be taking pictures?"

"Got my camera," she said, patting her bag. "Just snapshots, of course. The publisher will take care of the art, actually."

"Too bad you weren't here during the breeding season," he said as he led her out of the building and headed toward the paddocks.

"People keep telling me that," Liz improvised.

"Breeders want foals to be born as soon as possible after the first of the year," he explained, "because that's the official birth date for all horses in the Northern Hemisphere, regardless of their real day of birth. A horse born in the latter part of the year would be at a disadvantage against horses born six months earlier, so most of the breeding occurs between February and May. But you know all that."

"From Victor."

"From Victor. Come along. I imagine you'll want to see some of our prize beauties."

He took her into the main barn, a large building with a center pathway and stalls on either side. There were other animals running around the stalls, she noted—goats, cats and some lively dogs.

"They keep each other company," Lucas said. "Somehow having other animals around calms the horses who are very high-strung. But, of course, you know that, too."

Had she seen animals at Bosworth Stud? She had no idea. "Yes, of course, I'm afraid I know that, too." She quickly reached into her bag for her small camera and dutifully took a few pictures.

There was a group of people at the center of the stable, examining horses being paraded by green-jacketed grooms who had trouble keeping them calm.

One of the colts, however, had a mild, gentle personality. His sole interest seemed to be in playing a game of grab-the-shank with his handler.

"Here we are," Patrick Lucas said, going over to the animal and patting him on the flank. There was a burlap bag filled with carrots nearby, and Lucas pulled out one for the horse. "Wouldn't It Be Loverly, our latest investment."

Liz stopped cold. "I...I beg your pardon," she said, gazing at the big handsome colt. "Did you say Wouldn't It Be Loverly?" She recognized him from the star on his forehead.

"I know." Lucas said with a smile. "The name's a mouthful."

"I was a little surprised to see him here. He's from Bosworth Stud, and Will was the original purchaser. I attended the auction."

"You know Will, too." He gave her a charming smile. "Now why would Will have kept you a secret?"

"I'm afraid you'll have to ask Will. Perhaps it has something to do with the fact that he's a married man."

"It's hard to think that would stop Will."

"It would stop me," Liz said. "Now you must let me take a picture of you with Wouldn't It Be Loverly."

He glanced at his watch, then obligingly stood with his handler and the colt for a picture. "I'm afraid I've got another appointment," he told her.

"Yes, of course. I've really overstayed my welcome, I'm sure." She shook his hand and followed him to her car. "Well, thanks. It's a beautiful spread."

He leaned in at the open car window and smiled at her. "Perhaps we'll meet again in Ramsey Falls."

"Perhaps." She had lied to get in to see him, and if he were to show up in Ramsey Falls, she planned to be a million miles away.

She waved goodbye, checked the time and decided that she'd hit Tampa in time for dinner and that after that she'd head for bed. She had slept for maybe an hour or two at Brad's the night before, had napped on the plane and now she was having trouble keeping her eyes open. Perhaps that was why she didn't see the car turning into the drive as she headed out of Glenhollow. She swerved just in time, and as the driver leaned out of his window to curse her, she realized she was looking at Brad. She turned onto the highway and was quickly lost in late-afternoon traffic.

BACK AT THE HOTEL, after a light dinner, Liz crawled into bed and lay there, unable to sleep. It was still light outside, but that wasn't what kept her awake; it was seeing Brad out at Glenhollow Stud. He'd almost certainly ask Lucas about her. Then Lucas would learn the truth.

And worse, why had Brad turned up at Glenhollow? She had unashamedly listened in on his conversation with Will. Brad had seemed angry enough with his cousin. He'd even seemed innocent of the kind of real trouble his cousin might be in. But he also could have been playacting, knowing Liz could hear everything that was said in the house. Brad might be at Glenhollow because he was just as involved with Patrick Lucas and the Mob as Will obviously was.

Her telephone rang suddenly, breaking into her thoughts. She'd come to no conclusions about Brad, but knew he'd come to plenty about her. And the caller could be Brad or Lucas, and she had no wish to talk to either. Still, Liz picked up the receiver. It wasn't the first tight spot she'd be in, and if she were to follow through on the story, it wouldn't be the last.

The telephone operator was at the other end. "Mr. Bradford Kent is on his way up to see you, Miss Grady."

"On his way up?"

"Yes, ma'am."

Liz slammed the receiver down and flew out of bed. She ran into the bathroom and quickly doused her face with water. Her hair was rumpled. She grabbed a comb but didn't have much success taming it before she heard a quick, impatient knock at the door. Her mind was a blank. In fact, she had little choice but to stand back and take what he had to say. Then she might ask some questions of her own. She slipped into a terry-cloth robe, went to the door, unlocked it and pulled it open.

Brad stood there without a trace of a smile on his face, and when she saw his look of contempt, felt as if every ounce of will had drained out of her body.

"You storm out on me last night in Ramsey Falls and turn up today in Tampa. Amazing," he said, going past her into the room. "And there you were at Glenhollow Stud. You move pretty fast. You heard Patrick Lucas's name mentioned when I was talking to Will and decided you'd stumbled on a powerful story of corruption and wheeling and dealing. So did you convince Celie you had a story, or have you come on your own? I like the part about the book on stud farms you're writing. It has a nice, original touch."

"Brad—" she began, but he interrupted her.

"One thing's clear now. You'll do anything to get a story, even if it means destroying what we have between us."

"You know why I'm here," she said quietly. "And I'm curious about why you turned up at Glenhollow. I doubt it was just to see Wouldn't It Be Loverly."

"You know precisely why. It was to settle a gambling debt for Will."

"He apparently has a lot of good friends willing to cough up money for him," she said.

"He has a foolish, generous father. But I came down to convince Pat Lucas that, henceforth, the well is dry as far as Will is concerned."

"And that's all you think it is, just a gambling debt?"

"Obviously, since Pat Lucas saw the light."

"Just like that?"

"Liz, it's none of your business. There's no story. You're down here on a fool's errand. And I know damn well Celie would agree."

"As far as I'm concerned," Liz said, "there's a lot more to it than the gambling habits of one man."

"Forget it."

"Brad, I can't."

"Pulitzer Prize time, is that it?"

"Following a lead where it'll go, that's all."

He took a step closer and gripped both her arms. She closed her eyes and heard him moan her name. "I don't think that's all. There's one other thing—you and me."

His mouth came down on hers in a violent, hungry kiss—a kiss that was almost brutal in its attack. She felt herself go limp against him. He drew his lips away, still gripping her arms with such intensity that she could feel the pain cutting into her.

"Lord, I've thought of nothing else since last night. Of what happened between us, of how much I want you. Of how much I think you want me. That should be enough."

At that moment, with his hands on her arms and the way he looked at her, she thought their need for each other was enough. There could never have been anyone but Brad. If he hadn't come for her, she would have spent her life alone, of that Liz was absolutely certain. She ran her fingers through his hair and touched his ear with her lips. She would always want him.

His lips came down on hers again as he picked her up in his arms and carried her over to the bed. "Damn it," he said, "I came here to make sure you left Tampa with your tail between your legs." He stopped, his words and anger dying in his throat.

Liz reached for him. "Brad, don't talk. Not now."

He was over her, holding her captive. Their lips fused, held by the desire welling up, flowing out and mingling between them.

She felt his hand move to push aside the folds of her robe until her breasts were bared. She lay motionless, unable to draw a breath when he lowered his head to find the soft blossom that tipped her breast. His mouth on her flesh had the same devastating effect as before. She felt a ripple of electricity along her spine. A moan of animal pleasure rumbled through his chest. He was hard and warm, so warm that Liz felt his heat burn into her.

Without a word he eased himself off and stripped, then drew her robe away, tossing it carelessly onto the floor. There were no words now, no distances between them, no chasms, merely the already certain knowledge of what would happen. His mouth came down on hers once again with a desperation that equalled hers. They were one, she thought, arching into him, and all else would have to wait until some other universe appeared.

His tongue pressed home, roaming her mouth and moving back and forth, in and out again and again. Her body budded, her nipples hard and sensitive. The moist fury of his mouth and the force of his desire straining and pressing against her thigh was driving her over the edge. As he parted her legs, he poised over her, looking intently into her face as he entered her body. He held back for a moment, then pressed slowly, deeply home.

When he began to move he watched her, as though memorizing her reactions, her expression, her rapture. His eyes were smoky with a passion that enflamed Liz, and she began to move with him, matching his fervor. They rocked together, alone in a universe of their own invention. Then their new world exploded around them, shattering the moon and the stars into little shards of rock crystal.

Nothing would ever be the same again.

He had fallen asleep with one leg thrown over her and both arms around her, his weight heavy on her body, his soft breath warming her chest.

He stirred then and moved slowly before gazing down at her. "Hey," he said dreamily, "my memory isn't that good. Did I tell you how I feel about you?"

"No," she said softly.

"Oh." There was a long pause, then he put his head on her breasts.

"You rat," she said with a laugh, grabbing the pillow and drawing it down on his head.

"Okay, okay, I'll say it." He pushed the pillow away. "I know when I've been cornered." He held her in his arms and gazed deeply into her eyes. "I think you're the sexiest woman in the universe," he said. "And at the moment I don't give a damn why you're here. I'm just glad you are."

"I think," she said, cradling him in her arms, "I'm glad I'm here, too."

CHAPTER FIFTEEN

LIZ AWOKE in Brad's arms, her head resting against his chest. The soft, steady beat of his heart and the slow rhythm of his breathing touched her soul. He shifted a bit and murmured her name. "Move up here, love," he said in a sleepy, husky voice. "I need you again."

It was as the night before, a slow dance of touching, kissing, holding and moving together as though they were one. When their bodies joined, Liz wanted to take all of him into her so that there could be no question of the rightness of their love.

His breath was uneven and harsh, but his touch was tender. She experienced a swirling motion deep inside her and then a thrill that rocketed through her, at once exquisite and searing. He waited until her divine torment ended, then gripped her and anchored her as he moaned and rode his own crest.

Afterward, Liz closed her eyes and drifted uneasily toward sleep. For all their love, for all that the merest touch of their bodies could do to each other, nothing was settled between them. The chasm was no less deep than before, and Liz placed a high price on honesty and trust.

When she awoke, the sun was high. The room was suffused with light, the only sound the low hum of the air conditioner. Brad lay next to her, asleep on his side, his lips against her bare shoulder.

She smiled and was about to reach for him when the telephone rang. Brad stirred, but Liz picked the receiver up quickly, murmuring her name.

"Ms. Grady... Liz, just listen and don't bother answering me." She recognized the voice of Patrick Lucas.

"That for me?" Brad said, half asleep, his eyes still closed.

"No, for me," she whispered.

"I don't think you asked me the right questions yesterday," Lucas continued. "The only games I play are those where I set the rules. I value my privacy, and I don't want reporters sticking their pretty little noses into my business. It's as simple as that. You were really clever, Liz." She could almost hear his smile. "And nervy, too," he added. "I like that in a woman, which is why I'm passing on the message in a friendly phone call. Whatever you have in mind, give it up, here and in Ramsey Falls. I'm a patient man, but even my patience has its limits. Goodbye, Liz. I'd hate to think we might have to have a conversation like this again."

There was a slight click as he hung up. His voice had been pleasant, far from menacing, the voice of a man who was used to having his way.

She replaced the receiver, cast a glance at Brad, who lay quietly asleep, and with her hands clasped behind her neck, began to do some serious thinking. She had tapped into something concerning Patrick Lucas, after all. Will Vanderheyden, as owner of White Horse Farms, had purchased Wouldn't It Be Loverly. Supposedly stabled at Bosworth Stud, according to official records, the animal was actually being berthed at Glenhollow. And Lucas gave every indication of being the horse's owner.

Liz guessed that Will owed Lucas a gambling debt and that his way of working out that debt was to engage in money-laundering for the Mob. He'd purchased Wouldn't It Be Loverly for Lucas with cash given to him by the Mob. Now the horse was being used for stud purposes and was earning Lucas and his compatriots a lot of money.

She had just been threatened by Lucas, which meant there was a story. She'd have to be careful, and she'd have to do a lot of research, and Celie, undoubtedly already furious with her, would tell her she was fired. Well, at least she'd have the time she needed to track down the story—that much was almost certain.

Brad stirred. Liz gazed down at him. Trying to protect Will from the consequences of his gambling was something Brad had undoubtedly always done, and doubtless he believed Lucas was just a man trying to collect a bad debt from an incorrigible gambler. The idea of money collected from criminal activities making its way into Ramsey Falls would be as odious to Brad as it was to Liz.

"Did I hear the phone ring?" His voice was still heavy with sleep.

"Just a wake-up call," Liz said.

"Mmm," Brad said, reaching for her.

"I REALLY OUGHT to fire you," Celie said. They were seated in Celie's office. Outside, the afternoon sun blazed, though without the same ferocity as in Tampa.

Liz didn't even try to answer her. If she was in Celie's place, her reaction would be exactly the same.

"You calmly take off for Florida, and calmly return, as though you were on *Time* magazine, doing a story of earth-shattering importance."

"Celie, I left at four yesterday morning. It was impossible to call you then." Liz hesitated, aware of the slow flush covering her cheeks. "I . . . it was impossible to call you yesterday. This morning it seemed expedient to grab the first flight out and talk to you face-to-face."

"What information could possibly have come your way at four in the morning that you had to cut and run?"

"If you'll let me," Liz said quietly, "I'll tell you what I know, how I learned it, and why I ran."

Celie regarded her for a long moment, then reached for her telephone and asked her secretary to hold her calls.

"I know," Liz remarked with a tiny smile when Celia hung up. "It had better be good and I'd better be sure of my facts."

"I'm glad you've learned something in your months here," Celie said dryly.

Liz shook her head slowly, contemplating the distance she had come in that time. "It's amazing," she said slowly. "Just about four weeks ago I was covering what appeared to be a simple little story about a zoning dispute. I almost didn't go to see John Nelson. In fact, I only followed it up because of Wouldn't It Be Loverly. I wanted to find out who purchased him, just out of simple curiosity—"

"And because I told you to forget it," Celie put in.

Liz smiled but without mirth. "Well, the simple little zoning dispute has turned into a rather ugly story of money laundering of Mob money. And, incidentally, that money has found its way into several charitable institutions, including Pack College." She saw Celie blanch and clutch the arms of her chair.

"You're not making sense, Liz."

"Just listen to what I have to say, please."

Celie closed her eyes briefly, then said tersely. "Go ahead."

"Victor Bosworth is the biggest benefactor of Pack College," Liz said. "I've every reason to believe the money Will paid for his colt, Wouldn't It Be Loverly, was Mob money and that buying up horse stock is one of the many ways the Mob puts its tainted money into circulation. Well, the Mob has bought Victor's horse, and Victor has donated a lot of that money to his favorite college. Pack College's board of trustees is going to be embarrassed about that and so is Victor, though I'm sure that all along he acted innocently."

When she stopped, Celie got to her feet and faced Liz across her desk. Her face was still deadly pale. "Do you know what an accusation like that could cost this community, to say nothing of Victor? We're not just talking about *embarrassment*! This could *ruin* Victor."

"Killing the messenger doesn't change the message."

"Victor has spent a good portion of his fortune to fund educational projects," Celie said. "A fortune he inherited from his father, who earned it through the sweat of his brow."

"I believe that, Celie. I also believe Mob money has ended up at Pack College. Shall I remind you that I've been threatened, not once, but a couple of times—because I'm apparently putting my nose where it shouldn't be? I'm going to follow through, whether you agree to it or not."

"I can't think of it now," Celie said with an air of impatience. "I've got a lot on my mind. Right now there are lawyers to see, accountants to deal with—all the business involved with switching the *Times Herald* from a semiweekly to a daily. If you're going to stick around, Liz, I'll want your help in a lot of other ways."

"Celie, it's not a matter you can sweep under the rug," Liz said, and watched as Celie sat down, utterly deflated. "It's the way things have always been done around here," Liz said quietly. "You do almost anything to maintain the status quo, to keep everything and everyone in his place. Oh, yes, things are just wonderful the way they are. Sweep the nastiness under the rug. Celie, in many ways life in Ramsey Falls is a dream. The Scotties of this world are protected and allowed to go on making their mistakes as long as they don't seriously rock the boat. And so are the Will Vanderheydens. Except that Scottie is getting his act together because he saw what he was doing to himself and his family, and Will won't change. You and Brad and the judge will go on protecting him, refusing to believe he's a danger to anyone but himself."

"Liz, you can't come here and expect to change things overnight."

"It's not overnight, Celie. Let me put what I know and what my proposals are on paper. Turn them down, fire me, do what you want after that. It's not a story I'm going to sit on. I hope you're going to back me."

Celie gave an exasperated sigh. "Yes, of course, write me a memo. Put it all down on paper. I'll have Brad look it over to tell us whether it's a story that bears following through." She seemed to realize that she was doing just what Liz didn't want. She gave another sigh and waved her hand in dismissal. "Write it down."

Liz turned and ran from the office before Celie could say another word.

She went back to her cubicle and stood for a moment, staring at the small, friendly space. Her ivy plant needed watering, and she felt as if she had been away for a year. There were half a dozen pieces of mail on her desk and a copy of the current issue of the *Times Herald*.

She picked up the small watering can that she kept filled and tended to the plant as though it were her most precious possession. Then she sat down at her desk and reached for the toggle switch on her computer. The bright orange cursor flashed on. She'd compose the story much as she had told it to Celie. There would be months of research ahead, but it was enough for Celie, enough to question why a bar-restaurant should destroy a landscape for no reason at all except one man's gambling habit.

But she couldn't quite begin. Brad was on her mind. They had returned home on the plane together. Neither had mentioned Will or Lucas. All the way back Brad had been full of plans for their future together and Liz had let him talk. The moment she'd received Lucas's call, she'd known that loving Brad wouldn't stop her from following the story. To do so would destroy that tiny little thing in her that made her Liz Grady and no one else.

Now she'd have to tell him that she was going to write the story that would bring the perfect little world of Ramsey Falls crashing down in ruins. And she'd have to tell him before he talked to his parents or made plans for them both that would ultimately fail because, in Ramsey Falls society, she was going to be an outcast.

The cursor blinked steadily. The first sentence of her proposal popped into her head.

"It all began with a horse." *No, strike that.* "It all began with a beautiful view of the Hudson River in a town called Ramsey Falls."

It was nearly ten when she finished her report for Celie. She stretched, looked around the darkened office and realized she was alone there and that everyone else had left for the night. She turned back to her report, suddenly uncertain about what she was doing. She had written it, trying not to think about what Brad meant to her, what his smile was like, his laughter, his touch, the warmth of his kisses.

She turned and mindlessly punched the Print key on her computer, then stared at the printer as it whipped the memo out. When she heard a sudden, light tap on the door, she looked up, her first reaction one of fear. She hadn't forgotten the threatening phone call from Patrick Lucas and had no doubt he could reach her wherever she was. She sucked in her breath and held it, retreating behind her desk and sitting down as though it were the only way to be safe.

Brad opened the door and looked in at her. "Of course, where else would a dedicated reporter be at 10:00 p.m.? Come on, the social news can wait."

He came into her office and smiled as he placed a kiss on her forehead. Liz felt the numb place in her heart begin to have some feeling again but ignored it with cool resolve.

"I'm afraid I haven't been working on the social scene," she said.

His expression turned sober. "Liz, I thought you understood the way we handle things here."

"I do understand, but your method isn't my method. The fact is," she said, stuttering over her words and repeating herself, "the fact is, I think you're rushing to conclusions. About us, I mean. I've, well, I've had time to think over what happened between us. I really wonder if we have enough in common to continue a relationship.''

''You *are* Liz Grady, aren't you? The woman who came willingly into my arms not twenty-four hours ago? Not have enough in common to continue a relationship? I seem to remember quite a few moments when we had plenty in common. Liz, if you're talking about the differences in our backgrounds—''

''I'm talking about facing the truth concerning the way your cousin has been pushing people around. I'm talking about letting in the air—''

''No,'' he said, ''I don't believe that's what you're talking about at all. In fact, I'm beginning to believe you're just plain crazy, and so am I for standing here discussing continuing relationships that have to be discontinued because we have nothing in common.'' He reached for her and pulled her roughly to her feet.

''Brad, please.'' She tried to struggle against him, but he pinned her arms to her sides. ''Damn it, I'll scream.''

''Go ahead.'' His lips crushed on hers in a long, possessive kiss, forcing her mouth open. His tongue darted in, searching, seeking, settling a score with a driving, bruising pressure. She could feel his anger and couldn't fight against it. In a way she didn't want to. His touch was filled with a fury that made Liz want to cry. And then he moaned low in his throat and the kiss changed. It was no longer punishing. In another moment he released her arms and enclosed her in a loving embrace. His mouth dropped to shower her throat with kisses, his hands caressing her back in sensual circles. Liz experienced a wild, dizzying sensation of both soaring and falling at the same time. She raised her arms to cling to him and caught the triumphant look in his eye.

"No." She pulled away. "I said there's too much dividing us, Brad." She felt the breathless strain in her voice.

His look hardened. He muttered a low curse, and in a voice husky with emotion said, "You don't know what you're throwing away."

"The trouble is," she responded, "I do." She reached for the memo meant for Celie and solemnly handed it to him, waiting with white knuckles pressed against the hard surface of the desk while he read.

When he finished, his expression was full of cold fury. He folded the memo, stuck it into his back pocket and without a word turned and went over to her door. He hesitated a moment, then spun around. "I'll tell you something, Liz. What's separating us has nothing to do with Ramsey Falls or with Will or the judge or Thoroughbred horses. All it has to do with is you."

Then he turned and left.

BRAD FOUND Will Vanderheyden where he would always be at night—in the bar at the Shore Road Country Club, without his wife.

"I'd like a word with you outside," Brad said to his cousin.

Will put his drink down. "Hey," he said, nodding at his companion, a recently divorced woman whom Brad knew slightly, "I'm busy talking business here. Can't it wait?"

"Come on," Brad said, collaring his cousin and smiling an excuse at the woman. "He'll be right back."

Will, his face flushed, said in a low voice, "Take your hands off me, Brad, or I'll kill you."

"You can kill me outside."

"Be back in a minute," Will said to the woman in a low growl.

The exchange had been quiet enough, and no one in the bar, including the bartender, seemed to be aware of the heat beneath their words. Will, in fact, led the way out of the clubhouse through the kitchens to the rear gardens.

He whipped around to face Brad. "You ever do that again," he said through clenched teeth, "and I'll see you dead."

Brad laughed. In a swift move he grabbed Will's tie and pushed him against the wall, holding the silken material between tight fingers. "You stupid son of a bitch. I'm going to see you rot."

"What in hell are you talking about?" Will's eyes seemed about to pop.

"You and Lucas operating like a couple of gangsters to get a piece of land rezoned for a lousy bar-restaurant and telephone threats to Liz Grady because she wanted to call you on it."

"Oh, man, you're something. You're a bloody ostrich sticking your head in the sand. That's what I always liked about you. Mr. Clean, Mr. Pro Bono, the perfect lawyer up front. With Brad Kent on your case, you could take over the world and have everyone applauding you for it. Gambling's coming to Merriman County next year or the following year. It's inevitable. There are people around here who want it, need it. They're lobbying in the state capital. Man, I'm telling you. Open your bloody eyes. That piece of land on I-84 will be a gold mine."

"You and Lucas, that's what it's all about—gambling and Mob money and money-laundering. They all go hand in hand." For a moment Brad almost let go of his cousin, but it was Liz he was worried about, Liz who had opened her eyes a long time before he had.

"Listen," Will was saying, "I should have stopped her, but I didn't because of you."

"Don't even bother finishing the thought," Brad said.

"Lucas would've handled it for me, but I told him you had a thing going with her."

"Lucas called her, you damn fool, this morning in Tampa and threatened her if she followed through on her story." With a gesture of disgust he released his hold on Will and pushed him away.

"Look, take it easy," Will said, rubbing his throat. "You're in it now, so you might as well smile all the way to the bank."

"I thought maybe you were just stupid and got caught up in something," Brad said. "I figured you kept your gambling under control, but obviously Lucas bought himself something when he met up with you. Took over your debts, I suppose."

Will threw him a look of sheer hatred. "Maybe we should've roughed up Liz Grady after all. She's made a pansy out of you, and that's a big mistake."

"You slime." Brad hit Will's jaw in a sudden, unpremeditated flash. Will's eyes widened in surprise as he went down with a heavy thud. Brad didn't stick around to check the results. He went back into the clubhouse, through the kitchen and into the bar, where Will's date still sat over a drink.

"Your friend Willie had a little accident out back," he told her on his way out. "Maybe you ought to call a doctor."

It was nearly eleven when he made his way to Bosworth Stud and found Victor at his desk in the warm, book-lined, art-filled library. He was surprised to find Celie there, too, sitting opposite Victor.

"This memo is for you from Liz," Brad told Celie, "but I think you know the contents. I'd like Victor to see it first."

He threw himself into a chair while Victor adjusted his glasses and began to read. Victor's face, always calm, became hardened granite as he took in Liz's accusations. Then, finished, he silently handed the memo to Celie. Without a word he poured a glass of cognac from a decanter for Brad.

"I'm as guilty as Will and Lucas," Brad told him. "Nose to the grindstone, just doing my job. I always thought Will was an ass, a gambler and a fool, but a fool with a talent for making money. I should've looked deeper." Brad tossed the words out with as much bitterness as he had ever felt. He had allowed himself to become soft and disinterested over the years, and smug.

Celie glanced quickly through Liz's memo, then placed it on the desk. "A simple little story that began with a zoning dispute and with the sale of a prize colt to a prestigious breeding farm in Florida...."

"Paid for with tainted Mob money," Victor added. His face was ashen, and he sank back into his chair as if his bones had turned to water. "You're sure Liz knows what she's talking about?"

"She's been threatened by Patrick Lucas," Celie reminded him. "By Will Vanderheyden and by several anonymous phone calls."

"Will used the name White Horse Farms to buy Wouldn't It Be Loverly," Victor said. "He asked for anonymity, at least around town. Said the neighbors would be a little jealous if they knew he could raise that much money. I admit I didn't question him heavily when he asked me to keep it quiet. Will's always been a hustler, and it doesn't pay to ask too many questions of a hustler."

"And how was the check drawn?"

"Cashier's check. He said he sold some logging land to a developer. I had no reason to question the payment."

"Damn," Brad said, "we've been hustled under our noses and we would've gone on ignoring Will as long as he seemed to keep his nose clean. When he told me Lucas was putting the screws on him for some money he owed, I went down to Tampa like a fool and explained patiently that Will would pay up his debts. Lucas smiled and said no sweat, and all the time he knew Will was in deeper and deeper."

"Liz is absolutely right," Celie said. "We've insulated ourselves and we don't know the difference between justice and our own self-interest. We've run Ramsey Falls like a fiefdom. Do-gooders sometimes, but do-it-for-ourselves when it suited our purpose." She added after a moment when neither man made an objection, "Willie's a gambler and we've all closed our eyes to it. After all, he's the son of Thadeus 'Hanging Judge' Vanderheyden, who'll deal with you according to his whim. Sometimes it works, as in the case of Scottie, and just as often it doesn't."

"Wait a minute! Hold on!" Victor said. "We didn't knowingly break any laws. I haven't even touched the money I received for the sale of Loverly." He let out a deep sigh. "No, I haven't, of course. I gave it to Pack College. And that's the point Liz is trying to make. If it's true that Lucas is involved in money-laundering, Wouldn't It Be Loverly was purchased in order to legitimize money made in illegal ways. That money has gone to fund student programs at Pack College. I'll have to bring it up before the school's board of trustees. How in hell do I do that?"

"Tell them the truth. If the notion is any consolation," Brad said, "this isn't the first time an educational institution has been given tainted money, nor will it be the last."

"You know what Liz would say," Celie remarked.

Brad gave a brittle laugh. "I know just what she'd say."

"A lot of it's speculation, Victor," Celie said.

"Threatening phone calls don't add up to speculation," Brad pointed out.

"Damn," Victor said in a low voice, almost to himself, "along with all the other innocent victims, there's a very beautiful horse named Wouldn't It Be Loverly. That horse," he added with the air of a man used to having his own way, "is coming back to Bosworth Stud."

"When Liz's article appears, wherever that might be," Brad said, "Lucas might be very amenable to seeing Loverly back here."

"The article will see the light of day in the *Times Herald*," Celie said, coming to a sudden decision. "I'm going to ask Adriana to put off going to Columbia this year," Celie told Victor. "I'll want her to handle Liz's assignments until we go daily. Then we'll take on a couple more reporters. And when the story goes to press, Liz will move up to editor. It's the way I'd planned it, and now I realize I want someone at the helm who won't take no for an answer, not even from me."

"Hell," Brad said, "I'll personally go through every court case and zoning dispute for the past few years, and where there's been a miscarriage of justice—" He stopped. "We're setting ourselves up as arbiters again. Have Liz write the story. Momentum will carry it from there."

Brad eased himself out of his chair. The problem of what to do about Liz Grady wasn't anywhere near solved.

"Incidentally," Victor said with a brave smile, "I've decided to breed Brittany spaniels. I've always had a soft place in my heart for them. I've asked Scottie to take charge of the kennels."

"Is it really a soft spot for spaniels, or is it for Scottie and his family?"

"Maybe a little of both. I admit I wanted Adriana to be free to leave Ramsey Falls to continue her studies, but now that Celie has other plans—"

"She'll get there," Celie said. "I'll see to it. She has writing talent, and working on the *Times Herald* will be the best learning experience she can have."

Brad stood at the door and gazed warmly at his two friends. Victor shook his head. "I know, Brad, here we go again, arranging people's lives for them."

"As long as we don't put a shield around the Will Vanderheydens of the world," Brad said, "and protect them for our own selfish reasons, I think it's all right. There are going to be tough times ahead for all of us," he added, then saluted them and left. Whatever they might be, those tough times, he wanted Liz to know he stood by her.

For once, however, his lawyer's instincts on how to handle a problem, failed him.

CHAPTER SIXTEEN

MRS. KENT MATERIALIZED at the foot of the bed, dressed in an old housedress that Liz recognized after a moment as belonging to her mother. On Mrs. Kent, whose hair was expensively cut and coiffed, the flowered dress looked odd.

"What school did you say you went to, dear?"

"University of Chicago," Liz said, "on scholarship."

"Well, of course, Kents never go anywhere on scholarship."

"Not even Brad?"

"Oh, he was smart enough, dear. He graduated in the top ten, but Kents would never use up someone else's scholarship. After all, living in small apartments on the wrong side of Chicago with blue-collar parents, one understands. Good heavens, Will Vanderheyden wouldn't stand for it. All that lovely money he earns gambling. The Mob wouldn't hear of it."

"Then it's true?" Liz asked.

"What's true, my dear?"

"The Mob and Will and tainted money."

Mrs. Kent gave her a lethal smile. "Blue-collar fools. That's why you're where you are, living on scholarships, and why we're at the top of the pecking order." The housedress sprouted wings, and Mrs. Kent flew away, cackling.

Quarrelsome crows outside her open bedroom window woke Liz up abruptly, the dream fading so quickly that she had only a disagreeable sensation of having not slept well.

Liz pulled herself out of bed and was sleepily fiddling with the knobs on the shower when she realized it was Saturday morning, that she could have stayed in bed and that she had two days to get her act together. She had fallen asleep near dawn, wrestling until then with her indignation, her self-righteousness and her certainty that Brad had broken with her forever.

"What's separating us has nothing to do with Ramsey Falls or with Will or the judge or Thoroughbred horses. All it has to do with is you," he'd said to her.

What was separating them was the Ramsey Falls establishment against the Liz Gradys of the world, but she had learned that from the start, when Celie had put an embargo on half the stories she'd submitted.

Innocent of all charges but one was how she had summed up Brad's behavior on his cousin's behalf. He had taken Will at face value—or rather at his family's value. And because he loved his parents and his uncle, Brad had indulged Will, as they all had.

Damn, she was taking her mission too seriously. Ramsey Falls was about to celebrate its true tricentennial. Liz Grady was only a footnote in its history book. The town had undoubtedly survived such issues before and would go on, impervious to assault, for another three hundred years. And Kent boys would inherit dark blue eyes and narrow, aristocratic noses and a lot of self-worth, just as they always had. And Liz Gradys would fall in love with them and—if luck would have it—marry them.

She lifted her face to the shower spray. The water beaded over her, and abruptly the dream came back of Brad's mother wearing her own mother's housedress.

Then she thought about a small apartment in Chicago, where her two dearly beloved blue-collar parents lived. She thought about a massive pile of stone overlooking the Hudson River. The contrast was faintly ludicrous. She could no more see her parents walking into the drawing room of Kent Hall than the Kents at the kitchen table in Chicago.

Or perhaps she could see her father only too well, tucked into his best navy blue suit, decidedly uncomfortable in a strangling collar and tie, making his way into the drawing room at Kent Hall. And she could imagine her mother, who had a lot more poise and charm, feeling so disconcerted by her husband that she would stiffen and turn silent.

Was it so simple? Was she indeed a fool, a self-righteous prig, afraid to let Brad meet her faintly exotic family, learn the life she had come from, realize she'd always be rough around the edges?

Was she afraid of his family, of miles of marble floors and acres of antiques and a millenium of history?

She reached out and turned off the shower. As she quickly toweled herself dry, Liz already had her answer. *Compromise* had scarcely been a word in her lexicon until that moment, but it was certainly one she'd have to learn to love.

Celie would almost certainly be at the *Times Herald* offices that morning. She'd see her first and practice compromise over the way the story should be handled. There had to be a middle ground.

After Celie, she'd stop off to see John Nelson and bring him up to date on Will Vanderheyden. He'd be relieved to know that there would almost certainly be light at the end of the tunnel.

And following the visit to John Nelson, Liz knew of one more view of the river that needed checking out—a view shared by a large stone house and a far more modest one.

IT WAS NOON when Liz sat down on the stone wall overlooking the Hudson. The river reflected sun, sky and mountains with equal clarity. She wore jeans and a T-shirt illustrated with a drawing of a certain Mr. Thoreau.

She could hear the sound of hammering coming from Brad's new house. The exterior was complete. There were a couple of sun chairs on the open deck and a small table. Rhododendron bushes flanked the stairs, and azaleas and junipers had been planted around the deck. A fine green haze of grass and a sweet fragrance showed the lawn had been freshly mowed.

After a while the hammering stopped and Brad came out, carrying a huge piece of wallboard that shielded her from his view. He carried it around to the back of the house. Liz waited until he emerged on the other side. He was stripped to the waist. She drew her knees up and hugged them, studying him, his broad shoulders and slender hips and the aristocratic set of his head.

When he discovered her, he stood stock-still for a moment. Liz slid to her feet, suddenly shaky as she leaned against the wall for support. Neither smiled. Then, in another moment, he began to trudge toward her, stopping a few feet away. "Brought Henry David back to life, I see."

"He said it takes two to speak the truth—one to speak, the other to hear."

"I'm listening."

"It just occurred to me," Liz said, "that when I first met you, I thought you weren't at all good-looking, and now I wonder how I came to that conclusion."

"And I thought you were far too beautiful and decided Henry David wouldn't have you all to himself."

She gazed past him toward the house. "Lookin' good," she said. "You wouldn't be in the way of needin' a decorator, would you?"

"I've already refused the generous offers of a mother and a sister. Figured it needed the hand of the woman who's going to live here."

"And if she has funky taste?"

"If she loves me, she has funky taste, anyway."

"Brad, are we discussing what it is that separates us?"

He reached her in a couple of steps and gathered her into his arms. "I wanted to go to you, tell you that I love you, to tell you nothing separates us."

"But you didn't. You had to put up a wall or take one down."

"Liz, there were never any walls between us except of your own making. I've been waiting for you."

She felt tears in her eyes. "I saw Celie. I know what you're planning to do about your cousin and about Patrick Lucas. Will you believe me if I tell you I was coming to you no matter what happened, that I love you for always and forever?"

He kissed her. "I think we'll frame your friend Mr. Thoreau in gold leaf and hang him over the fireplace. Funky enough for you?"

"Oh," she said, laughing as she threw her arms around his neck, "What a terrible idea, and wouldn't it be lovely?"

Montana Man

BARBARA DELINSKY

When you think of Harlequin Temptation, it's hard not to think of Barbara Delinsky. She was there from the start to help establish Temptation as a fresh, exciting line featuring extremely talented storytellers. The title of her very first Temptation—*A Special Something*—describes what Barbara has continued to bring to you over the years.

We thought it was high time to officially recognize Barbara Delinsky's contribution to Harlequin. And by happy coincidence, she gave us *Montana Man* for publication in December. We couldn't have hoped for a better book to carry Harlequin's Award of Excellence or a better gift to give *you* during the holiday season.

It's tempting to say that, of Barbara's eighteen Temptations, *Montana Man* is the most moving, most satisfying, most wonderful story she's ever written. But each of her books evokes that response. We'll let you be the judge in December....

AE-MM-1

Have You Ever Wondered If You Could Write A Harlequin Novel?

Here's great news—Harlequin is offering a series of cassette tapes to help you do just that. Written by Harlequin editors, these tapes give practical advice on how to make your characters—and your story—come alive. There's a tape for each contemporary romance series Harlequin publishes.

Mail order only

All sales final